DUEL ON THE DUNES

The four men were fifty meters from the plane when the Russians opened up on them. In less than four seconds, the entire team was dead within sight of the plane that would have whisked them to safety. Jinx and BJ sprinted to the ramp and hurled themselves aboard . . .

The ship was hit badly, but still flying. Bits of steel and carbon fiber chunks whipped around the cargo bay as rounds from outside hit the composite walls of the V-22. The ship lurched as the wall behind the door gunner blew in . . .

Berkley Books by
James B. Adair and Gordon Rottman

The WWIII: Behind the Lines Series
TARGET TEXAS
TARGET NUKE
TARGET IRAN

WWIII: BEHIND THE LINES
TARGET IRAN

James B. Adair and Gordon Rottman

BERKLEY BOOKS, NEW YORK

WWIII: BEHIND THE LINES
TARGET IRAN

A Berkley Book / published by arrangement with
the authors

PRINTING HISTORY
Berkley edition / May 1991

ISBN: 0-425-12729-X

A BERKLEY BOOK ® TM 757,375
Berkley Books are published by The Berkley Publishing Group,
200 Madison Avenue, New York, New York 10016.
The name ''Berkley'' and the ''B'' logo
are trademarks belonging to Berkley Publishing Corporation.

PRINTED IN THE UNITED STATES OF AMERICA

10 9 8 7 6 5 4 3 2 1

*We wish to thank Jim Morris,
our editor at Berkley,
for his never-ending patience*

★ Prologue ★

It was the eye of the storm. The first gale had passed over Europe from the East, blasting it beyond recognition, grinding it beneath the treads of thousands of Russian tanks. The current calm was only a respite, though, not a release. Now the storm would return, changing course and speed, turning south to Iran.

Still stung from defeat in Germany, the U.S. Army came home to lick its wounds and brace itself for the next shock. It was not long in coming.

BJ Kirkley and Richard "Jinx" Jenkins had survived the fight at Ft. Hood, Texas, on the first day of the war. They had survived the war in Germany. Thousands had been less fortunate.

Company G, 143rd Infantry, Kirkley's Long-Range Reconnaissance Company (LRRP) was a shadow of its former strength. Many teams had gone deep behind the Soviet lines never to be seen again. Others had been shot to pieces but recovered. The men of Company G had spent years building their unit. Now they had weeks, if that, to re-create it.

Jinx's Military Intelligence unit had fared better than the LRRPs. A gas attack had killed a few, but otherwise the only injuries were professional, their naïveté the only other death.

1

In their enemy's camp, there was jubilation. The Red Army had expelled the Forces of Darkness from Europe. Lt. Colonel Aleksei Bodnya's elite Spetsnaz troops had showered themselves with distinction in their attack on Ft. Hood. They had done well against the enemy's special-purpose troops in the Soviets' rear areas.

Soon Americans and Soviets would all meet again in the arena of battle. This time they would fight in a sea of stones.

★ 1 ★

Valentin Morozov fought the urge to prop his polished boots up on the table's edge. A Guards Army commander had to maintain an image of an iron disciplined perfectionist devoid of any need for personal comfort. He knew the image was false, though. The glass of sweet tea was warm in his gnarled hand, and his *ponchiki* (hot sugared doughnuts) were piled high on a silver platter on the table's center.

You are getting old and soft, Morozov, the veteran tanker thought to himself. The room's comfort was subtly tempting him to let down his guard. Despite the room's warmth and the overstuffed chair's softness, he was not among friends. Not necessarily among enemies, but definitely not friends either.

Across the ornate hand-rubbed table were his three adversaries, all lieutenant generals like himself—but younger. And each was doing his utmost to prove his toughness to the others. Youthful fools, thought Morozov, watching them swill down their vodka and deeply inhale lungs full of American cigarette smoke.

Since the passing of Comrade Gorbachev's more enlightened leadership, the new regime had made it clear that the excessive consumption of spirits was again in vogue. This change had been announced by the actions of the

3

state's new rulers rather than by pronouncement. Morozov's preference for tea was considered quaintly old fashioned.

His youthful comrades' taste for American cigarettes was another new fad. Train car loads of liberated cigarettes had been shipped in from the American military's vast warehouses in the former Federal Republic of Germany. Morozov had read in the Soviet Army's journals about the American military's shameless self-indulgence and consumerism. The articles were accompanied by long lists of luxury goods and recreational items discovered in the military collective stores and warehouses. Even he found some of it hard to believe.

Regardless, many of the supplies had found their way into the *Voyentrog* (Army Navy stores serving military officers), the state's way of thanking the armed forces that had not directly participated in the liberation of Germany.

The Soviet armed forces had again protected the *Rodina mat* (the motherland) from aggression. But the American military's preoccupation with comfort still perplexed him. Had they not actually expected to fight a war?

Thoughts of his own comfort brought him suddenly back to the present and the young officers seated across the table. Morozov thought of them as youthful, though they were in their forties. He was ten years senior to the eldest.

Idiots! They all knew why they were here in Tbilisi. The entire Headquarters of the Transcaucasus Military District had been preparing for this day for months. The reduced-strength divisions had been brought partly up to strength with reservists before the war in Germany. In recent weeks, battalion "packets" of combat-experienced motorized rifle and tank troops had been shipped in from Germany and assigned to the divisions. The Soviets placed great emphasis on combat experience, one of the reasons for the prolonged Afghanistan campaign. Now it was time to stop boasting and goading and take things seriously.

Each of the officers had served in Afghanistan as division or brigade commanders. Morozov idly permitted his mind to drift for just a moment to a popular soldiers' song sung from *Afghanya*. The line spoke of "hepatitis's yellow stare."

God, it had been a terrible war, but they had all learned so much! And it had changed the stagnant, bureaucratically burdened army as well. Junior officers were now expected to demonstrate initiative. Soldiers had more of a voice in subunit affairs. Tactics had been refined and their organizations were more flexible. It had even become fashionable for middle-grade officers to experiment with unofficial tactical concepts within their units.

But these young fools still have to prove to one another how manly they are, Morozov ruminated. Too bad they couldn't have been in Germany. That fight had certainly not been Afghanistan. Their losses in Germany had been appalling, much higher than forecast. And for those losses, there had been repercussions on the planning staff of the Western Strategic Direction. The Soviet military hierarchy did not actually possess the total disregard for loss of life depicted in the West. Soldiers, like tanks and aircraft, were a difficult-to-replace combat resource. Actually, he was thankful for this assignment in the Transcaucasus Military District in South Central USSR.

But these youngsters! They proved the stereotype of Soviet officers. They all had inflated egos. They could not have gotten where they were if they had been shy. He realized he was little different, only older now and more cautious.

And that is why I am here with these youthful dogs of war, he reminded himself. They would charge forth, disregarding their exposed flanks, tearing at the throats of their enemies. Old Morozov would follow in their wake of destruction with his second echelon army, waiting until the young men got themselves into trouble. Then he would meticulously extract them from their overzealousness. Or, like the old lion circling the younger hunters of his pride

as they made rushing charges at their prey, he would outflank them and suddenly appear in the enemy's rear.

The door set in the far wall suddenly swung open, and
in stepped Colonel Vinogradov, the youthful military district chief of staff. Behind him was Colonel General V. M.
Sukharev, the district commander. Morozov set his glass
on the table and began to stand with a silent groan.

"Be seated, Comrades," Sukharev said quickly as his
subordinate army commanders began to rise from their
chairs. "We have much to discuss and little time." It was
typical of his terse style, Morozov thought.

"Effective tonight at 00.01 hours Moscow time, Soviet
Contingent South is activated along with the 1st Southern
Front," Morozov said and smiled. "That is us."

Sukharev's dream, indeed that of every Soviet senior
officer, was coming true. He would command a wartime
front. His deputy commander would remain behind to assume command of the Transcaucasus Military District and
ensure that it trained the new conscripts, formed new units,
and managed the vast amounts of war materiel fed from
state depots. It would also supply the deployed front and
its ever-hungry armies with replacement manpower, supplies, and equipment.

The youngsters were now all eyes and ears, hanging on
every word their front commander spoke. Sukharev dove
into his briefing without preamble.

Just as he will attack, thought Morozov.

"The situation in Iran has degenerated to a degree that
provides the opportunity the General Staff has been waiting for," Sukharev began.

"The Iranian rebel forces of Lieutenant General Ali
Mossadegh are preparing to conduct an offensive intended
to secure Bandar 'Abbās, the key Iranian port on the north
side of the Strait of Hormuz. Mossadegh's forces consist
of almost one fifth of the total Iranian military. As you are
aware, the reason for Mossadegh's split was the Iranian
government's move into the Soviet sphere. Mossadegh, a

radical Shi'ite fundamentalist, feels that we are as great a
threat to Iran as the Americans. His motto is 'Neither East
nor West, but Islam.' ''

Sukharev stopped for a moment, looking thoughtful. ''I
suppose that saying Mossadegh is a radical Shi'ite fundamentalist is a redundant statement!'' he said smiling. Morozov could tell his commander was enjoying himself. The
other officers laughed as he continued.

''We have been selling arms to the Iranians since 1989
to rebuild their military, which was close to collapse in
the aftermath of the Iran–Iraq War. Although they are suffering from severe economic problems, the Iranians are
easily able to pay for the weapons and services with oil.''

This was all old news to the assembled army commanders, but Sukharev pressed on. ''Mossadegh accepted the
transfer of weapons. What soldier would not?'' The army
commanders laughed again. ''But when Iran was convinced to cease their provocative anti-Soviet radio broad-
casts to the Muslims in Soviet Central Asia, Mossadegh
began to protest to the parliament. As the economic and
technical ties between the *Rodina* and Iran solidified, Mossadegh became more outspoken. He was summoned to
Tehran by President Hashemi Rafsanjani himself to explain his views. Mossadegh refused, for obvious reasons.''

As in the old days of the USSR, Morozov remembered,
such a summons could well be one's final trip. Iran was
now no different.

Sukharev paced across the room, his subordinates' eyes
following. ''Mossadegh announced the creation of the
Islamic Republic of Kerman in the southeast of Iran—
Kermanstan.'' Sukharev laughed at his pun. Morozov only
hoped that ''Kermanstan'' would not turn into another version of the ''stan'' that he and the others had endured.

Sukharev continued with more recent events. ''Mossadegh's forces moved westward and to the south to
strengthen and enlarge the territories under their control.

More military units joined his forces. The loyal Iranians managed to hold Bandar ʻAbbās at the mouth of the Persian Gulf and to keep the roads open to the northwest. They are hard pressed, though, since they must maintain many of their most effective forces on the border with Iraq.ʼʼ Sukharev looked around the room. This next bit of news would surprise his commanders as most, except old Morozov, were allowing their attention to drift.

ʻʻThe Iraqis are making aggressive noises once again at our request. We have, of course, offered them more arms for the performance of this service. By tying up key Iranian forces on the Iraq border, they are unable to deal effectively with Mossadegh. We have maneuvered them into a situation where they have no choice but to accept our generous offer of military assistance.ʼʼ

That reawakened them, thought Sukharev.

ʻʻMossadegh is receiving some supplies from Pakistan,ʼʼ he went on, ʻʻnot so much because they fully support him, but simply to further destabilize Iran with which they are no friend. Kermanstan is also backed by China, one of the first countries to recognize the state.ʼʼ

If it was not the Americans stirring up trouble, thought Morozov, it was the damnable *Kosoglazyi* (slant eyes).

ʻʻIf the rebels take Bandar ʻAbbās, the Chinese will be able to supply them by sea,ʼʼ Sukharev went on. ʻʻOur forces will move into Iran following the same routes we did in 1920, 1941, and 1946.ʼʼ They all knew this was not the first time Soviet forces had entered Iran. Perhaps this time, due to America's inability to draw on international support after their European debacle, the Soviets would stay.

ʻʻFourth and 45th Armies will advance southeast along the Zagros Mountains toward Bandar ʻAbbās, our ultimate objective. Comrade Morozov's 76th Guards Army will compose the front's second operational echelon. The 34th Air Army will deploy into forward airfields to support our advance. The 2nd Southern Front, advancing out of the

Turkestan Military District, has the main objective of securing Kerman in eastern Iran, Mossadegh's capital.''

Syukharev gave each commander a hard look. "Comrades, there is little doubt that the Americans will attempt to intervene, perhaps making a major effort." Morozov noticed a tiny smile on each of the officers' lips—they too would now have their chance at the *glavny rag* (the main enemy). "We will, of course, first be threatened by their usual limp ultimatum. This will buy us additional time to establish ourselves."

"Very well, Comrade Front Commander," the 4th Army Commander interrupted, addressing Sukharev by his full title. "When are we to begin operations?"

"The armies are to commence operations in two days," Sukharev replied casually. "Fourth and 45th armies will cross the Iranian frontier at 0900 hours, as will the 2nd Southern Front out of Turkestan. Suitable Iranian welcoming crowds have been arranged." Sukharev peered dramatically at his watch and looked around at each of his four army commanders. "Army operations will begin in two days, but front operations have already commenced."

★ 2 ★

Sepahbod (Lieutenant General) Ali Mossadegh humbly followed the other worshipers, their heads bowed, into the Great Mosque of Kerman. From its tall thin minarets, the muezzin called the faithful to their evening prayers—*"Allah akbar!"* This most favorite of mosques was his religious headquarters, not far from his military headquarters. The Friday night prayers, *namaz*, were important to him. It was here, on a Friday night three months before, that he and his key followers declared a *baya* (oath of allegiance) to the Brotherhood of the Path—*ikhwan al-tariqa*. At the same time they formed the Islamic Republic of Kerman and declared it *dar al-Islam* (abode of peace), a land where absolute Islamic law was in force—The Path. The remainder of Iran, and the world as far as Mossadegh was concerned, was *dar al-harb* (abode of war).

Friday was equivalent to the Sabbath in Judaism and Christianity. But neither Saturday nor Sunday was the Muslim day of rest. Saturday simply because it was the Jews' Sabbath. The Sunday day of rest, instituted in Muslim countries by colonial powers, was shunned by the Muslims as a Western, Christian legacy.

Ali Mossadegh, whose military training began under the Americans during the late Shah's regime and was later continued by the Soviets, had learned his real skills as a

10

mujahid (soldier of God) during the long Iran–Iraq War. Mossadegh considered himself to be the *mujaddid* (re-newer) and the *Mahdis* (The Expected One).

It was said that at the beginning of each century, Allah would send a *mujaddid* to his Muslim community to re-store true Islamic practices, to rejuvenate those who had wandered from The Path. All before Mossadegh's self-proclaimed ascension to the *mujaddid* was *jahiliyya*, a pe-riod of ignorance. With the arrival of this *mujaddid* came the removal of foreign and non-Islamic influences and their accompanying corruption of the community. It was a *ijti-had*—a reinterpretation of Islam needed to revitalize and purify the community.

In order to achieve this, the Koran, the literal word of God, approved and even encouraged a militant and revo-lutionary force. Mossadegh knew he had been chosen as the tool by which Allah was to set the community back on The Path and rid it of the foreign devils now blighting the abode of peace.

Several dozen *Mahdis* had appeared in the last century. This mattered little now. The events Mossadegh had set in motion would assure him a place in history.

The night air was chilly and the sky clear. Allah had graced them by decorating the sky with a heavenly swath of brilliant stars.

They are jewels in the night sky so bright that the de-voted have no need for lights to find their way to the mosque, Mossadegh thought, then began reciting quietly to himself from the Koran: ''He is God alone. God the Eternal. He begets not and is not forgotten. Nor is there like unto Him alone.''

Not entirely lost in religious thought, Mossadegh was quick to observe the attentiveness of the guards placed on either side of the ornate entrance. In deference to Allah they appeared to be unarmed, but each had an automatic pistol concealed in his clothing, within easy reach. Other guards with more substantial armament were deployed in the shadows cast by the outer courtyard's small trees. More guards patrolled the streets around the mosque. Mossadegh touched the grip of the .45 caliber automatic hidden in the folds of his robe. He drew comfort from the big pistol. Even though it was American made, he respected its hitting power. He realized that his troops were armed with American, Soviet, or European-made weapons. Such was the order of the world. Weapons were not permitted into mosques by practice, they were a place of peace. Mossadegh was no fool, though, and had survived only because he took liberties with both his military and religious practices.

All worshipers removed their shoes before entering so as not to defile the mosque with ritually impure substances. Like the other faithful, he performed the ablutions at the fountain that cleansed the body—face, mouth, hands, and feet—and spirit, to bestow the ritual purity necessary for divine worship.

The two guards surveyed the women entering the mosque's side entrance. Women were not permitted to worship with the men, but a secluded section was set aside for them in most mosques. Entered through a separate door, the women's section was partitioned from the larger men's area in the main covered courtyard by a light, intricately hand-carved wooden screen. In many Islamic cultures, the women were not expected to participate in observances in the mosque. They were restricted to their homes and received only limited education.

Mossadegh thought otherwise. The women of the Islamic Republic of Kerman were encouraged to return to the mosques, though keeping themselves in *purdah* (seclusion).

A female attendant watched over the small pile of prayer rugs stacked against the back wall. After removing her sandals, each woman picked up a rug and quietly padded to her place. The women were not to be seen nor heard by the men. They were to do nothing to distract the men's attention from their worship—ever.

Each spread her rug and knelt, taking pains not to even rustle her long black *chador*. Many of the women wore a white headpiece in mourning for their men killed in the war. The robes covered the women from head to foot and included a face veil. Though the *chador* had fallen from use in the Shah's Iran, women had donned them as a symbol of opposition to the Shah and for anonymity during antigovernment demonstrations.

Khomeini had attempted to make the wearing of the *chador* compulsory, a law successfully resisted by the women. Mossadegh, though, had convinced the mufti, specialists in Islamic law, to deliver a *fatwa*, or formal legal decision, declaring that wearing the *chador* was mandatory in the Islamic Republic of Kerman.

Though encouraged to return to the mosques, the women in Mossadegh's Kerman were restricted from the legal professions and from holding government office. Such was the *nahda*, the renaissance of Mossadegh's Kerman.

Capt. D. I. Kunaev unrolled his own prayer rug, ensuring it was evenly aligned with his neighbor's. For the hundredth time, he swallowed his pride. The sacrifices he made for the Motherland were daily becoming more difficult. Of all the tasks he had been called on to perform, this posing as a woman was the most humiliating, aside from being the most dangerous! An Iranian Shi'ite woman at that! Even though he had long ago forsaken its teachings, the religion in which he had been raised was debased by this charade. He kept his hands concealed as best he could in the *chador*'s long sleeves. His accomplice had told him his large hands would be a certain giveaway.

Lt. Tinya Ahmad was another matter. He knew that she was a Kurd from western Iran and that she spoke several languages. She had been raised as a Muslim like himself, but she was very different from the other women that Kunaev had known. She was so much more outspoken, and

when she spoke, she expected to be listened to. Tinya
Ahmad was self-assured and well educated. She was also
cold blooded. He had no doubts that she would execute
this mission.

What Captain Kunaev didn't realize was that Tinya, aka
Fatima Ahmad, had spent part of her twenty-four years in
Austria. Her outlook and attitude, so direct and strange to
Kunaev, were basically that of a Western European
woman, made more complex by her earlier Muslim upbringing. There was more to her than a Western cosmo-
politan perspective, though. The fires of a Kurdish
nationalist burned hotly within her breast, leading to a
complex meshing of values. Her abilities as a GRU agent,
attached to the 5th Directorate—Spetsnaz, were unusual
for any woman, and even for most men. They came from
hate.

Fatima's uncle was one of two men assassinated with
Abdolrahman Qassemlu by an Iranian hit team in Vienna
in 1989. Qassemlu had been an Iranian Kurd opposition
leader. He had been the principal figure in an effort to
bring together the Kurds of Iran, Iraq, Turkey, and the
Soviet Union. His goal was to form a united Kurdish front
against the common enemy—all non-Kurds.

Fatima had been with her uncle since her father and
mother had been murdered during the Iran–Iraq War. They
and many of their Iraqi Kurd coconspirators had died at
the hands of the Iraqi Army. The Iraqis had been simply
responding to a recurring threat developing on the northern
flank of their war zone. Unable to release the needed troops
from the front to quell another suspected Kurd uprising,
they had employed the most manpower-conservative means
available—mustard gas.

Fatima's uncle had taken the strong-willed young girl
with him to Austria where there was a small but politically
active Kurdish community. She possessed a high degree
of intelligence and with proper training could serve the
cause in a more administrative manner. Her uncle was a

man of peace and sought the independence of his people through diplomatic means. This role she accepted. A young Kurd girl in a strange land, she followed her uncle's wishes as was expected. She was enrolled in a university and excelled at her studies. A whole new world opened up to her. She learned from her professors and from her fellow Austrian students. She was sometimes confused by it all—even the Democratic Party of Kurdistan, for which her uncle worked, was pro Iraqi. But she threw herself into the work and into her schooling in a futile effort to forget the cruel deaths of her parents, to forget the age-old injustices inflicted on her people, to forget the barren land she so loved and sorely missed.

That all changed on the warm July afternoon when her uncle and another man were gunned down with Abdolrahman Qassemlu by Iranians. She and other Kurds attempted to piece the organization back together. Fatima grew only more confused. Who ordered the killings? Who was really working for whom? Who could be trusted? No one, she finally concluded.

Her life changed one night in a small quiet Vienna café where she often studied. The August night had been chilly and damp. He was a handsome young Kurd from northern Iran. He, too, was studying in Vienna. Could she help him with his German? Charmed by this young man, she soon became his friend. They began to date just like the young Austrians, a concept alien to Kurds. They became lovers.

She wanted to do more than the old men in the organization. Something more meaningful for the cause. Something that would make a difference.

He wanted her to meet a friend. Someone that might help. His friend was a chief secretary in the Soviet Embassy, in reality a head agent and captain in the GRU—Chief Intelligence Directorate of the General Staff. Fatima was at first skeptical. The Soviets had been no friend of the Kurds. She had been taught to distrust all non-Kurds.

Her lover and recruiter, also a GRU lieutenant, was prepared to deal with her reluctance. Indeed, the young Kurd had been brought in from the southern Soviet Union specifically to accomplish this recruitment.

The sudden reassignment had disrupted his work as a courier and key contact with various Kurd groups in Iran and Turkey, none of which had the slightest idea they were being aided by the Soviet Union. Not that he complained. The opportunity to travel to the West, to study, and to be treated to Fatima's favors more than made up for his initial inconvenience.

The chief secretary, an understanding woman in her early thirties, met Fatima often in the little café. In the Soviet Union, there were people who could help her, the woman explained. People who believed in the goals of the Kurds. People who sought to help the persecuted minorities suffering at the hands of the imperialists, capitalists, and religious fundamentalists.

She had only to demonstrate the will to do what was really needed of her, and her people would achieve the freedom they so desperately sought. They had known she would accept the offer to finish her education for free.

Fatima's two years in Moscow were spent under the tutelage of the Fourth Faculty of the Military–Diplomatic Academy of the General Staff. She never once entered the academy's Greek-colonnaded museumlike building on Narodnogo Opolchenia Street. Nor did she ever enter "The Aquarium," the GRU headquarters on the edge of the Khodinka airfield. She did not even realize she was assigned to the academy, much less that she was being trained as a GRU agent.

Instead she lived in a small apartment with two other girls, one an Iranian Kurd like herself, the other an Armenian from Turkey. A perpetually bitter woman, the Armenian had little to do with the two Kurd girls, for which they were grateful. She sometimes reminded them that it had been the Kurds who had served as the bought tool of the Ottoman Turks, slaughtering hundreds of thousands of Armenians in the Twenties.

Fatima went to school daily in an obscure unmarked office building. She thought of it as a political-science school, an image cultivated by the faculty. The atmosphere was not much different from that at the university in Vienna, except the students never discussed their backgrounds and used assumed names. She was popularly known as Tinya, the Russianized version of her name.

It was all so exciting. The students were from strange, faraway countries, but all had two things in common: They were from among the oppressed ethnic minorities of their native lands and were Muslims. Many of the subjects were the same as those she had studied in the West: history (though sometimes different from what she had been taught in Vienna), mathematics, language, and world cultures. Other classes were different, though, and sometimes even fun. They learned about simple codes and encryption, dead-letter drops, pistol shooting, simple sabotage techniques, photography, sketching, map reading, surveillance, intelligence-collection requirements, cover stories, how to cover one's movements, how to tail someone and how not to be tailed, and secret rendezvous. Fatima enjoyed this last form of training the most, what her instructors called *yavka*. She was actually able to arrange *yavkas* with her lover in his apartment. His roommate always found an excuse to be out. They jokingly called it their secret house—*yavotchnaya kvartira*—the GRU's equivalent to Western intelligence services' safe house. He, too, was undergoing further training. The faculty was, of course, aware of these *secret* rendezvous. They were part of the program designed to keep the restless girl settled and happy—for now.

She was frightened by the war in Germany, but the Soviets were victorious, as her fellow students had expected. The training suddenly intensified. They were told that some of them would soon be departing. Her lover came to her one night and sadly told her he was leaving. He was going somewhere far away to do what they had all been prepared for. It pained her, but she knew they all had a duty to perform for their respective peoples.

Two weeks later her instructor–mentor called her to his small office. Her lover, in the performance of his duty to the Kurdish cause, had been captured by rebel Iranian forces in the southeast of Iran, the newly formed Islamic Republic of Kerman. He had been executed, beheaded.

Her lover was actually employed at the Turkestan Military District's GRU Intelligence Directorate's intelligence center, coordinating agent border crossings into Iran. He was unaware of his tragic "demise."

Fatima did not cry. She accepted the pain silently like any Kurd woman. And like any Kurd, she wanted revenge; she pleaded for revenge. An old Kurdish saying went: "If you stand at your door long enough, the bodies of your enemies will be borne past." Fatima had not the patience to wait as long as the old saying suggested. Tinya was ready for the mission the GRU had been planning for her for more than two years.

Captain Kunaev watched scores of men file into the mosque's roofed main courtyard and begin to unroll their prayer rugs in straight rows, side by side. He slid his hand into the special slit under the loose sleeve on his right side. The Czechoslovakian Vz.61 *Skorpion* machine pistol hung against his side on a thin leather sling. Tinya had one similarly concealed. The compact weapons were on safe now, but by merely flicking the selector lever to "20" they would be capable of full automatic fire. In true Czechoslovakian simplicity this indicated that squeezing the trigger would empty the twenty-round magazine at the rate of 750 rounds per minute, or in less than two seconds. The diminutive .32 caliber cartridges were hardly more powerful than a .22 long rifle, but the designers felt that the high degree of muzzle control the low-powered cartridge allowed would enable the weapon to achieve multiple bullet strikes on the target, reasoning that five or six little bullets did more damage than two or three big ones. He had decided to forgo the silencers. The noise would add to the confusion and panic he relied on to aid their escape.

He and Tinya each additionally carried two RGO fragmentation hand grenades and a Makarov PM 9mm pistol, to use if necessary while reloading their Skorpions. He quickly stole a sideways glance at Tinya. She was looking at their target. Her *hijab* (veil) was dropped to one side of her bowed head, revealing her eyes. There was not the slightest sign of emotion on her attractive face. Attractive, yes, and desirable. High cheekbones, full lips, a shapely jaw line. Her sensually rounded hips had not gone without his notice, but there was something about her eyes that bothered Kunaev. When she looked at him, he saw the hard edge of hate. Not for him, but hate did lie half hidden in those gray-green eyes, always searching for something or someone to direct it at. He thought it odd that she had chosen to wear a white mourning headpiece—a nice touch. Kunaev only hoped that the other thirteen men of his strike group were properly positioned to cover their escape.

He made another effort to locate the informant among the men unrolling their prayer rugs. There he was. Kunaev would concentrate his attention on him. If he had betrayed them, it might show in his actions or his expression. If something were to go wrong, the informant would be one of the first to die. Kunaev would see to that. Tinya could take care of the renegade Iranian general, of that, too, he was certain.

Mossadegh entered the roofed courtyard from under the surrounding arcades, decorated with elaborate patterns of molded and carved stucco. He passed his retainers and entered a fenced-off *maksura* (enclosure) originally reserved for the community's leader to protect him from assassination during a time when the blade was the weapon of choice. Near the *maksura* were small decorated niches—*mihrabs*—set in the deep, covered arcades on the mosque's wall facing Mecca, the *kibla* side. The *mihrabs* indicated the direction for the prostrations of canonical prayers.

The worship began. Kunaev bowed with the women. Each prostration included the reciting of prescribed prayers. The worshipers bowed the required four times, touching their foreheads to the disk-shaped tablet on the stone floor and rising after each prostration. The final bow brought the worshipers upright, their eyes closed.

Kunaev and Tinya, as one, smoothly continued to their feet as the imam (prayer leader), standing beside the pulpit with his arms outstretched and facing in the direction of Mecca, began to recite the *shahada*, the confession of faith.

"There is no god but Allah." At the same time, they slowly drew the Skorpions from the slits in their *chadors*. No one had yet noticed. Even the guards' eyes were closed in worship.

". . . and Mohammed is His Messenger!" intoned the imam. In one flowing motion Tinya brought the Skorpion up to eye level, with the wire stock still folded forward, her arms outstretched.

The imam recited the first of two *taslim* (peace greetings). "Peace be upon all of you." Tinya flicked the selector lever to "20."

". . . and the mercy and blessings of God!" There was no hesitation. As they had practiced, both squeezed their triggers as one.

The decorative wood screen shattered, sending varnished splinters across the courtyard. Never releasing the trigger, Tinya followed her target as he scampered across the floor on all fours toward one of the *mihrabs*, until he crashed into the low fencing, already splintered from the stream of bullets. Bits of coarse white cloth leapt from his robe across the broad of his back. Dark blood followed.

Kunaev fired a brief burst at Mossadegh's chief of staff,

who was kneeling to the left and rear of his commander. The man's arms were on his knees, his torso bent slightly forward, exposing the area just under his left arm, opening the way to the heart. The first rounds struck there, and Kunaev allowed the machine pistol's recoil to walk the stream of bullets up the man's neck and side of his head. The carotid artery was punctured, spouting a pulsating stream of blood. Kunaev swung the Skorpion to the right as the man fell on his side, jerking as blood spewed across his white robe.

The others had flattened on the flagstone floor for the most part. A few were scrambling to their feet. He saw one reaching for a pistol. He found his next target lying among those on the floor, his hands clasped over his head. Kunaev centered the sights on the interlaced fingers and again squeezed the trigger emptying the remainder of the magazine. Hair, skull fragments, blood, gray matter, and fingers exploded from the informant's head. Dead men tell no tales, and a traitor could not be trusted anyway.

Tinya dropped the empty Skorpion on its sling and pulled out her pistol. Outside, Soviet assault rifles hammered. The other women were on the floor screaming; most of the men were, too. She started for the door, pulling out her yellow scarf. Kunaev drew his own 9mm and shot the general's bodyguard with the pistol. The man was still looking for a target. Kunaev backed toward the door as Tinya darted through doubled over low, the Skorpion bouncing on its sling. Her pistol hand was thrust forward. She waved the recognition scarf with the other.

She went down on one knee to the right of the door beside one of the two guards felled by the assault rifles fired from across the broad side street. Kunaev pulled out a grenade, yanked the pin with his right thumb, and threw it into the squirming crowd on the floor. Jerking out his own scarf, he bounded over the prone women and through the door. He was just in time to see Tinya blow a hole through a still-twitching guard's neck.

Vicious bitch, he thought. *Ba-wam!* He crouched to the left of the door and whipped the other grenade in. Tracers zipped down the cobblestone street from the far end. His machine-gun team positioned there could take anyone attempting to come around the front corner of the mosque. Two RDG-1 black smoke grenades bounced into the street, thrown by the two-man team Kunaev had stationed in the shop. Tinya threw one of her grenades through the door. *Ba-wam!*, his second grenade exploded inside.

Kunaev was now on both knees, holding his pistol in a two-handed grip and aiming at the door. Tinya reloaded her Skorpion. When she was through, he would reload his weapon while she covered him. *Ba-wam!*, her grenade went off.

A bleeding figure stumbled out the door. Kunaev fired twice at its upper chest from less than a meter. The robed body crashed into Tinya, knocking her against the wall. She hammered viciously with the Skorpion at the dead woman's head as the body rolled limply to the pavement. Recovering herself, she snapped her machine pistol's cocking handle to the rear, chambered a round, and glared across at Kunaev. She is totally consumed with wildness, he thought, and with hate.

"Go!" he screamed. The billowing smoke cloud had developed sufficiently to conceal them. He reloaded his own Skorpion and, crouching low, plunged into the acrid black smoke, giving one last look at the empty door. Several rapid-sharp explosions banged from in front of the mosque, part of his diversion. It suddenly crossed his mind that he had forgotten to bring extra shoes for himself.

Ali Mossadegh did not want to move. His back and shoulders felt as though someone had pounded him with a hammer—hard. His left arm felt lifeless. He knew he had been hit in the shoulder, maybe more than once. The nape of his neck stung. His legs and hips burned with fire from grenade fragments. The American-made Kevlar body armor vest had saved his life, permitting him to continue in the service of Allah on Earth. Men and women cried and moaned. He dared not move more than he had to, except to wiggle the .45 automatic out from under his robe. He heard steps and mumbled words of concern. Hands grasped his body. "He lives!" they shouted. "*Allahu Akhbar!* God is most great!"

As Mossadegh blacked out, his thoughts were of getting his hands on those infidel Russian bastards!

★ 3 ★

"What's up, Pat?" whispered Platoon Sergeant Benjamin Joseph (BJ) Kirkley as he let himself into her room in the BOQ. Captain Pat Paterson waved her hand toward the small refrigerator as she talked into the phone.

"Yeah, you heard right, Sal," she said. "Captain Bradford is no longer my main squeeze. I let myself into his apartment yesterday morning to give him a breakfast surprise."

BJ was peering disappointedly into the fridge, muttering to himself. "Nutin' but diet soft drinks . . . no beer. How does she survive?"

"Wellll," continued Pat, "he was lickin' and stickin', and I don't mean no Green Stamps!"

BJ selected an orange diet soda and wandered over to Pat's desk. Much to his delight, he discovered a small greasy bag of stale French fries. "Now I've got two of the basic food groups," he exclaimed to himself. "Fruits and vegetables—orange soda and fries!"

"No, I don't know what the little slut's name is!" Paterson said, motioning for BJ to take a seat, "Oh, wait, yeah, I do! He said it over and over. Her name is Baby, oh, Baby!"

BJ burped.

"Maybe it's love, honey. I know she respects him, anyway. How do I know she respects him? She kept saying, 'Oh, God, oh, God!' ''

BJ made a gagging sound, pretending to poke a finger down his throat. He picked a catsup packet up off the floor and began to squirt it over the cold fries. Tomatoes are veggies, too, he reasoned.

"Nah, I don't want to get even. Besides, what am I supposed to do, call counterintel and tell them he's passing military secrets to her? They were just talking about the space program when I let myself out." Pat's voice deepened in imitation of her former boyfriend, " 'Yeah,' he said, 'we have ignition!' ''

BJ finished inhaling the fires and tossed the crumpled bag into a wastebasket by the desk.

"It was no big deal, Sal! There's only about three hundred miles of dick on this post!"

BJ immediately held his hands up about two feet apart and gave Pat a questioning look. She shook her head no. He began narrowing the interval in six-inch increments with Pat shaking her head each time. He was down to the length of a finger when she finally nodded yes. BJ displayed a look of mock disappointment.

"No big deal is right!" he scoffed. "I can give you a better deal than that!"

"Yeah, there's someone else here. He's trying to make me a better offer. Remember that weird LRRP sergeant I told you about. Yeah, the one that helped me save Fort Hood when the Russkies hit us. Nah, no way. Besides, he's only an enlisted swine!"

"Just as I thought," groaned BJ, "class prejudice!" He pulled an Army demo knife from its belt carrier, opened the blade, and pretended to slash at his left wrist.

"I've got to go, Sally. This jerk's overcome with grief and's trying to kill himself in my room," Pat said without emotion. "Yeah, when you're hot, you're hot. More than mortal men deserve! Besides, how would I explain it to the MPs? Bye, Sal."

She hung up the phone and peered at her friend through tired, red eyes. "My ass is whipped, babe. We did a twenty-klick march this afternoon." She peeled her thick green socks off and began to rub her right foot. "Our new battalion commander is a real hard ass. Thinks we're infantry instead of military intelligence!"

"My pitter-pat goes heart heart for you," crooned BJ in mock sympathy.

"Yeah, I guess that's nothin' for you long-range recon types. You do that before breakfast, right?"

"Right, but they seldom bother us with breakfast," replied BJ.

"Do you give foot massages, babe?"

"Yeah, and do backs and . . ."

"And fronts, too, no doubt," she interrupted. "The feet will be just fine."

BJ scooted his chair over to Pat and began to slowly work over her right foot with his strong fingers.

"What brings you into civilization, anyway? I haven't seen you in two weeks."

"They gave me and some of the other Selection and Training NCOs a couple of days off," BJ answered. "We've been hittin' it hard."

Pat let her head drop back. "That feels so good it ought to be illegal." She closed her eyes a moment. "I know why you're here, babe. Ol' Pat always has the latest poop, right?"

"Right, Pat. So what's the story?"

"Company G, Long-Range Surveillance, 143rd Infantry, formerly of the Texas Army National Guard, is moving out to Fort Irwin, California, for desert training."

The news didn't faze BJ. "Got any idea when?"

"About a week. You think it's got something to do with that shit goin' down in Iran?"

BJ lowered her leg to the floor and picked up the other. "It sure as hell ain't' to teach us how to build sand castles."

* * *

"Hey, boss, we're moving again," shouted Sergeant Jenna Collingsworth as she breezed through the office door. The six-foot blond tossed her BDU cap onto her desk and bounded into Major Richard "Jinx" Jenkins's small office.

Jinx swung his swivel chair around and dropped the field manual he was reading on his desk. After his long absence, he was still trying to absorb the Army's new doctrine. The three weeks of intense combat in Germany had shown him that he still had a lot to relearn about the Army. It wasn't the same Army he had left in 1974 when he had transferred to the CIA's Paramilitary Branch. The much tabbed and highlighted copy of FM 34-130, *Intelligence Preparation of the Battlefield*, was part of his catch-up effort.

"And we were just getting settled into lovely Fort Bragg," Jinx declared.

Jenna dropped a fax message on his cluttered desk top. "Read it and weep, sir."

"Message number 03-0467, dated 18 March, U.S. Army Special Operations Command (Airborne)," Jinx read out loud. "588th MI Detachment (Special Operations Support) will relocate to Fort Irwin, California, no later than 22 March. Temporary duty status. Movement coordination instructions to follow."

"What's happening out at Fort Irwin, sir?" asked Jenna.

"That's the National Training Center where each tank and mechanized infantry battalion in the states rotates through every eighteen months. They take on an Opposing Forces unit trained and equipped to duplicate a Soviet motorized rifle regiment. They usually get their asses kicked by the OPFOR."

"That's real interesting, sir, but what're we going out there for? To play the part of the GRU? I've always wanted to be a Russian spy," Jenna quipped, pulling a strand of her hair under her nose in an impression of a femme fatale.

"Got no idea, hon. How about stirring up Major New-house? He needs to know so we can get this show on the road."

"I've already sent one of the guys over to JFK Center to round him up. He was going over to their library to do some research," said Jenna. "When's Colonel Taylor going to be back from wherever?"

"MacDill Air Force Base. He's taking the Joint Special Operations Deception Course. He'll be through Friday, so he's going to have to meet us at Irwin," said Jinx. "I'll call him this evening."

Looking at the manual on Jinx's desk, she remarked, "You really take this shit seriously, sir."

"Well, I'm now second in command of this lash-up. I better be able to speak the language!"

Jenna turned to leave but spun around in the door. "That's all desert out there in California, right?"

"Yep, sand and rock. Why."

"Have you been reading the Intelligence Summaries that USASOCOM's been putting out? All the stuff about Iran?" asked Jenna.

"Yes, of course."

"That's all sand and rock, too, right?"

"Most of it."

"I think I'll drop by the PX tonight and pick up some number fifteen sunscreen. It won't do to have this fair skin freckled!"

"Indeed," Jinx told the retreating buck sergeant's finely crafted backside. He picked up the manual again and propped his feet up on the gray metal desk.

Maybe I should have gotten her to pick a tube up for me, he thought.

"Colonel Rutland, sir."

"Ellis, I've some news you're not going to like," boomed Colonel Jason MacKinnon's deep voice over the secure phone. As commander of the 75th Ranger Regi-

ment, MacKinnon was Rutland's boss. Lieutenant Colonel
Ellis Rutland commanded what was left of the 75th Ranger's 3rd Battalion. Both units were at their home station,
Fort Benning, Georgia.

"Yes, sir."

What now, thought Rutland, more OPFOR support for
the Illinois National Guard's 33rd Infantry Brigade? He
was attempting to rebuild his battalion after severe losses
supporting III Corps in Germany. His unit, however, was
in high demand to provide OPFOR elements to act as Soviet Spetsnaz in support of the 33rd Brigade's training in
rear-area security. The Army had learned much in the all
too brief European Campaign, and the need for more effective training of rear battle forces was one lesson they
had learned the hard way.

"I just had a conference call with USASOCOM's Deputy Chief of Staff for Plans, Policies, and Force Management and his counterpart at U.S. Special Operations
Command at MacDill Air Force Base," continued
MacKinnon.

What now? thought Rutland.

"We're going to form a Fourth Ranger Battalion, Ellis!"

Oh, shit, Rutland groaned to himself. He had been a
newly promoted captain in the 1st Ranger Battalion at
Hunter Army Airfield, Georgia, in 1984 when the 3rd Battalion had been formed. Both the long-established 1st and
2nd Battalions had been required to provide cadres for the
new battalion. The resulting turmoil had all but made the
existing battalions nondeployable and threw their training
goals way out of kilter.

"That's certainly good news, sir!" Rutland responded
brightly. Fucking empire builder! he thought. We've been
busting our collective asses for a month and a half to rebuild this outfit and now he's tickled pink that he's going
to get another battalion and screw up all our efforts.

"Ellis, I have your last Unit Status Report before me, but it's not broken down by company."

Here it comes, though Rutland, damn it!

"Which of your companies is most ready to go, personnel and training wise?"

"That would be Bravo Company, sir."

Damn, damn, damn, Rutland bawled mentally. He's going to leave it alone to placate me and pull Rangers out of the other two companies for the new battalion.

"Ellis, we're pulling the entire company along with a company each from the First and Second Bats, plus a cadre from each of the battalion headquarters companies."

That was too much, thought Rutland. "Damn, sir! A whole company! I'm going to have to start over from scratch, and that's going to disable all three battalions!"

"Easy, Ellis! Something big's up. None of the battalions are good to go right now. They were all mauled in Germany. You know that. They want a battalion on-line and ready to go . . . now! They figure this is the best way to throw one together fast." MacKinnon paused. "Ellis, the Joint Chiefs of Staff are in on this. Something big is up," he repeated.

"Yes, sir," sighed Rutland. They were right, you can't fight city hall or regimental headquarters. "When do I release them, and can I tell them where they're going?"

"Movement and permanent change of station orders will arrive tomorrow. They need to be prepared to depart next Monday. That gives you one week, but you need to have an advance detachment ready to go Friday. They're going to Fort Irwin." The colonel paused a moment, "Ellis."

"Yes, sir."

"I was told to nominate my best commander. You're going with them. You're now my Fourth Battalion Commander."

Rutland hesitated the expected moment before answering. "Thank you, sir. I'm honored by your confidence in my abilities. I'll do the best I can."

"I know you will, Ellis," MacKinnon said solemnly.

"Ellis, you know a situation is developing in Iran. I want you to be prepared for a Southwest Asia deployment."

"Yes, sir, I half expected you to say that because of Irwin."

"Well, you've got a lot to do, Ellis. We'll send some expediters over tomorrow to help you get things moving. Be prepared to attend some meetings, Ellis, this is going to be big!"

"Yes, sir, thank you, sir."

Mother of mercy! Ellis whined to himself, Why me! As if Germany wasn't something big! Mother of mercy!

The column of sand camouflaged high-mobility, multi-purpose wheeled vehicles—Humvees and Honda dirt bikes snorted out of the New Mexico desert and up the sand road. The road was little better than a trail. The six specially modified Humvees, called desert mobility vehicular systems—DMVS—were festooned with bundled desert camouflage nets and assorted heavy weapons. They wheeled into a line and parked at two-meter intervals behind the collection of Quonset huts. The four dirt bikes pulled up beside them. The little collection of Second World War huts was one of Ft. Bliss's outlying training camps. The Ft. Bliss main post cantonment area was in Texas, but most of the huge post was actually in New Mexico and abutted the White Sands Missile Range. The three or four soldiers in each of the high-tech vehicles dismounted, carrying their rucksacks, weapons, radios, and other gear. The dust-covered group were clothed in mottled sand-and-brown desert camouflage uniforms, matching boonie hats, face scarfs, and goggles pulled down around their necks so as not to reflect sunlight.

A similarly uniformed captain, canned soft drink in hand, stepped out of one of the old Quonset huts. A sign proclaimed the building to be Headquarters, Company A

(Operational Detachment B-11), 1st Battalion, 5th Special
Forces Group (Airborne).

"Hey, Sam!" shouted the soda-armed officer. "The CO
wants to see you and Andy ASAP."

Captain Samuel Herrion was slapping his hat on his
trousers legs, generating clouds of dust. The other captain,
Andrew Wittwer, caught up with him. "I wonder what
Nutting wants now?" asked Herrion.

"Probably wants to talk to us about that deuce and a
half we ran off the road yesterday," muttered Wittwer. "I
told you that damned air-defense unit would report us.
We're the only outfit on Bliss with desert-painted Hum-
mers."

"Yeah . . . well, let's go face the music," said Herrion. "You got another of those, Frank?" Herrion asked
the captain with the canned drink as they passed him in
the door.

"The CO's got an ice chest of 'em by his desk." He
followed them into the commander's office.

The two captains looked at each other and entered the
dusty company headquarters. Everything here was perpetually dusty, even the chow. To their surprise, all six of
the company's A-team commanders were present.

"Help yourself, guys," said Major Hugh Nutting,
pointing at the sweating ice chest. A pedestal fan hummed
in the corner serving only to keep the hot dry air and the
dust moving.

After the can tops were popped and everyone had taken
a seat, Nutting stood and walked around his desk. Most
of those assembled were expecting the C.O. to present a
training-status report, but instead he said, "We're standing down early, guys."

The seven Green Beret captains looked at one another.
"Day after tomorrow we're going to Fort Irwin. Our
temporary-duty status will remain the same. We're taking
everything with us. The rest of the battalion will join us

there from Fort Campbell, maybe the whole group for all I know.''

He waved his hands at the chorus of questions. When everyone had quieted down he said, ''You all know what's going on. We've been giving you daily updates on the Iran situation. That's our principal mission, that's our part of the world. We've all worked hard to perfect the desert mobility concept. . . .'' He looked around the room, fixing each man with his gaze. ''Now maybe we'll have an opportunity to see if it really works!'' The group of dusty officers chuckled. ''I'll let you know more when I find it out myself, but for now let's get the vehicles cleaned up and ready for transport. We're going to have a bunch of commercial contract flatbeds pick them up on main post Wednesday at 0700 hours. Frank's made up a list of work assignments. Let's do it, guys!''

Considering how battle-fatigued they were and how long the flight back to southern Georgia had taken, the battalion fell into formation sharply enough. Company officers surveyed the troops while sergeants shouted orders. The troops, still in their camouflage battle uniforms, finally stood at attention, their weapons slung over their shoulders, their eyes staring straight ahead.

The only sound, aside from the distant drone of transports, was the unit colors snapping in the brisk Georgia breeze.

Good soldiers, their commander thought. They had all been through much in the course of the short war. They had seen more action than many other soldiers.

''The battalion is formed, Comrade Commander,'' reported Guards Major Serafim Goncharov, saluting.

Guards Lieut. Col. Aleksei Bodnya, hero of the Soviet Union, looked out over his command, the 800th Guards Independent Special-Purpose Battalion.

What is in store for us next? he wondered. He knew that the war was far from over. Where the next phase would be fought, when it would begin, and the form it would take were questions that rolled back and forth through his mind. That his battalion would be committed was a given. He also knew why they fought—to defeat the *glavny rag*. For this reason it was a just war, a peoples' war. How his nation's leadership chose to fight it and their ultimate objectives were no concern of his.

His life, since his early adolescence, had prepared him for his role. His sole purpose in life, as far as the State, the Party, the Armed Forces were concerned, was to accomplish any task assigned him. Bodnya recalled the military oath he had proudly sworn so long ago: "I pledge to defend the Soviet Socialist Republics courageously, skillfully, with dignity and honor, without sparing my blood and life in securing complete victory over the enemies." This he had sworn to do, and this he would do.

He also remembered the passage that spoke of what awaited him if he failed: "If I break this solemn vow, may I be severely punished by the Soviet people, universally hated, and despised by the working people."

He sometimes thought about the dignity and honor phrase. He glanced over at KGB Capt. K. V. Yakushev, his unit's Special Section officer, a master at extracting information from those so unfortunate to fall under his care. Dignity and honor referred only to how effectively Soviet servicemen accomplished their missions and achieved the goals of the State and the Party, not to their personal conduct. His pale-blue eyes scanned the ramrod-straight soldiers.

"Hunters of the 800th Spetsnaz Battalion," Bodnya began, "a new challenge awaits us in our battle against the forces of darkness. You have honored the *Rodina mat*—the motherland. You have honored this unit. You will have ample opportunity to continue to do so in the very near future!" He saluted his soldiers, his little speech over.

"I serve the Soviet Union!" they shouted as a body and followed with three deep, roaring cheers.

"Comrade Chief of Staff," Bodnya said, turning to Major Goncharov, "have the companies unload the unit equipment and assemble it for transport. We will depart in two hours."

"It is done, Comrade Commander!" snapped Goncharov, saluting. He turned and ordered the company commanders to report to him.

Now, if they will only provide us with suitable replacements to make good our losses, he thought. Almost seventy dead and wounded on the last day of the Battle for the Liberation of Germany. They had lost a few more in the two months spent ferreting out renegade West German *Bundeswehr* units and the disorganized resistance movement.

Please make them give us good Russians and Slavics, he prayed, no more *chernozhoph* (black asses) from the Soviet Central Asian republics!

As the company commanders gathered around Goncharov, Bodnya noticed another small cluster forming around a short, mustached individual in the 1st Company. Guards Senior Ensign Pavel Kovpak was motioning toward a stack of five-liter petrol cans on the edge of the concrete apron. The unit would be here only a short time, but Kovpak and his clique of loyal sergeants were already dabbling in the local black market. Petrol was a scarce commodity among the local citizens.

Let them have their little adventure, thought Bodnya, it will serve to keep them out of more serious trouble. They will have plenty of that soon enough.

★ 4 ★

Brigadier General Ronald Galvan watched through the curtains as the crowd of officers filed quietly into Ft. Irwin's new theater.

They're a mixed bunch, he thought. Most were uniformed in BDUs, but one large group wore the desert camouflage colors. Those in the desert camouflage wore green berets bearing the white-edged black flash of the 5th Special Forces Group.

A pity that they removed the colors of the Vietnamese flag from the group's flash, thought Galvan, but that was the post-Vietnam Army for you.

Another group of officers wore the Rangers' black beret. The 4th Ranger Battalion had been thrown together so fast that they still wore the flashes of their former battalions.

Four officers took seats toward the back. Their maroon berets identified them as members of the two long-range surveillance companies. They were new to this collection of special operations forces and probably felt a bit like outsiders, as did another small group clustered together at one side of the room. They, too, wore BDUs, but their berets and badges were different. Two of the officers wore the scarlet berets of the Combat Control Teams, the Air Force's pathfinders. One had an Air Rescue Service maroon beret, another the Air Weather Service's gray beret, and three wore black—Tactical Air Controllers. Most were assigned to the 1724th Special Tactics Squadron at Ft. Bragg, and all were airborne qualified.

Three other officers were removing their Marine "covers," but they weren't Marines. Galvan knew that two of the three were from the Naval Special Warfare Group 1 at Coronado. The other had just arrived from the Philippines to represent Naval Special Warfare Unit 2; an in-theater planning and logistics staff that would support SEAL Team 1. With them sat two Marine officers from the 3rd Surveillance/Recon/Intelligence Group, a new organization supporting III Marine Expeditionary Force.

There were other officers present as well. They represented the various military intelligence, electronic warfare, and engineer detachments that would support the special-ops forces. There were also representatives from the 4th Psychological Operations Group, 95th Civil Affairs Group, 112th Signal Battalion, 528th Support Battalion, all U.S. Army Special Operations Command (USASO-COM) units from Ft. Bragg. All wore airborne maroon berets.

The two reps of the 160th Aviation Regiment (Special Operations) from Ft. Campbell, Kentucky, sat with an officer from the 1st Battalion, 245th Aviation Regiment. The 160th "Night Stalkers" had been badly chewed up in Germany, and most of their units were still in England supporting the 10th SF Group. The 1st of the 245th was an Oklahoma National Guard special-ops aviation unit mobilized to augment the 160th.

The Air Force's 1st Special-Operations Wing (SOW) at Hurlburt Field, Florida, was represented as well. Galvan, in his long Special Forces career, had nothing but admiration for the 1st SOW's gutsy special-ops aircrews. He had worked with them on dozens of exercises and operations. Back in 1983 he had been a liaison officer between XVIII Airborne Corps and the 1st SOW during Operation "Urgent Fury," the Grenada invasion. Galvan had been

in the international airport on Barbados where many of the
supporting Air Force units had staged. The hotshot fighter
pilots had been worried about the air defenses on Grenada.
They were especially worried about surface-to-air missiles
and the possibility of Cuban or even Soviet air interven-
tion.

A lieutenant colonel, sporting jump wings under his
command-pilot wings, had barged into the terminal followed by a small flock of majors and captains, all from
the 1st SOW's 16th Special-Operations Squadron. Galvan
had seen their ugly but dangerous looking AC-130H Specter gunships land earlier. If there was ever a combat aircraft that was vulnerable to modern fighters and missiles,
it was the Pave Specter.

The special-ops pilot had walked up to him, removed
his sunglasses, and offered his hand. ''You the Army liaison guy?''

Galvan, himself then a lieutenant colonel, was just as
informal. ''Sure am, what ya need?''

''Wing said on our orders that we could get rental cars.
There any left? We wanted to do some sight-seeing before
our op tonight.''

That exchange just about summed up the attitude of the
1st SOW's aircrews. Special Forces troopers felt more than
confident when supported by the 1st SOW's many and
varied aircraft. They had performed equally well in Panama in 1989.

Col. Keith McCalla, his deputy commander, caught his
attention. ''It looks like they're all here, sir. Are you
ready?''

''It's show time, Keith. Let's get this dog and pony
show over with.''

McCalla walked confidently onto the stage. Galvan noticed one last detail about his audience. There was not a
single female present. That was unusual in today's Army.
Not even any of the support units were represented by
women. After all these years of working shoulder to shoul-

der with highly competent women, both officer and enlisted, he still felt somehow uncomfortable about women in uniform.

Maybe it's my Hispanic upbringing on my father's side, he thought. Well, you're going to be a long way from San Antonio now, amigo, let's hope we're not getting ourselves into another Alamo.

The unit commanders and operations officers of Galvan's new command ceased their conversations as McCalla strode onto the stage. "Gentlemen, General Galvan, Commander, 5th Special Operations Support Command."

The officers rose and snapped to attention. Galvan walked onto the stage wearing a pressed desert camouflage uniform with a single black star newly sewn on both collars. Over his left breast pocket were the combat infantryman's badge, master jump wings, and scuba diver's badge. A black leather general officer's belt, with its bright gold U.S. coat of arms emblazoned circular buckle, was around the hard flat stomach he had worked long and hard to keep. His spit-shined jump boots had stepped over the still-twitching bodies of many brother officers on his path to this position. He had held the right positions in the right units and agencies as commander, staff, and joint-specialty officer.

It was his performance as the latter that had actually assured him this assignment. He had spent much of his career on the joint duty-assignment list, when he was not attending the requisite advanced studies and Special Forces unit assignments.

The purple haze many officers called it—the mixing of Army green, Air Force sky blue, Navy blue, and Marine forest green. But the "track," the combination of the right "ticket punches" and the required schools, Foreign Area Officer Course, Special-Operations Staff Officer Course, Command and General Staff College, Armed Forces Staff College, and the big plum, National War College, had gotten him his star.

And now here he was, about to command the largest collection of joint special-operations forces ever assembled for a wartime operation. He took his position behind a podium bearing the emblem of 5th Special-Operations Support Command (5th SOSC). "Good morning, gentlemen."

"Good morning, sir," chorused the some seventy plus officers.

"I don't believe that I've ever seen such a collection of bad asses assembled in one place at one time." The assembled special-ops officers chuckled. "I had to assure the theater manager that I'd pay for any damages, so I want you boys to behave yourselves!" More quiet laughter.

"I've asked all the unit commanders, down to company level, to be here today and to bring their operations officers. I want everyone to be fully aware of what we will be asked to do in the very near future." He paused for effect a few moments before continuing.

"You were all briefed last night by Colonel McCalla on the current situation in Iran. Now I'm going to tell you what we're going to do about it." The lights dimmed on cue, and the movie screen glowed with the 5th SOSC emblem, fading into a multicolored map of Southwest Asia, the U.S. Central Command's area of responsibility. The map covered Pakistan, Afghanistan, Iran, the Arabian Peninsula, and Saudi Arabia. To Saudi Arabia's north were Jordan and Iraq—Israel, Lebanon, and Syria were not included in the Command's charter. To the south were the United Arab Emirates, Oman, North and South Yemen, and other small oil-rich countries. Across the Red Sea were Egypt, Sudan, and the civil war- and famine-torn countries of the Horn of Africa, Ethiopia and Somalia.

Raising his right hand, Galvan asked, "How many here have participated in any of the 'Bright Star' or 'Gallant Eagle' exercises?" Most hands went up. He was referring to U.S. Central command's two major semiannual exercises. Bright Star was conducted in odd-numbered years in Egypt and involved major troop deployments to the region. Gallant Eagle took place in even-numbered years at massive Ft. Hunter Liggett, California. It included a large-scale field training exercise by divisions of the XVIII Airborne Corps. At the same time, other Central Command units participated in "Gallant Knight," a supporting command post exercise, at their home stations.

"Well, gentlemen," his dark eyes shot over the audience, "this one is going to be somewhat bigger. We call it 'Gallant Caravan.' Our portion of it, the special-ops portion, is 'Gallant Archer.' "

"If we go, gentlemen, it's initially here." The red dot of his hand-held laser-light pointer fell on Oman's northeast coast. "Most of us'll be airlifted into Sib International Airport, twenty-six kilometers west of Muscat, the capital.

"As most of you are aware, Oman is on extremely good terms with us and the British," Galvan continued. "From there we move to Hazm Number Two, a sultanate of Oman Air Force field just over a hundred kilometers west of Muscat. I'm sorry to report to our blue suiters that there's not much to it, but we already have an engineer unit in place and working to upgrade it. Regardless, this will be our rear-operations base."

The red dot moved up the coast of the Gulf of Oman to the *Ru'us al Jiba*, the rugged Musandam Peninsula flanking the southern entrance to the Persian Gulf, the Strait of Hormuz.

"Though separated from Oman itself by more than one hundred kilometers of the United Arab Emirates, the Musandam Peninsula belongs to Oman. The sultan of Oman's army has reinforced Musandam with a full brigade, and we have a special-operations-capable U.S. Marine expeditionary unit in position in the Gulf of Oman, outside the Persian Gulf. The Marines are prepared to execute a landing *exercise* there if the need arises.

"Our forward-operations base will be at the Khassab Airfield, another Omani Air Force base. It's near the tip of the Musandam Peninsula and has been extensively upgraded with U.S. funding. From Khassab, it's one hundred and twenty kilometers by air to Bandar 'Abbās, Iran, on the north side of the Strait. Before I get to what we're going to do once there, I want to briefly discuss where we fit in to the big picture.''

The slide changed to a confused wiring diagram titled "Command Structure–U.S. Central Command–Operation Gallant Caravan." It was also marked "SECRET-NOFORN"—no foreign dissemination. All the slides carried this designation. Galvan let his shoulders fall into an exaggerated slump, and his head bowed.

"Gentlemen, don't let this plate of worms frighten you. I don't understand it either, but my staff assures me that it's all okay!'' His audience laughed at his effort to keep things on the light side. There would be plenty of time before long to get really serious.

"As you know, our overall headquarters is the U.S. Central Command [USCENTCOM], what used to be known as the Rapid Deployment Force, a unified command joint staff of all four services at MacDill Air Force Base, Florida. Each service contributes its own component, which in the case of the Army is the Third U.S. Army headquartered at Fort McPherson, Georgia. Third Army is set to go. The deputy commander of Forces Command [FORSCOM], who controls all Army units in the states, has put on his second hat as Third Army commander, and his advance headquarters has already deployed to the region.''

Another slide appeared, reversed. Galvan's little red light pointer jumped from box to box. The soft laughter from his audience caused the general to look more closely at the slide. His eyes rolled back in his head as he realized it was backward. A young captain scuttled offstage toward the rear of the theater, headed for the projection booth. A minute later, the screen went dark. The house lights began to come up just as the slide, repositioned, came back up on the screen. The slide was titled "Contingency Structure–Third U.S. Army–Operation Gallant Caravan." Galvan wrestled the irritation off his face and went on.

"If we have to go, four major corp-size commands will eventually fall under Third Army, the XVIII Airborne Corps headquartered at Fort Bragg, North Carolina; III Corps from Fort Hood, Texas; the Marine's III Expeditionary Force; and the British Land Forces–Persian Gulf, which will come directly from England."

The slide changed once again, this time reading "Contingency Structure–Joint Unconventional Warfare Command Central–Operation Gallant Archer." Galvan read it carefully before he turned back to the assembled officers.

"Once deployed, 5th SOSC will form the basis for Joint Unconventional Warfare Command Central [JUWCOMCENT] to control all special-ops forces in the region. This, gentlemen, will not only include all the units represented here today, but certain U.S. follow-on forces plus British and Omani special-ops units." Galvan surveyed his audience to see their reaction. These men were professionals, and they were used to joint service and combined-forces operations with other countries, but he could tell by their sideways glances at one another and a few thumbs-up signs given to friends seated across an aisle, that they knew full well they were about to be a part of the largest special-operations forces effort in history.

The last slide melted away, and a map of Iran with the Persian Gulf to the south replaced it. It was simply marked "Operation Gallant Caravan–Phase I." The young captain returned and sat sheepishly in his cushioned theater seat. Galvan never missed a beat of his briefing.

"The XVIII Airborne Corps will go in first to secure Bandar ʿAbbās and throw out an airhead. They'll be staging out of Saudi Arabia and Oman with the 82nd and 101st Airborne Divisions. The 82nd will jump in to secure an airhead around Bandar ʿAbbās and the 101st will helicopter air assault into Bandar ʿAbbās itself and secure the port. The 10th Mountain Division will be flown in to expand the airhead line. A couple of days later the 24th Mechanized Infantry Division and 194th Armored Brigade will arrive by ship. They've already departed, by the way, and the airborne divisions are now preparing to airlift to the region.

"Elements of the 3rd Marine Division, staging directly from Okinawa, will land at different points on the Iranian coast, Bandar-e Lengeh west of the Strait, Qeshm Island in the strait itself, and Bandar-e Jask east of the Strait. The red dot indicates each landing site. Their convoy is now assembling at Diego Garcia in the Indian Ocean."

"Tactical air support should be plentiful," Galvan continued, nodding toward the Air Force types in the audience. "The 3rd Tactical Fighter wing from Clark Air Base in the Philippines is in the process of deploying to Saudi. The Seventh and Third Fleets have three carrier battle groups and two recently reactivated battleship surface-action groups either in the Indian Ocean or on their way."

Galvan turned and faced his audience, his light pointer held in front of him like a riot baton.

"Now, this is where things get sticky, gentlemen. For years our scenario models for a Soviet incursion into Iran have allowed us two basic options: The so-called northern defense calls for establishing an east–west defense line south of Tehran and north of Kashan. It's anchored on the Zagros Mountains along Iran's western border with Iraq and curves gradually back to the south toward the city of Kerman in eastern Iran." He turned and traced a line on the map with the red dot.

"Soviet forces are advancing out of the Transcaucasus west of the Caspian Sea, Turkistan east of the Caspian, and Afghanistan, just as we long projected in our scenarios. The advantages of the northern defense are that it allows us to meet the Soviets well north of the Strait in terrain with limited maneuver space for them and favorable to us for a defense in depth.

"This option has been denied us by three factors," he explained, ticking off each one with his fingers. "One, the unexpected Iranian invitation to the Soviets to intervene in their civil war, which already places their advanced forces close to the northern defense zone. Two, the fact that the rebelling faction is principally located in the Kerman area and Pakistan border region on our east flank and that they are fighting not only the loyalists, but will fight both us and the Soviets with equal fervor. And three, Congress's refusal to finance the C-17 transport, which would have allowed us to put the required equipment and resupply tonnage into central Iran's small austere airfields. The C-17 could have landed on these, but C-5s and C-141s cannot." His tone reflected his bitterness at Congress's severe budget cuts during the early Nineties. The McDonnell Douglas C-17 jet transport had been an early casualty.

"So, gentlemen, by default and by the combined but uncoordinated actions of our enemies, Iranian, Soviet, and Congressional," Galvan paused for more laughter, "we're forced to adopt the less-desirable southern defense. This requires an overland movement to get our tanks, infantry fighting vehicles, and self-propelled artillery to a defensive line running from the Zagros Mountains along the Persian Gulf coast to the vicinity of Kerman. With hope, we can take Kerman from the rebels, because it's the primary airfield in the forward area. We need it to air land material to sustain the defense. This is another task for the 82nd and the 4th Ranger Battalion."

He heard a faint growl from among the Rangers and grinned. "The southern defense also forces us to deploy on ground that gives the Soviets a wider area of contact and lots of maneuver room, more than in the north. That means we'll have to defend a wider front in less-favorable terrain. It also makes it more difficult to maintain a defense in depth."

Capt. Wally Schultz, commanding officer, Company G,

143rd Infantry, looked at the Air Force major seated next to him. The man's eyelids were drooping, his head was slowly tilting backward, his mouth opening as his head tipped farther and farther back. Schultz smiled. Long briefings with many slides had the same effect on him. The major's head was precariously far back now.

"Third Army has placed a high degree of emphasis on the employment of special-operations forces in order to slow the advance of the Soviet main force, disrupt their rear support, degrade their command and control capabilities, and attack their exposed flanks, we hope, force them to protect those flanks and rear areas by drawing units from the main force. We'll also have to assist with protecting Third Army's own exposed east flank from the rebel forces. In effect, we're to be used as combat multipliers, enabling our maneuver forces to conduct a more effective defense. It's a tall order, gentlemen, but I know we're up to it."

This little impromptu pep talk was answered by applause and some shouted hurrahs from the Rangers.

The slide again changed, showing the same map, but this one depicted an established southern defense line and broad blue broken-lines arrows lancing north.

"Phase II begins with the arrival of III Corps by fast sea lift. The Corps's 4th and 5th Mechanized Infantry Divisions and 2nd Armored Division will counterattack the Soviets at the most advantageous point." Many of the officers were looking at one another. Galvan could see some mouthing "Three Corps?"

"I'd better take a moment and explain what's happened to the Army's structure since Germany, gentlemen. I see a number of perplexed expressions out there." He paused a moment. It's not easy to talk about your own army's defeat, especially on the eve of an extremely difficult and risky operation of this magnitude.

"As we all know, III Corps was badly mauled in Germany, as were V and VII Corps. Two of III Corps divisions that are slated for Iran were not deployed to Germany. The 2nd Armored was, but it's been rebuilt, literally by pulling equipment, troops, and even entire battalions from other divisions. Five Corps is now back in the states and is undergoing reconstitution. Seven Corps is still in England as part of our defense agreement with the British. One Corps up at Fort Lewis, Washington, can't be touched. They're strictly reserved for Korea, and North Korea is rattling its sabers loudly. For these reasons, III Corps has been selected as our heavy corps for this little exercise.'' He again scanned the audience, which had settled down.

Any second now, Schultz thought. The major's head was tipped all the way back, his mouth hanging open. He was right. A few seconds later, the major's head dropped backward and his neck cracked like a set of knuckles. The major, suddenly awake, gasped, ''Jesus!'' and grabbed the back of his head and pulled it forward, massaging his neck with his fingertips and grimacing. Schultz stifled a laugh. The major looked over at him, a sheepish look replacing the grimace. He shook his head, and Schultz smiled and nodded. Onstage, the lecture went on.

''Arriving the same time as III Corps will be III Expeditionary Force's other division, the 1st Marine Division from Camp Pendleton, California. We hope for them to execute a landing somewhere on the Persian Gulf shore farther up the coast from our western flank, perhaps at Bushire. They'll either draw off enemy forces or, failing to attract that sort of attention, will move inland and cut the westernmost highway running through the Zagros. Also arriving, by airlift, will be the National Guard's 29th Light Infantry Division. They'll permit the release of the 24th Mechanized for more offensive actions.

''There is one other principal land force I wish to address—British Land Forces–Persian Gulf [BLF–PG]. This is a plum we had never counted on in past exercise scenarios, an operational reserve. The BLF–PG is now preparing for sea lift to Oman where they will remain until needed by Third Army to counterattack a Soviet breakthrough or exploit an operational opportunity. They're composed of two provisional divisions, the 6th and 7th Infantry with two brigades each. The 6th has 1 Infantry Brigade and 12 Armored Brigade. The 7th is made up of 5 Airborne Brigade and 19 Airmobile Brigade. Reserved for attachment to either division as needed is 3 Commando Brigade, Royal Marines; or it can perform independent operations in support of III Marine Expeditionary Force. We were able to get this substantial force because we agreed to maintain VII Corps in the U.K.

"Now, what's in store for us? Well, of course we can't go into too many details about one another's missions, but I do want to give you an overview." The screen reverted to a modified southern defense map. It was divided into unconventional warfare operational areas (UWOAs).

Everyone was seriously quiet now. Wally Schultz looked around to see if his ops officer was asleep. Captain Ranwanz was awake, leaning forward to get the only really important information in the briefing.

"The 5th SF Group has four principal missions: One, execute direct-actions missions against enemy forces advancing on the main highways running from the northwest and into our defenses, especially on our western flank in the mountains. Two, deep direct-action and reconnaissance missions in the enemy's rear areas. Three, direct-action missions against the rebel forces on our east flank. And four, establishing contact with and jointly conducting operations with certain indigenous ethnic minority groups. Additionally, you'll be involved in various recovery operations.

"The 4th Ranger Bat will be assigned some particularly nasty missions to eliminate selected critical targets. That's all that needs to be said for now. Our two long-range surveillance companies will operate well forward of the Front Line of Own Troops [FLOT] in order to provide early warning on the routes the enemy is using and their composition, plus acquire targets for air interdiction.''

Schultz nodded. Nothing too bizarre so far.

''Naval Special Warfare Group 1 has a full schedule of Iranian naval targets on and off the coast as well as support for the Marine's amphibious operations. I believe there are some more oil rigs being used for military purposes that need removal.'' He was referring to retaliatory strikes made on Iranian military oil rigs back in 1987 and 1988. ''The 1st SOW will have a full agenda supporting these operations in many ways. We're all counting heavily on our blue-suit friends.'' Galvan handed the pointer to an aide and stood center stage.

''That's it in a nutshell, gentlemen. I do not need to tell you that the Strait of Hormuz is the fulcrum of the region. It is the single most important choke point in the world. Almost thirty percent of the free world's oil consumption passes through the Strait. The danger is simple, gentlemen. If we're not there, the Soviets will be.''

Schultz stopped outside the theater's main entrance and looked at Capt. Chuck Ranwanz, his operations officer. A pair of sleek Blackhawk helicopters roared over. Their counterparts from Company H, 122th Infantry of the Georgia National Guard joined them. They were XVIII Airborne Corps's long-range surveillance (LRS) unit.

''Is this some shit or what?'' Ranwanz asked the other three LRS officers in his soft Southern accent.

''Yeah, it's a big deal,'' mumbled Schultz. The other officers only nodded. Their unit, the most recently formed LRS company, had yet to see combat. ''It's almost as big a deal as Germany. What bothers me is we had an established logistics structure there. Where we're going, halfway around the world, we don't have diddly shit!''

The two Company H officers looked sobered by that observation. ''Well, at least we don't have to worry about any of our so-called allies wimping out on us this time,''

remarked the Company H ops officer. The West German
surrender had been a bitter pill indeed.

"You have some friendly advice?" asked the Company
H C.O. Schultz could see the man wanted to talk, to maybe
get a little encouragement.

"Yeah. Meet you guys at the officers' club at 1900
hours?"

"Sounds good to us. We need to get back to the company area and alert the troops." The four LRS officers
darted across the dusty blacktop just ahead of a company
of Rangers that trotted up the street, blocking the way.
Outfitted in new desert camouflage, their white sidewall
haircuts evident even under their helmets, the Rangers were
chanting something about living a life of danger.

★ 5 ★

"What're we waitin' for, Beej?" grumbled staff Sgt. Norm Sterling, one of the 2nd Platoon's six recon team leaders. "We jumped through our ass to get over here, and now we're sitting around on our butts!"

"Hurry up and wait," reminded one of the prone scouts without removing the desert camouflage floppy hat covering his eyes.

"There it is, man," muttered PFC Tyrone King. The big black man sat up and repositioned the gray and green rucksack he'd been using as a pillow.

"We're waitin' for a ride, guys," responded BJ, "like we've been doin' for the last week an' a half."

BJ's 2nd Platoon was sprawled under the shadow of a C-130's wings. Like the LRRPs, the transport wasn't going anywhere. Due to a failed fuel pump, it sat parked on the edge of a packed earth parking area. Darab airfield was only a secondary dirt strip 250 kilometers northwest of Bandar 'Abbās. In the distance, through the clouds of dust whipped up by scores of aircraft landings and takeoffs, they could see the 10,400-foot Kuh-i-Qibla Mountain, the highest in the area. The airfield was a hive of activity. C-130 Hercules transports landed and took off constantly. Helicopters rushed in and out. Mountains of pallets stacked with ammunition contain-

51

ers, ration cases, spare-parts boxes, and all sorts of general supplies, rivaling Kuh-i-Qibla, were situated on every level space not needed by aircraft or trucks. Desert-camouflaged trucks ran back and forth, stirring up still more dust.

Everybody seemed to be doing something, BJ thought, everybody but us.

"Hey, Beej!''called Tom Estes, an assistant team leader. "What ever happened to that Simon Rusty guy?"

"Simon who?" asked BJ, turning around to face Estes as he tried to remember if it was someone who had been in the unit.

"Simon Rusty or Rosty or somethin'. That guy that Khomeini wanted offed because of the book he wrote."

"Salman Rushdie," said Norm Sterling. "Khomeini sentenced him to death for blaspheming Islam in *The Satanic Verses* on February fourteenth, 1989."

"How did you remember the date?" some faceless body asked from under his hat. "That was a long time ago."

"It was Saint Valentine's Day," muttered Sterling. "Just stuck in my head."

"Well, what happened to him?" Estes asked again. "The rag heads ever nail him?"

"The last I heard he was in England and had an SAS bodyguard," responded another body from behind a rucksack.

"Man, I'd sure hate to have every Muslim in the world after my hide," contemplated King.

"Every Muslim in the world *is* after your hide, dumb ass," gently reminded one of the scouts.

"Who knows," said BJ. "He just dropped out of sight. Besides, the Iranians have more pressing concerns at the moment." This was greeted with several snorts and chuckles.

"Hey, BJ." It was King.

"Yeah."

"Who has long blond hair, big boobs, and lives in Sweden?"

"I don't know. Who?" asked BJ.

"Salman Rushdie."

It was a second or two before the entire platoon burst out laughing.

Company G, 143rd Infantry's odyssey had begun when the long-range surveillance unit's 200 troops, sixteen assorted vehicles, CONEX cargo containers, and pallets of rucksacks and duffel bags were flown out of Travis Air Force Base, California, by a series of C-141 Starlifters. After numerous refueling stops across the Pacific, they finally arrived at Sib International Airport in Oman.

After two days in Oman, a quartering party, 1st Platoon, the Communications Platoon, and an element from the Operations and Intelligence Section (O&I) were flown to Khassab Airfield on the tip of the Musandam Peninsula. The recon teams passed the time practicing immediate-action drills and acclimatizing themselves by "exposure to the elements," as Master Sergeant Hagger, the Ops NCO put it.

Everyone believed that 1st Platoon was in isolation and preparing for a mission. Another day passed before the remainder of the company was lifted to Khassab. No one was surprised that 1st Platoon was not there to greet them, The TOC (Tactical Operations Center) and Commo Center seemed active, though. The TOC and Comm Center were in the operations area, along with the isolation facility, which was, in this case, a collection of dusty hexagon-shaped "GP smalls" (tent, general purpose, small).

Unless you had business there, it was all off limits. The isolation facility was where each recon team was cloistered away to plan its mission. The only people who could have contact with a team in isolation were the O&I Section members, the team's platoon leader and platoon sergeant (simply to aid them in obtaining supplies and other admin-

istrative matters), and selected individuals from the
Commo Platoon. The teams did not talk to anyone about
their mission, especially not to the other teams. The fewer
people who knew the mission's details, the better for all
concerned. Even the company commander had limited access to the teams once they entered isolation.

BJ's 2nd Platoon had expected to go into isolation as
soon as they arrived. Instead they sat sweating while waiting for something to happen. At least they had cots, a
luxury unavailable at Sib International. They were also
quartered behind some hills away from the airfield, insulating them from the constant aircraft noise. Team training
continued as always.

The word was passed their first night at Khassab that
they were restricted to the billeting area. Before dawn, a
continuous stream of C-130s lumbered in and out of the
airfield. The flights lasted all day. Before long, the LRRPs
had made several unsanctioned recon missions in the hills
overlooking the airfield. The recon teams observed hundreds of troops debark from the transports and assemble
into helicopter-size loads. Through their twenty-power
spotting scope, BJ's men could make out the Screaming
Eagle shoulder patch of the 101st Airborne Division. In
the afternoon, clouds of helicopters arrived. Like organized ants, the desert-camouflaged air-assault troops
boarded the UH-60s and CH-47s.

The sticks of helicopters would take off together, assemble into long lines, and head north, dropping low over the
waters of the Strait. Activity continued through the night
at the same tempo. Flights of choppers would return to
pick up more troops as transports continued to roar into
the field. The sound of aircraft turbines was incessant.
Sometimes they heard jets overhead, and occasionally a
flash was seen over the hills to the north, out in the Gulf.

On the morning of the third day, Company G was roused
out before daybreak. The tents were struck, equipment
packed, and vehicles loaded. The word spread fast they

were going into Iran. Another quartering party and two of the Commo Platoon's two-vehicle base radio stations were flown out first. They had to be up and running in order to maintain contact with the committed recon teams. Most of the Headquarters Platoon and 3rd Platoon went out before noon. The 2nd Platoon found itself again waiting beside the airstrip. That did have its advantages. More troops, mostly support units of the 101st, were being lifted in from Oman. Some of the LRRPs managed to mingle with them, and the word soon spread about events in Iran.

Two full brigades of the 82nd Airborne Division, the "All Americans," had executed a mass parachute jump to establish an outer perimeter outside of Bandar 'Abbās. The night drop had cut off the main roads into the port city while the 101st Airborne conducted an air-assault operation into landing zones on the outskirts of the city. The 101st had lost a lot of helicopters. Shot-up UH-60 Blackhawks and CH-47D Chinooks were being repaired by maintenance crews on one side of the airfield. The 82nd Airborne's other brigade had been airlifted in at dawn.

The 2nd Platoon had been flown over late that afternoon. The troops took turns peering out the few windows at the waters of the Strait 1,000 feet below. The bluer-than-blue water reflected flecks of golden sunlight, a welcome relief from drab rocks and dust. The plane flew over a few ships, the troops excitedly calling out the few types they recognized. Those at the windows all shouted a thunderous "AIRBORNE!" as the plane's shadow crossed Iran's rugged shoreline. They quieted down considerably when they saw just how rugged the mountains were.

"Good morning, Major Jenkins. We've been going over your 201 file."

Uh oh, Jinx thought, whenever they start going over your records, you know you're in trouble.

"You seem to have a great deal of experience working as a military adviser with indigenous peoples."

"Yes, sir," Jinx answered, "that's what the agency's paramilitary section does."

The colonel with the red arrowhead and black dagger USASOCOM patch smiled. His expression seemed to Jinx to be a mixture of amusement and frustration. The Active Army seemed to rediscover unconventional warfare about once a decade. This time it was called SO/LIC—Special Operations/Low-Intensity Conflict. Recalling what special-ops forces had accomplished in Panama, Jinx wondered, low intensity for whom? Outside the converted warehouse still another C-130 touched down on the dusty Hazm Number 2 strip in northern Oman.

"Your experience and your availability seem to make you the ideal candidate for a special operation we have in mind."

Jinx's heart skipped a beat, and that old feeling came back, that excited, nervous, disemboweled, abandon-hope-all-ye-who-enter-here feeling. He got that feeling every time someone unveiled a new operation—or concept.

A lieutenant unrolled a large map and pinned it on the easel. Jinx reflected how odd it was to see an SF lieutenant; they must be getting shorthanded, but, then, he was here, too. The map was a composite of three map sheets covering the area southwest of the Caspian Sea, including western Iran, eastern Iraq, eastern Turkey, and the Soviet republics of Armenia and Azerbaijan. The lieutenant then unrolled an acetate overlay and taped it to the map.

"The operation is called Mustafa," the colonel said, moving over to the map. "Simply put, it is to establish contact with a group of Kurdish nationals that live about here." He pointed to a valley in western Iran near Bakhtaran.

A captain took up the lecture, "The group is a relatively new force. They are led by one Mohammad Ahmad. Unlike many of the Kurdish groups, Ahmad's group is not aligned with either side. They seem to be autonomous and concerned only with the establishment of a Kurdish nation that would include parts of eastern Iraq, western Iran, and a piece of eastern Turkey.''

The colonel looked at Jinx, waiting for questions. Jinx continued to stare at the map. Because there were no questions, the colonel went on.

"Ahmad is a traditionalist. He calls his group the *Hamawand,* the Wolves of Kurdistan. There is an explanation of that name in your background packet. Ahmad is a proud, charismatic leader. His troops seem to be dedicated, and their lack of affiliation makes them very attractive as an insurgency force behind the Soviet lines. Our preliminary contact with them has been positive.''

"Thank you, Captain. Jenkins, we want you to work with these Kurds, arm them, and advise them in fighting the Iranians and the Soviets.''

"Sir, isn't this more a job for an SF A-team?'' Jinx interrupted.

The colonel looked over at the lieutenant, who answered, "Usually, sir, yes, but this fellow Ahmad would not permit an entire team, at least not initially. He wants weapons and ammunition but no foreign personnel. He said he would let one man come to show his people how to fire the weapons.''

"What weapons does he want?'' Jinx asked. The butter bar must be somebody's nephew, they're even letting him speak.

"The usual high-tech stuff. Stingers, TOWs, cruise missiles.''

The whole group chuckled at the captain's joke, although there was much truth to it.

"Anyway, we have arranged to send one man to show them the equipment and persuade him to accept an A-team. You will be brought up to speed on the weapons, and we have an interpreter who will accompany you.''

Once more into the breach, dear friend, Jinx thought, and fill it up with your unknown dead. The feeling in his guts was strong now, almost a knot right up under his diaphragm.

"How many of them are there in this group?" Jinx asked.

"Unknown," the captain answered. "We think about five hundred."

Jinx nodded. About a battalion.

"They're armed with a hodgepodge of weapons, mostly Soviet rifles and machine guns, some RPGs, and a few small arms of western European origin."

"That doesn't surprise me somehow," muttered Jinx. "For all the Europeans talk of peaceful coexistence, they're awfully fast to turn a franc or mark in Middle East weapons deals."

The captain smiled, "The Kurds are excellent mountain fighters and pretty good horse cavalry."

"Horse cavalry?" Jinx asked.

"The terrain around their area is mountainous, and distances are great, horses and mules have always been the primary means of transportation in the region."

Jinx nodded. This was not the first time he had worked with horse troops.

"Jenkins, Captain Ramke will work with you on your preparations. Consider yourself in isolation as of 1600 hours this afternoon."

The colonel stood and shook Jinx's hand. "Good luck!"

The brass all gathered up their papers, put them in their briefcases, and left. The captain remained.

"Why don't you gather up your stuff, sir, and meet me back here at 1600?" the captain suggested.

"Right," Jinx replied. "See you then."

Well, so much for the new action Army, Jinx mused as he walked back to his quarters. Looks like I'm back at the same old stand.

"So what's cookin'?" Jenna asked, never looking up from her typewriter as Jinx trudged into the TOC tent. The

TOC was empty except for Jenna, the others were probably at chow.

"Looks like I'm off to B. F. Iran," Jinx answered, "and I don't mean Inspect and Repair As Necessary." When he answered, Jenna's face changed to a look that Jinx had not seen before, a look of concern and maybe something else.

"To do what?" she asked, her voice echoing the concern on her face.

"To liberate the oppressed Kurds and show them how to visit destruction on their enemies."

Jenna kicked the chair back from the typewriter and stood up. "I want to go!" Jinx laughed, then stifled it when he saw she was serious.

"Sorry, dear heart, this is a solo trip," Jinx said, matching the seriousness of his answer to hers. "Besides, you wouldn't be able to teach these Kurd guys anything."

"The hell I couldn't," she barked. "I know as much about weapons as anybody!"

"That's not what I meant, Jenna," Jinx answered. "I mean that these guys are serious Muslim chauvinists. They would never pay any attention to anything a woman said, especially a blond, white woman who was a foot taller than them." Jenna looked hurt and resentful.

"Hell, they may not listen to me," Jinx added. "I'm a foreigner and a nonbeliever."

"Male chauvinists!" she mumbled in disgust and peered hard at Jinx. "You know, my sister just had a baby."

"I didn't know you had a sister," said Jinx, surprised at the sudden change of subject. Maybe the girl wasn't taking this too well.

"Yeah, they don't know what sex it is. It has a dick *and* a brain!"

Jinx didn't know whether to laugh or try to stay serious. She sank back into the chair and slumped forward on the desk, holding her head in her hands. "Rats! So when do you take off?"

"This afternoon."

"Jesus," she blurted, "what's the hurry?"

"They want to make sure I know what' I'm doing with the weapons they're sending. Stingers and so forth."

Jenna didn't say anything for a second, but sat staring out the door, annoyance flickering across her face. She finally looked up and stood and walked around the desk.

To Jinx's great surprise, she took his hand in both of hers and squeezed it. "You be careful, now, hear?" she said, her voice strained. Her bright eyes seemed unusually wet.

Jinx squeezed her hands and touched her face. "Hey, don't worry about me. I'm too ornery to kill!"

She laughed, regaining her usual perky self. "That's true!"

Jinx suddenly felt very uncomfortable. The morning before mission isolation was no time to try to put a relationship on a different level, even during a war. Hell, especially during a war!

"Well, I gotta gather up my stuff," Jinx said, lamely looking for a way to get out gracefully. "I'll stop back before I take off."

"You better!" Jenna said, turning back to her typing. As he left the TOC, Jinx thought he saw her wiping her eyes.

Christ, he thought as he crossed the dusty unit area to his tent, that's the one thing I don't need right now, romantic involvement, and with someone half my age!

Senior Lieut. Yan Babikov surveyed his other nine T-80 tanks from the hatch of his own, which was already loaded on the ChZAP-524G tank transporter towed by a huge MAZ-537 tractor in various stages of on loading. None of the frantically working tankers dared look in his direction for fear of attracting his attention—and wrath. Babikov ruled his subunit rather than commanded it. His tank crewmen did not call him the Little Führer and his tank company Babikov's Panzer Division for no reason.

The one man in the company who did not fear his commander's ceaseless raging trotted across the churned-dust ground and climbed onto the transporter and up the tank's side. Saluting, Senior Lieutenant Petrovich, the company's deputy commander for technical affairs, laid the clipboard with its attached repair authorization form in front of Babikov.

"Comrade Commander," the maintenance officer shouted over the roar of the thousand-horsepower gas-turbine engines, "the cracked road wheel has been replaced on tank 532."

"Have all tank crews completed their technical service inspections?" asked Babikov, never taking his eyes off his subunit's activities.

"Exactly so, Comrade Commander."

"What is the status of tank 537's gun stabilization controls?" Babikov glanced down only long enough to sprawl his name in the upper right corner, approving the authorization form. Petrovich had already signed his name at the bottom authorizing the action.

"Operational, Comrade Commander."

The tank battalion had covered just a little more than 160 kilometers in the past ten hours. The asphalt road, suffering from the passing of countless combat vehicles, had inflicted its own damage on their tanks and the crews. Now they were loading onto the massive transporters for another ten hours of travel, but they would cover more than twice the distance. With hope, this shuttling of units would allow defects and equipment failures to appear and be corrected prior to engaging the enemy. The long hauls in the transporters would also give the crews and tanks a rest. The crewmen would sleep in the transporter's crew cab. The crew would rotate manning the turret-mounted antiaircraft machine gun. It was still a long way to Shiraz. Beyond that southern Iran city were the Americans.

The on-loading site was an oasis of logistical support. The tanks were refueled a company at a time at the TAPZ-755 fuel distribution point. The regimental maintenance company operated a technical inspection and repair point. Medics were on hand to care for any minor injuries and illnesses. A PAK-200 field kitchen turned out hundreds of liters of pressure-cooked *kasha*, an undistinguished thick, hot soup of meat, fat, and vegetables supplemented by rye bread. Soldiers, too, needed fuel.

A sand-painted T-80 snorted its way up a transporter's rear ramps in reverse, its turret turned to the rear. A black-uniformed soldier in front of the tank rapidly waved his left arm up and down, signaling the driver to halt. The tank's treads were misaligned with the ramps. He then motioned the tank forward with his right arm. Try it again.

"Five-three-nine! Who is driving that tank?" snapped Babikov.

"Reserve Lieutenant Prokopyuk, Comrade Commander!" responded Petrovich. "He is loading all of his platoon's tanks himself, he does not trust his driver-mechanics!"

"That I can understand, Comrade, but can we trust him?" Babikov made a quick notation in his ever-present black notebook. "He is no more experienced than the rest of these reservists!"

"Just so, Comrade Commander!" agreed Petrovich. "We have trained them well enough in maintenance in the time permitted," he quickly added. He knew Babikov believed there was never enough maintenance training. "What I am concerned with is the limited time we had to practice gunnery and battle drills."

Tank 539 made another effort to mount the transporter. Babikov turned from watching its stuggle. "I thought I would never hear worries about gunnery skills from my technical-affairs officer."

Petrovich suddenly felt he had made a tactical error. The Little Führer was a maintenance zealot.

Babikov saw the anxiety in the officer's face. "Never mind, Petrovich. Your concerns mirror my own. Our tanks may operate at full capability when we meet the Americans, but let us hope we can hit them!" He again turned his attention to Lieutenant Prokopyuk's tank as his 2nd Platoon leader again attempted to load the vehicle. "When these reservists were on active service a few years ago, they trained on old T-64 tanks."

"Exactly so, Comrade Commander."

"Tell me, Petrovich," Babikov turned to his maintenance officer, "what are the similarities between the T-64 and the T-80?"

"They possess essentially the same driver and fire controls. The guns operate the same. Even the fuel filler caps and maintenance access panels are in the same positons."

"And what are the differences?"

"The T-80 itself is greatly improved in many small details, but the engine is the greatest improvement along with the capability to fire the AT-8 antitank guided missile from the main gun."

"So I do not see the source of your concerns," Babikov replied.

"Exactly so, Comrade Commander. I am certain you are correct and my fears are groundless." But, thought Petrovich, gunnery skills and crew coordination have deteriorated over those intervening years. Time will no doubt tell all.

Tank 539 successfully jerked its way onto its transporter followed by the crewmen to secure the anchor chains. High overhead, the thin white threads of jet contrails embroidered a delicate lace against the blue sky.

"What the fuck is this? A paid vacation?" shouted the irritating voice.

"Shit," muttered one of the relaxing LRRPs under his breath, "it's Mr. Sunshine!"

"What the fuck's going on here, Sergeant Kirkley? What are all these misfits doing laying on their asses?" shouted the voice.

BJ turned down the page of his book, slid the slim paperback, *Death Commandos #33, Massacre in Manila*, into the leg pocket of his BDU, and looked up at his platoon leader, 2nd Lieut. Glen Tippard.

The lieutenant's lips were twisted into a thin, tight line, a habit he displayed when angry. Since his assignment to Company G, he had been perpetually angry, hence his nickname, Lieutenant Tightlip.

The rest of the platoon ignored the lieutenant, which seemed to infuriate him even more. He opened his mouth to shout them all to their feet. "On your . . ."

"Now, sir," said BJ, jumping to his feet, "I need to talk to you about somethin' important." He flipped his desert hat onto his head and walked slowly toward the aircraft's nose, sticking his hands deeply into his pockets. The lieutenant followed in a huff.

BJ had learned early in his career as an NCO that one could say pretty much anything to a junior officer, even use strong language, so long as a few "sirs" were thrown in and the officer was not embarrassed in front of the troops or other officers. You could do the same with senior officers, but you had to smile a lot more.

Lieutenant Tightlip had been assigned to Company G while they were at Ft. Hood. He was considered by the older hands to be a throwback to some of the officers the unit had endured in the late Eighties. He had come straight out of the Officer Candidate School and Infantry Officer's Basic Course at Ft. Benning, Georgia, referred to by NCOs as the Ft. Begining School for Boys.

Not that they were not good officers; in fact, most of them were good. But, as with any group, there were some bad ones and they were a real problem. Not bad because of incompetence, corruption, or other serious faults, but, well, just dickheads.

Too many of the junior officers were eaten up with the macho image. Their solution for any problem was to come on like a hard ass. They were more concerned about physical training than tactical proficiency. They tended to lose sight, if they had it to begin with, of the mission. They seldom stepped back and listened to cooler, more experienced heads. They knew it all. In recent years another problem had developed. Too many of the new officers acted like yuppies, for Christ's sake! Sergeant Hagger had wanted to remove lieutenants from the unit's TOE—table of organization and equipment—but he reasoned that they had to start off somewhere.

Lieutenant Tippard had reported to the Company with a Ranger-style white sidewall haircut. He was appalled that no one else in the unit had the same. Captain Ranwanz had taken the young shavetail aside and told him to let his hair grow. The Ranger white sidewall haircut was inappropriate for an LRRP unit, an OPSEC—operational security violation. It waved a flag that the unit was different, special. LRRPs needed to keep a low profile.

Tippard had gone immediately to the commander. "Sir, Captain Ranwanz just told me my hair was too short and to let it grow out! Can he do that?"

Captain Schultz again explained the rationale behind the rule and added, "Besides, you'll probably pick up more girls if you have a normal haircut."

BJ would try the subtle approach first in his effort to put the lieutenant on the right tack.

"God damn it, sir, what the fuck are you tryin' to do?"

Tippard's mouth was not quite hanging open, yet.

"We've spent years trying to make this unit into what it is! Most of these guys have been through some real shit in Germany! The newer ones made it through a hellish selection and training program. Only about forty percent that tried out for this unit made it. And now you come along and try your best to fuck it up—sir!'' BJ was pissed now.

Tippard defensively crosses his arms, a real sign of weakness. He would have been better off placing his hands on his hips, but not by much. ''Sergeant, I feel those troops' time could be better spent preparing for the mission!''

Always let them have their say, BJ thought, but not for too long.

''Don't *sergeant* me, sir!'' BJ shot back. ''They've been busting their asses ever since we hit the ground in Oman. Let 'em relax a little. I can assure you they'll get a good workout soon enough!'' BJ eyed the officer. ''That's not the problem, sir,'' he went on, slipping into a calmer tone. That always gave the officer the mistaken impression that you were willing to negotiate or that you were actually a rational person. ''An LRRP unit expects its troops to operate in small, independent teams. They're entrusted with crucial missions and expected to make critical decisions on the ground. You don't jack with them! You don't treat them like recruits! And this ain't the Goddamned Ranger School, sir!'' BJ took a breath. Christ, was he preaching or what!

''Well, look, BJ . . .'' began Tippard, dropping his arms to his sides—they usually avoided the ''sergeant'' crap after an outburst—''I only wanted to . . .''

''That's okay, sir,'' BJ interrupted. Always stop them from making excuses or apologizing, especially apologizing. You never wanted them to think you had accepted an apology. You didn't want them to make excuses either. That tended to affect their self-esteem when they thought about it later. Besides, there were other ways to get rid of a troublesome lieutenant.

BJ slipped into the ''we'' form of address. He was at the point that he now wanted the officer to feel that he really did support him, that they really were on the same team. It prevented the officer from becoming too alienated.

"Sir, we've got to treat these guys like responsible individuals all the time. Not just when they're out there on a mission. All the fuckin' time! We've got to show we trust them, show 'em we have confidence in 'em, all the fuckin' time, sir! All the fuckin' time!"

"Yes, I see what you mean, BJ, it's just that I'm not used to a unit like this," Tippard said earnestly.

Shit, thought BJ, there he goes again. What a wimp!

"Having just come out of OCS, well, it's an entirely different environment, you know," said Tippard. "I'd expected to be more involved when I found I had orders for an LRRP unit. I'd thought that it was more like a Ranger unit."

Yeah, thought BJ, that's the problem, everyone thinks that about special-ops units. Lance missile units and 105mm batteries are both artillery, but they're different, too.

"Anyway," continued Tippard, "it was a shock that the platoon leaders never went on missions, that all we did was the paperwork."

"Well, that's the nature of the game, sir," said BJ. "The teams have got to do their own thing, and guys like you and me have to do ours, which is support them."

Now you can end the conversation on a mellow note, BJ thought, establishing the "we're in this together" attitude.

"Look, sir, you're doin' okay, sir." *Liar, liar, pants are on fire!* BJ thought, recalling the line from the old kids' song. "Just stick with me, listen to the other NCOs, and you'll do just fine!"

BJ had been slowly walking the lieutenant away from the C-130. That way when he turned to go back to the platoon, the lieutenant would most likely keep going in the direction he had pointed him and maybe even find something constructive to do. This was easier to do if there was a group of other lieutenants clustered somewhere. He probably would have gone over to them, but, unfortunately, there were none. There wasn't even an officers' club to point him at.

"Now I'm goin' back and make sure the guys have their shit packed and are all set to go when we get the word, sir."

"That sounds good, Sergeant," said a more self-assured Tippard. "I'll go and check at airfield operations if there's any word on our transport. I'll let you know if I find out anything."

"Yes, sir, we'd appreciate that. See you later, sir!"

Yes, go forth my child. Christ! Like fuckin' putty in my hands! thought BJ. Fucker would choke on his own spit!

"Oh, Sergeant Kirkley," the lieutenant called, "I almost forgot what I came to tell you! Get the men ready to move out. We have new orders coming in, something about Soviet armor."

"We're ready anytime, sir," BJ answered brightly and gave him a cheery wave.

He turned and walked back to his platoon. At least they had kept their mouths shut when he walked off with the lieutenant. No "here it comes now," or "shit's gonna' hit the fan." He had them trained well. Those kinds of remarks made it only more difficult when it came to tuning-up a lieutenant.

"Hey, Sergeant Kirkley, what was that all about?" Coker asked. Coker was a good team leader, but he could sometimes drive you crazy with questions.

"Nothin', Cokehead," replied BJ as he resumed his prone position. "just another TLD."

"A what?"

"Typical Lieutenant Deal," muttered Sterling.

Christ, these El-Tees, thought BJ. They act like this is some kind of game. They try so hard to put on a professional show and then go off on some weird tangent and forget to give you the orders. Now, those two Russian

Spetsnaz, the ones who they had tangled with at Ft. Hood and in Germany, those guys were pros.

"I'm fuckin' horny!" suddenly shouted an unidentified body propped up on a rucksack. A nearby LRRP, sprawled face-down on a poncho, quietly rolled over on his back. No one else commented, except Coker, of course.

"You know what I could go for, Sergeant Kirkley?" Coker chimed in. "I wonder what Iranian tail's like?" He always called BJ sergeant, even though he was only a stripe lighter.

"They don't make their women wear veils for nothin', Cokehead," observed one of the radio operators.

"Why don't you just double-time over to those three broads down there and see if they'll trade you a blow job for some rations?" grumbled Sterling. Three Iranian women clothed in dusty black robes were picking through the trash alongside the road. They looked like black crows.

"Gee, you really think they would, Sergeant Sterling?"

"Yeah, Coke, why don't you get two blow jobs and bring one back for me?" Hickey suggested.

Coker rose to his feet and started ambling down the edge of the taxiway toward the women. He had two brown plastic MRE (Meal, Ready to Eat) bags in his hand. The three women had worked their way farther down the road.

"I bet the little prick does it," Saul Moser said.

"No way," John Armstrong, Moser's radio operator, said. "They probably don't even know what a blow job is!"

"More likely he'll talk them to death."

"Beej, you'd best stop him," said King. "He might start an international incident or somethin'!"

"You mean we might offend the Iranians? Oh, dear!" responded Estes.

"Coker ought to stick to self-abuse," Sterling laughed.

"At least then he'd be doin' it with someone who loves him."

"Masturbation, aye, there's the rub!" Hickey added.

As the others continued to lewdly speculate on Coker's sexual habits, BJ returned to his paperback.

I wonder what those two Russians are up to? BJ wondered, remembering the last time he had seen the two Spetsnaz. They're probably terrorizing the shit out of some poor Germans now.

★ 6 ★

Ahmad Kemal cradled his West German-made G-3 assault rifle across his lap and settled his back against the blanket-padded rock outcropping. He had just scanned the rugged mountainside to the northwest with his binoculars. This was a task for which he had stood, not so much as to better observe, but simply to stretch. He had been perched on this low hill as a lookout since early morning. The noon prayers had long passed. He had participated just as the other *mujahiddin*—Soldiers of God and followers of the Brotherhood of The Path—had done in the valley below, doing his best to estimate the direction to Mecca when he heard the calls to worship on the light breeze.

Ahmad Kemal's unit, the Iris Brigade, was the westernmost of the hosts of the Brotherhood. The Brotherhood's brigades were named after the "armed" flowers in the poem the great sultan, Murad Khan II, had long ago written in honor of Adrianople, comparing the town and its springtime environs to the appliances of war. It was from here that the armies of Islam launched their attack on Constantinople, held by the infidel Byzantines. *"The iris had girded its saber on its thigh. . . ."* In 1453 the Byzantine capital fell to a brutal Islamic assault and suffered a sack lasting three days and nights.

"The victorious troops entwined the arm of possession

71

*around the neck of their desires, and binding the luster of
their hearts to the locks of the damsels. . . .''* as Khoja
Sa'd al-Din's poem, *The Conquest of Constantinople,* so
nobly described the rape of the flower of Byzantine
women. Kemal fervently hoped to share in a similar epic.

The Iris Brigade had thrust far westward as the vanguard
of two other brigades; its goal Shiraz, the capital of Fars
province and key regional communications center held by
the misguided brothers. Ahmad Kemal, of course, did not
realize this. He did know that the drive had been stalled
when one of the supporting brigades was withdrawn to
Kerman to face the Russian horde striking out of the north.
His and the other brigade now waited to fling themselves
onto the godless Russians advancing from the northwest
or the satanic Americans approaching from the southeast,
whichever should attempt to first take Shiraz for themselves. The fact that the misguided brothers had stopped
the Brotherhood did not bother Kemal in the least. Nor did
it occur to him that what the loyalists had inflicted on the
Iris Brigade was nothing when compared with the devastation a confrontation with the godless Russians or satanic
Americans would bring.

The Iris Brigade had advanced this far to Zarghan in
their armored personnel carriers, trucks, buses, and handful of tanks, only to be stopped thirty kilometers from their
prize. The misguided Iranians had fought better than they
had expected, and their morale had suffered. And now
they sat in the Kur Rud River valley waiting. Below Kemal was the brigade's supply company, the repair and
technical element, and part of the transport column, clustered among the mud huts of some, to Kemal, dismal,
nameless village.

He wiped the beads of sweat from his brow and peered
at the sun, now hidden behind a ragged cloud. It was at
that moment that he *felt* the sound. He listened but heard
nothing. Then he felt it again. The faintest of—what? A
vibration, a deep humming? It was there, just beneath the

sounds detectable by the human ear. It rose again to be momentarily detected by his senses. Kemal grabbed the binoculars and swung them toward the mountains. Nothing. Laying his rifle on the ground he rose to his knees still scanning the far slopes. There! Between two steep peaks, a notch in the mountains, like the spread thighs of a woman. Two small specks. They rapidly grew as more appeared behind them! Helicopters! He dropped the field glasses and grabbed his rifle. Grasping the operating handle on the weapon's left forearm, he yanked it back, chambering a round. He could *hear* the sound now. Turning toward the village, he pointed the G-3 skyward—*BLAM! BLAM! BLAM!* He could see fellow *mujahiddin* in the streets turn toward him as the sound of the shots reached their ears. He waved his arms frantically and fired three more shots. Men began running to their posts.

Kemal turned and was stunned to see the first of the big, ugly flying machines almost upon his hilltop. Rolling onto his back, just as their Chinese adviser had taught them, Kemal pointed the rifle almost straight up and began squeezing the trigger as fast as he could. The first two helicopters roared over spouting fire as they launched rocket salvos into the village. Kemal's shots had no apparent effect on the monsters. Rolling to his side he changed magazines as more of the demonic machines were rapidly approaching. He again pointed his rifle to the sky and began to pull the trigger.

The machine gunner anxiously watched through a side port as his temporary replacement hammered a burst of tracers into the Iranian atop the hill. The fool, who had been laying on his back shooting into the air, disappeared in a cloud of dust. Ricocheting red tracers bounced off the surrounding rocks at odd angles.

The gunner swung the PKB machine gun into a forward locked position and turned with his palm held up. The machine gunner grudgingly dropped two cigarettes into

Guards Senior Ensign Pavel Kovpak's outspread hand.
Smiling over his huge mustache, the ensign shouted, "Man
your weapon, gunner! We are fast approaching the landing
area where you may yet have opportunity to prove your
prowess with the machine gun!" Swinging around, one
hand clinging to an overhead spar, Kovpak bellowed,
"Stand by, comrades!" at his twenty-nine *ikhotniki*—
hunters—crammed into the Mi-8's troop compartment. He
glanced over at his 1st Squad commander, poised in the
transport helicopter's left side door. The battalion commander had forbade any platoon or company commander
to be among the first men out the door during an assault.
They were too valuable. That directive was just fine with
Ensign Kovpak. He had other plans for his military career,
and dying for the *Rodina* in this shithole of a country was
not among them. The khaki-colored ground was rushing
up fast. "Stand by!" he again shouted over the howling
engines.

Excellent shooting! Guards Lt. Col. Aleksei Bodnya
thought to himself with enthusiasm as a passing helicopter's rotor wash revealed the Iranian's riddled body from
under the small dust cloud. Perhaps this assault-helicopter
squadron was better trained than he had expected.

Bodnya's command helicopter was hidden in the rear of
the formation. Survivability of the command elements was
crucial to him. There was a time to lead from the front,
but only when his subordinate commanders faltered. He
rose from his crouch from which he had watched through
the side port and looked through the front canopy between
the pilots. The shabby village of mud huts careened off to the
left at a steep angle as the helicopter banked sharply to the
right. The other helicopters continued ahead.

As his leveled out for its landing at the foot of the hill,
he could see the six camouflage-painted Mi-8s bearing the
1st and 4th Companies of the 800th Guards Independent
Special-Purpose Battalion settle down amid swirling clouds

of dust. Partly screened from the village by a low rise, the *ikhotniki* leapt from the troop doors and fanned out in ragged lines. They stumbled through the dust and trotted up the rise as the helicopters lifted off, their turbines screaming. The two Mi-24 combat helicopters screamed over the village again, this time from the southwest, perpendicular to the line of tan-uniformed troops. Their 23mm automatic guns blazed as they sent more 57mm rockets into the mud huts. They exploded in clouds of black smoke and mud-colored dust. Tracers rose harmlessly to meet them. The Mi-24s had served their purpose, to draw fire as the troop helicopters lifted off.

Bodnya's small command group leapt out of the helicopter behind the security squad. They all went to the ground as the Mi-8 lifted off behind them. Back on their feet, they rushed among the jumbled boulders at the hill's base. The command group and security took up positions and began to set up their radios. Bodnya, Captain Noskov, his 1st Officer–operations, and a single radio operator continued up the rocky hillside to a better vantage point. Looking to the southwest Bodnya could see two more Mi-8s inserting two platoons from the 3rd Company near the road. A kilometer away, they would double as a flank-blocking force preventing any of their quarry from escaping and as a security force ensuring no reinforcements would arrive from that direction. The 3rd Company's other platoon was being dropped off on the road to the northeast with a similar mission. Another Mi-8 roared over low after dropping off a recoilless gun team atop the hill. It banked hard to the left losing altitude fast. Landing near his own helicopter, he could see soldiers of the Supply Platoon shoving out ammunition boxes. They had no more than bounced onto the ground when the helicopter lifted off. Everything was going exactly according to plan.

Be more cautious now, he sternly counseled himself.

"Here!" he yelled at his two companions. The radio operator dropped on one knee beside him and checked the tuning on the backpacked R-107 radio. Captain Noskov immediately made a fast circuit of the area with his AKSU-74 submachine gun at the ready. He wanted no surprises. Bodnya was more concerned with the attack's progress. Through his big B-8 binoculars he could see that the assault companies had reached the boulder-strewn crest of the low rise. Visibility was none too clear, the helicopter-generated dust had not yet settled. The AGS-17 automatic grenade launchers, two with each company, were being set up among the rocks. Their crews fed the clumsy belts of 30mm rounds into the tripod-mounted weapons. The dangling ammunition belts draped around the crews' necks may have been difficult to handle, but the troops preferred them to the weapon's even more awkward drum magazines. The *ikhotniki* had already opened fire with their AKS-74 assault rifles and RPKS-74 light machine guns. The first of the AGS-17s began to fire short, ranging bursts into the village, its rounds making small puffs of dirty white smoke as they burst in loose groups. The dull popping of their detonation reached Bodnya just as the 73mm SPG-9 recoilless gun, positioned just below the hill's crest, banged its first round into the village. It would cause little physical damage, but these Iranians were rear-service troops, Bodnya reasoned, and it might have a valuable psychological effect. Large white clouds of smoke blossomed from among the assault troops as shoulder-fired RPG-16 rocket launchers began to add their devastation to the fusillade.

Bodnya motioned for the handset. "Jackal Five, this is Jackal One Four. Come in Jackal Five."

The handset crackled loudly. "This is Jackal Five," responded Captain Yurosov, 1st Company's commander. Bodnya realized that the crackle wasn't static but small arms fire.

"Report, Jackal Five!"

"We are in position; return fire is light. I have only one man hit that I know of! Over."

"Continue mission! Over. Jackal Eight, come in."

More crackling was heard behind Senior Lieutenant Dubovik's youthful voice. "This is Jackal Eight. Same situation as Jackal Five, but I have three hit that I can see! Over."

"I do not see your grenade launchers firing. What is the problem? I want them firing now! Over." He had expected no answer to his rhetorical questions and received none. He did receive results.

"It is done! Over!" came Dubovik's curt response.

Only seconds passed before the 4th Company's AGS-17s began to pump rounds into the huts. Dubovik was a good Spetsnaz officer, thought Bodnya. He was having some trouble shaking his new company out though. Only weeks before, it had been the battalion's Scout-Diversionary Platoon, a reaction-force subunit, but their strength had been increased to that of a company when they received substantial reinforcements for their new mission.

"Jackal One Three, come in."

"Jackal One Four, this is One Three," responded Major Goncharov. He was in direct command of the two assault companies. The crackling was not as loud because he was behind the two companies' firing line. "Enemy fire is light. I will signal as planned when it slackens. The soldiers appear in good order. Over." His chief of staff sounded so relaxed that anyone listening in on the radio would think this was no more than a map exercise.

Bodnya received reports of no action from the 3rd Company's two blocking/security-force elements. The 73mm recoilless gun continued to fire. The helicopters had departed for now.

There appeared to be little return fire from among the mud huts. Fires had broken out, creating more gray smoke than flames. Some Iranian vehicles were fiercely burning, releasing dense, oily black columns of smoke. A red flare, fired by Major Goncharov, arched into the dust- and smoke-filled sky. Riflemen rose from behind their rocks and formed irregular lines as they disappeared down the far side of the rise, firing short, full automatic bursts from the hip. The machine guns, rocket launchers, and grenade launchers remained in place, increasing their rate of fire to cover the assault troops and firing over their heads.

"Jackal Six, this is Jackal One Four," Bodnya again spoke into the handset. "Stand by!"

"This is Jackal Six. Standing by." No crackling noise accompanied that transmission. He raised the binoculars to his eyes. On the far side of the village, between the gaps in the huts and columns of smoke, he could see the first of the Iranian rear-service soldiers running toward the ravines and rock rubble sloping toward the Kur Rud River. They had no place else to flee. More appeared as the assault companies blasted their way through the burning huts. Many were unarmed, having dropped their weapons in their blind panic to escape. The supporting weapons had ceased fire when the Spetsnaz entered the village. The dull thump of hand grenades was carried by the breeze. Some of the supporting weapons crews began to displace forward, others moved to cover the village's flanks.

The village was fast emptying of confused Iranians, those who had survived the assault. The *ikhotniki* of the assault companies did not pursue. With startling suddenness the ravines and rock piles to which the Iranians fled erupted in a barrage of assault-rifle and machine-gun fire. The green flare signaling the fire assault arched into the panicked Iranians now caught in the open in a crisscross of tracers. The 2nd Company, Jackal Six, had made its presence known. The assault companies joined in the slaughter from the rear. Machine guns set up on the village's flanks cut down anyone fleeing from the fire sack in that direction. BG-15 grenade launchers, mounted under assault-rifle barrels, added their deadly fragmentation bursts among the stricken Iranians. It was the classic hammer-and-anvil tactic, long used by Soviet forces hunting bandits, terrorist groups, and enemy divisionists. It

worked equally well against enemy rear-service troops inexperienced in sophisticated tactics.

The 2nd Company had been infiltrated the night before.
Landing by helicopter some twelve kilometers to the east,
the company had executed a difficult approach march
across rugged country in total darkness and silence. They
had crossed the Kur Rud River with no little difficulty and
occupied their ambush positions well before dawn. During
the morning they had reported by radio the activity and
dispositions of the targeted enemy grouping—information
on which Bodnya's staff had finalized the operation's plan,
briefed the subunits, and even conducted a quick rehearsal
prior to launching the mission. Captain Shepelev would
receive a suitable decoration for leading the successful ac-
complishment of the 2nd Company's formidable task.

Bodnya lowered his binoculars, having little desire to
watch the carnage any longer. He had seen worse, though,
in Afghanistan: unarmed bandits—civilians—butchered by
Spetsnaz and paratroopers, but he still had no stomach for
such wholesale slaughter. He had witnessed his share of
brutal reprisals in Germany as well. The companies began
to report in as the firing dwindled, rose in volume momentarily, and finally trickled to a stop.

"Let us go forward," he muttered to his two companions. Silently they picked their way down the hillside.
Passing the command group and security squad, which fell
in around Bodnya in a loose square, they walked the 700
meters to the village. A handful of lightly wounded soldiers were assembling at the ammunition stockpile. The
Feld'scher—medical specialist—and his orderlies were already treating them. Bodnya stopped to offer a few words
of praise and encouragement. Other soldiers from the assault companies were heading toward the small ammunition stockpile to draw their subunits' resupply. Fires in
the village were spreading and more smoke bellowed into
the sky. Occasionally single rifle shots were heard from the
village's far side.

Major Goncharov met Bodnya at the edge of the village. His tan uniform was dusty and smudged with ash, as were his face and hands.

"Comrade Major!" exclaimed Bodnya, feigning disgust, "you are expected to set an example for the *ikhotniki*! This is no way for my chief of staff to appear!" The security squad laughed. The Spetsnaz were no different from other soldiers in this regard, attempting to relax now that the immediate danger had passed.

"I beg your forgiveness, Comrade Commander!" Goncharov responded with an exaggerated frown. "I was only emulating the precedent set by the assault companies!"

"Very well, Comrade Major, order a full inspection in ten minutes!" announced Bodnya. The command group and security laughed, all except Capt. K. V. Yakushev, the battalion's KGB Special-Section officer.

Becoming more serious, Goncharov pointed at a larger hut on a side "street." "That is the rear-services headquarters. Captain Milstein, bring two soldiers and come with me. We will see what we can find of value." The battalion's 2nd Officer–intelligence indicated two *ikhotniki* and followed Goncharov. The rest of the command group continued through the smoldering huts. Bodies of Iranians were strewn among the burning trucks. Soldiers were disabling the undamaged vehicles by setting the fuel tanks alight.

Near the far side they found Captain Yurasov of the 1st Company. On seeing Bodnya, he stopped and reported. "Comrade Commander, the 1st Company has three confirmed dead and six wounded."

"Have the bodies of the dead been recovered?" Bodnya asked. They never left a dead soldier behind if at all possible. It was a tradition the Spetsnaz and paratroopers had adopted in Afghanistan. As in that terrible country they knew here too that unrecovered bodies would be mutilated. The same applied to wounded and soldiers separated from their subunits. They all knew that every effort would be made to recover them. For this reason all of the Spetsnaz involved in air-assault raids carried two small smoke flares attached to their equipment, to mark their location for searching helicopters. The emphasis the Soviet Armed Forces placed on the recovery of soldiers often came as a surprise to Western armies, which thought they had little regard for human life. That may have been true at one time, but as with so many things, Afghanistan had changed that. The Afghan rebels had brutally murdered soldiers left on the battlefield, especially Spetsnaz, paratroopers, and helicopter crewmen. The Mi-24 combat helicopter, designed principally as an attack aircraft, also had a large troop compartment. The aviators had found this capability invaluable for the recovery of downed aircrews. When its replacement, the Mi-28, was designed without a similar troop-carrying capability, a cramped two-man compartment, devoid of seats or windows was incorporated into its design specifically for the rescue of downed airmen.

Yurasov glanced at Captain Yakushev. "We have a live prisoner, a lieutenant, Comrade Commander."

Yakushev, who had been surveying the destruction with ill-concealed disgust, suddenly showed interest in the conversation. To him the Spetsnaz were nothing more than a band of murderous hooligans, bent on killing everything within their reach, often depriving him of his needs. "Where is he, Comrade?" he asked, obviously making a valiant attempt to restrain his anticipation.

"This way, Comrade," replied Yakushev looking at Bodnya with a pained expression. "He has been shot in the legs and has lost a great deal of blood," the young captain added, as if that would make any difference to the methods that the KGB officer would select to obtain information from the wretched soul.

Bodnya made a point of appearing unconcerned. While quite unpleasant in his interrogation methods, Yakushev would furnish results—always. And results were all Bodnya wanted, even if his Special-Section officer did seem to derive perverse pleasure from his duties. Yakushev holstered his pistol and followed the 1st Company commander to one of the few huts not yet on fire. He pulled a triangular file from his trousers pocket to replace the Makarov pistol. The KGB officer's Farsi-speaking interpreter followed.

Continuing on to the edge of the village, the command group came upon the fire sack, or perhaps killing ground was a more fitting description. Some eighty or more Iranian bodies were spread across the rocky ground. Most looked more like bundles of bloody rags than fallen soldiers. The *ikhotniki* were meandering across the area dispatching the severely wounded with single rifle shots, recovering weapons, searching bodies for documents, looting the dead, and accomplishing other after-the-battle duties.

Satisfied with the results of his unit's operation, Bodnya turned to make his way back to the helicopter landing area where the assault helicopters would extract his battalion. He suddenly halted when he heard an all too familiar voice from within a painfully filthy hut.

"Dump the rice out on the floor and piss on it," the voice ordered. "I do not care if I ever see another grain of rice!" The unit had been subsisting principally on the local economy. A greasy blanket covering the doorway was suddenly flung open and out stepped Senior Ensign Kovpak, his arms filled with canned food. His submachine gun was hanging by its sling from the crook of his arm where it had slipped off his shoulder. Almost blundering into Bodnya, Kovpak stopped and peered over the cans, his eyes twinkling, the submachine swinging back and forth.

"Ah! Comrade Commander! Eh, you are invited to take supper with the 1st Company this evening!" The little Ukrainian was never the least troubled when caught in the act of pillaging. To him it was his duty and right.

Bodnya looked down at his long-standing friend. "And what are we having for supper, Comrade Ensign?"

Kovpak craned his head back so his eyes could focus on the cans' labels. "It appears fish, Comrade Commander!"

"Very well, I and my staff are honored to accept your kind offer!"

"Eh, staff? Why, yes, of course, Comrade Commander!" A youthful junior sergeant, with a pasteboard case of canned food under one arm and his assault rifle slung over his shoulder, came through the door. With his free hand he was attempting to button his fly after complying with his platoon commander's order. He stopped short when he saw Bodnya and the battalion staff standing before him. Kovpak turned to him, "Comrade Sergeant, there will be seven extra places for supper tonight."

"Eight, Captain Yakushev will be attending as well," corrected Bodnya.

"Yes, make that eight, Sergeant," said Kovpak, barely preventing one of the cans from slipping from his arms.

The sergeant, his mouth hanging half open after finding the battalion staff standing in front of him, was still trying to button his fly. "It is done, Comrade Ensign!"

"And, Comrade Ensign," said Bodnya, nodding at the Walkman earphones Kovpak was wearing, a souvenir from their visit to Ft. Hood, "I think the radio headset is inappropriate in a combat situation!"

"Exactly so," resounded Kovpak.

As Bodnya turned away, he heard the cans clatter to the ground and a blaze of jazz music as the earphones were yanked off. "*Ikhotniki*, you!" Kovpak shouted at a passing soldier. "Do you not have anything better to do than shooting more *chernozhoph*? Pick up those cans!" Bodnya thought that Kovpak occasionally allowed his priorities to become confused.

The staff remained silent during the exchange. They all knew their commander confided more in the peculiar little

Ukrainian ensign than any of them. A most unusual relationship, but he was their commander.

"Jackal One Four, this is Pelican One Zero," the radio spoke. The operator quickly slapped the handset into Bodnya's outstretched hand.

"This is Jackal One Four." The thumping of approaching rotors could be heard faintly over the crackle of spreading flames.

"We are inbound to your position. Will arrive in ten minutes. Situation report, please." Bodnya recognized the voice of the assault-helicopter squadron's commander.

"The operation is completed. The landing area is secure. Look for the recognition signal." The two big Mi-24s roared over, minutes in advance of the troop helicopters, and began to orbit the area. Bodnya thought they looked like giant nightmare insects searching for prey, which indeed they were. Bodnya recalled the machine-gunning demonstration during their approach to the landing area.

"Commander, I wish to congratulate your unit on the excellent machine-gun marksmanship I witnessed during the landing. I would not have believed such accurate shooting from a moving helicopter if I had not seen it for myself!"

The squadron commander turned to the right and shrugged his shoulders at his equally perplexed copilot. After watching his crews in an air-to-air defensive shooting exercise, he had sadly concluded that the only way one of his machine gunners would shoot down a helicopter was to empty his weapon inside his own craft. Still, a compliment was a compliment.

"We serve the Soviet Union, Comrade! I will pass your congratulations on to the aircrews. Pelican One Zero, out." He had long ago found that the safest course of action was always to agree with a Spetsnaz officer, especially with one offering a compliment, a rare occurrence in any case.

* * *

Far away to the north, in Esfahan, the capital of the province bearing the same name, events were being placed in motion at the forward command post of the 1st Southern Front. Bodnya's battalion's successful raid was a very small element of an elaborate operational plan and its equally complex companion deception plan, Operation Storm Front. A hidden map's location was revealed by the unfortunate rebel Iranian lieutenant under the ministrations of Captain Yakushev. It offered the final bits of information the Soviets needed to finalize their operational plans.

★ 7 ★

Lieut. Col. K. S. Drachev watched with satisfaction as the last of the 2S9 120mm assault guns rumbled off the big camouflage-painted An-12 transport. Its four turbo prop engines were still whining as the squat tracked vehicles off-loaded. Over the transport's wings the sun, almost touching the rugged western horizon, appeared as a big orange ball, magnified by the dust-filled sky. The ball simmered in the aircraft's hot exhaust vapors.

The whole of the 247th Guards Airborne Assault Regiment was now on the ground. While not the first of the 104th Guards Airborne Assault Division's three regiments to be lifted into Shiraz International Airport, it had accomplished the off-loading of the almost 100 transports required to lift it in record time. Drachev's regiment's advance guard had already departed to the north, toward Zarghan and one of the rebel Iranian brigades in the area.

Scores of BMD infantry combat vehicles, the smaller airborne version of the BMP armored-personnel carrier, were lining up in march formation alongside one of the two 4,270-meter-long runways. Soon the regiment's main body would follow the advance guard. They were paratroopers, but unlike their Western counterparts, they possessed the secondary ground mobility that allowed them to maneuver with the speed of motorized rifle units, protect them from small arms and artillery fire, and provide substantial additional firepower. Each squad's BMD mounted a 73mm antitank gun, an AT-5 antitank wire-guided missile, and three machine guns plus the squad's own weapons.

The rebel Iranians had already been met and defeated, or at least stalled, by the loyal Iranians. If the loyal Iranians had accomplished that feat, from what Drachev had seen of them, he felt certain the rebels would be no great opponents for his highly trained regiment. He knew, too, that Spetsnaz and air-assault troops had been raiding the rebels' rear areas and even hitting the combat battalions. The brigade was being steadily picked away. Now air strikes were being directed at them. That would soften them up even more. At this rate there would be little left to oppose his regiment.

Drachev's unit had spent the past month at one of the desert training-methodology centers in the Turkestan Military District's huge Kara Kum Desert. There they had been one of the few units to train with the Laser Fire and Hit Simulator system known as the *Besstrashiye*—Fearless. Similar to the American MILES system, the Fearless was composed of a low-power laser emitter fitted to each paratrooper's rifle and a harness with laser-detector disks attached. When the gun fired a blank round, the laser would "fire" and the detectors on the opposing soldiers would register "hits" by sounding a "beeper". His *desantniki* had become extremely proficient in subunit tactics and the ability to survive their small exercise battles.

The operators of his crew-served weapons were none less proficient after running countless live-fire exercises. His AGS-17 grenade-launcher gunners had become so experienced that he had complete confidence in their ability to place effective suppressive fire on enemy antitank, wire-guided missiles.

His regiment was tactically proficient, physically toughened, and acclimatized for this country's harsh environment. Drachev had little doubt the *Vozdushno-Desantnye Voiska* (Airborne Assault Forces) would achieve victory over the rebel Iranians. Drachev walked toward his BRDM-2 RU command vehicle. Victory was virtually assured. He looked over his shoulder to the darkened east. After they dealt with the Iranians, they would turn and crush the American invaders.

"Well, that's just fucking great!" muttered Colonel James Larder as he flipped the sheet of flimsy fax paper onto the field table. He stared at the PERINTSUM— Periodic Intelligence Report—as if willing it to disappear. The wind outside the tent had picked up after sunset. In the background could be heard the never-ending low whine of the power generators.

Major Larry Simpson looked at his boss, the Deputy Chief of Staff, Intelligence almost apologetically. The XVIII Airborne Corps' G2 was not in a good humor.

"Sir, we knew they were going to put the 104th Airborne Division in some place, sooner or later. Ever since national assets reported them to be staging in their base at Kirovabad."

The national assets he spoke of was satellite reconnaissance. Major Soviet troop moves had always seemed to confound them. The 104th Airborne was based in the Turkestan Military District, from which the 2nd Southern Front had launched its offensive into northeastern Iran. Yet the division was conducting an operation in support of the 1st Southern Front from the Transcaucasus Military District's 1st Southern Front. It made no difference, though, as the 104th was under the ultimate control of the Southern Theater of Military Operations headquartered in Tashkent. It could be committed wherever the theater commander-in-chief desired. The Americans of course "knew" this, but still, such moves always seemed to confound them.

"That's going to make it impossible for us to grab Shiraz as we planned," complained the G2, "not with the forces we have available."

The major said nothing.

"Damn it, we needed Shiraz, too! It's the most advanced airfield we expected to lay our hands on. Now the Soviets have it as a forward base!" He paused in thought for a moment. "How far has the 24th Division gotten, Larry?"

"The bulk of the division's landed at Bandar 'Abbās. The 1st Brigade is already on the road to Shiraz, near Fasa."

Larder picked up another fax sheet. It listed the locations of known enemy regiments and brigades, the smallest units in which corps-level staffs were generally interested. The list had been compiled from analyzing the satellite imagery and supplemented by airborne electronic-intelligence—ELINT—aircraft. For the dozenth time during the long frustrating day the G2 wished that the SR-71 Blackbird strategic reconnaissance aircraft had not been deactivated in 1990. It simply took too long for satellite imagery to be analyzed and filtered down.

Down the sheet's left side were four-digit grid coordinates of the enemy unit's center of mass. Following their designation was a brief summary of their dispositions (what they were doing) and their location in relation to Shiraz, on which they were centered. Three Soviet regiments were U/I, unidentified, two moving, one defending. Two Iranian brigades were defending, and an unidentified Iranian brigade was held in reserve.

Also listed were the two rebel Iranian brigades defending around Zarghan. Larder thought the situation had the potential to become quite confused.

It was believed that the Soviets and Iranians were preparing a defense to meet any U.S. move to take Shiraz until their heavy forces reached the area. Then they would no doubt transition to an offensive mode. Two of the Soviet airborne regiments, mounted in their BMDs, were moving to engage the two rebel brigades in the north. They, the rebels, were assessed as being of only limited effectiveness due to previous engagements with the Iranians and continuing Soviet air-assault attacks and air strikes. As battle was joined into between the Soviets, their allies, and the rebels, extensive troop moves were expected to take place on both sides. The Soviets might well be preoccupied by this battle. Perhaps XVIII Airborne Corps could capitalize on the speed and mobility of their armor and aviation to take the Soviets by surprise.

"If we can get an armor-heavy brigade in there before the Soviets have the chance to establish a good prepared defense, we can kick their ass," surmised the G2, almost to himself.

"No doubt, sir," responded the major with perhaps too little enthusiasm. He had served in V Corps' Collection Management and Dissemination Element in Germany. He had heard almost identical words from another G2.

He could not see the grinding armored-personnel carriers churning sand and gravel, or the red and green flags flapping from their staves atop the vehicles, or the wild-eyed glares of the *mujahiddin*, but he knew it was all there. The pitch-black darkness concealed the visual scene from him but not its sounds. The squeal of treads, grinding gears, deep rumbling of powerful engines, and shouts of the *gourhbanin* (sergeants).

Sarhang (Colonel) Shaul Bazargan listened to his proud Iris Brigade as it advanced to meet the godless Russian invaders. The spearhead of The Brotherhood, he was certain the Iris Brigade would give its all. What bothered him was that this spearhead did not possess the weight of the shaft, which would allow it to fly true with penetrating force. His brigade and the other, the Carnation Brigade, were alone, without additional artillery other than what little remained; without air support; without reserves to reinforce and exploit; and equally important, without logistical support. Even during the war with Iraq they'd had the necessary support. Sometimes not enough, but at least some. Here there was none.

Bazargan had been commissioned early in the war with Iraq, the rank of *setvan sevon* (3rd lieutenant) almost forced on him while he still attended the university. He had known the ecstasy of victory and the terror of defeat. He had seen incredible blunders and brilliant tactical feats. The sacrifices of the *Basij-e-Mustazafin* (literally the "Mobilization of the Deprived"), the peasant and working-class volunteers who died in droves on the Faw Peninsula: Their sole motivation was simply the liberation of Kerbala, a Shi'ite shrine in Iraq. And, of course, for Allah. Immortal life begins with death. Committing oneself to a holy war—*jihad*—assured one's immortal salvation in the next world. It is this belief that causes Muslims to desire martyrdom, especially when destroying the *kafir*—infidels.

Bazargan, too, believed in such self-sacrifice, and had many times come close to achieving martyrdom. But Allah still had need for him on Earth. It was for this belief that he had thrown his lot in with The Brotherhood. He felt, as did many other officers, that Khomeini's Islamic revolution had been bastardized into something else. The people had been led from the intended and true "path" of Islamic law. They needed to be set back on course.

Yes, Allah still needed him on Earth; there was much left to do. Only, the tools he had been given to serve His need were few indeed. The Iris Brigade had lost almost a quarter of its strength in the clashes with misguided brothers. Their remaining strength had dwindled away as the Russians snapped at what little support he still had. They had become even bolder and were striking at his combat units. Like the Iraqi special forces, they came in daylight and night, sometimes when and where expected, but more often when and where not.

Now the Iris Brigade was preparing to face the Russians, the Lesser Satan, on their own terms. Dawn would see the godless ones before them. Allah still had need for him on Earth, but apparently not for much longer.

The Americans had every possible electronic-intelligence collector up when the Soviets clashed with the rebel Iranians. A 64-foot-long KH-11 reconnaissance satellite watched the battle unfold from 180 miles up. Nick-named Keyhole, the 30,000-pound satellite had been maneuvered into the proper orbit days before. Its high-resolution search-and-find cameras focused on the action. Five television cameras recorded the scene and down-linked their real-time pictures to a ground station.

A Boeing E-3A Sentry AWAC—Airborne Warning and Control aircraft—orbited safely many miles to the south-east. Its down looking radar images were video recorded for later analysis. This would provide a visual "history" of the Soviet employment of their air support. A mass of data would be stored on the Sentry's IBM 4-Pi CC-1 high-speed computer. Much would be discovered about Soviet air tactics, attack formations, response times, and the types of targets they were directed to.

To the east another greatly modified 707, an E-8A JSTARS—Joint Surveillance Target Attack Radar System—aircraft flew a huge racetrack-shaped course. Its side-looking phased-array standoff radar provided a real-time window deep into the battlefield. Detecting moving and stationary ground targets, a joint staff of Air Force and Army console operators processed the collected information in-flight. From there it was downlinked to Joint Tactical Information Distribution System, where it was fed to both Air Force and Army ground stations for rapid distribution to customer headquarters. Digitized computer maps and graphics were integrated into the video-taped radar data. Operators, who could monitor broad areas or scan small sectors, tagged specific units for tracking. Targeting information could be displayed in ground tactical-operations centers and intelligence cells either real time or played back time, compressed for later, more detailed analysis.

A high-flying TR-1 reconnaissance aircraft surveyed the battlefield with its Advanced Synthetic Aperture Radar System. It imaged targets and downlinked the data to ground stations that turned out deep targeting data in less than twenty minutes.

RF-4C recce aircraft boldly darted into the fringes of the battle area to photograph the action. The Army kept two OV-1D Mohawks airborne, their SLAR—Side-Looking Airborne Radar—downlinked to ground stations and providing a filmstrip image of vehicle movements on a near horizontal plane. RC-12H Improved Guardrail aircraft monitored and recorded both sides' radio transmissions and radar emissions.

An impressive quantity of data was collected. In fact, tremendous amounts of aerial photos, videotapes, SLAR, and ELINT printouts piled up in the various collection cells. Analysts slaved over the masses of materials: evaluating, analyzing, processing, posting, filing, and disseminating. The staffs discussed, augured, plotted, and surmised over the intelligence products they received. The intelligence collectors and analysts were being worn down before their battle even began.

★ 8 ★

The pain woke him. It started in his lower back, then made its way up and across his shoulders. He rolled from one side to the other searching for a position that would ease the aching. There was none. The long day's ride had taken its toll on his body.

"Please, God, another twenty minutes," he begged, his voice smothered by the sleeping bag. From outside, he heard a laugh.

"I myself have asked God for another twenty minutes," Ishan Fuad said brightly, "but not to sleep! Come on, my friend, the mountains call us."

Jinx pulled his turban out of the hole at the top of the sleeping bag, letting in a breath of chilly air, then pulled down the canvas zipper pull. Rolling out of the down-filled bag, Jinx's breath caught in his throat. The air was cold, near freezing, but the view was what riveted him.

They had climbed the steep ridge as the sun had started down and abruptly vanished the way it always did in the mountains. After dark, they had continued on for another four hours, leading the animals on foot as they made their way in the dark up the narrow, twisting trail. By the time they had reached the crest and made their little camp, Jinx had been too tired to look around.

Now he could not stop looking. The mountains that

94

spread out before them were rugged, steep, pitiless, and magnificent. Far below, in the narrow valley, irregular patches of green marked the small fields where the Kurds grazed their flocks. The mountains across the valley were purple in the haze. A few thin clouds drifted down the narrow valley, looking more like smoke.

The sight reminded Jinx of his first look at the Grand Canyon when he was six years old. His father had driven all night to beat the August heat in their old unairconditioned '53 Chevy. They got to the canyon just at sunup. His dad, wired from the all-night drive, had dragged his mother and him over to the observation point. That awesome sight had thrilled and scared him. Now he felt the same awe and fear.

No wonder these people are so tough, he thought, you either get tough here or die. I wonder if they ever get used to the view?

Fuad had a fire going and was kneeling over it, tending a small pot.

"Jesus, Fuad, what a place!" Jinx exclaimed, then grimaced as he realized he was invoking the wrong deity. "Sorry Fuad, I meant Allah."

The big Kurd laughed. "Do not worry, Jenkins, I grew accustomed to hearing your American women invoking the name of the prophet Jesus when they, too, were overcome by awe."

"Uh huh," Jinx chuckled, "I see." He stretched to work out the kinks in his back, then reached into his rucksack pocket for the packet of freeze-dried coffee and the cup stashed there. Bending over shot another twinge up his back. In his heart, Jinx hoped there was a special level of hell just for mules.

Fuad looked around and smiled, then frowned when he saw the coffee packet. "My friend, you are not going to force me to watch you drink that awful concoction, are you?"

"What," Jinx asked, "this coffee?"

"That is not coffee, my friend," Fuad replied, lifting his pot out of the fire and stepping over to Jinx. "This is coffee. Share it with me."

The smell of fresh-brewed coffee wafted up from the little pot. It was a smell fraught with memories of warm Sunday mornings, exotic sidewalk cafés, expensive room service, and gorgeous mountains half a world away. Fuad made coffee in the Turkish tradition, black as hell, strong as death, and sweet as love.

"Thanks, Fuad," was all Jinx could manage, the flood of images swirling away.

"The stuff in that foil package is no more coffee," Fuad went on, "than a camel is an animal or an Arab is a human being."

The depth of the man's animosity was startling to Jinx, even after his cram course in Kurdish history. The Kurds had been at war with the Turks, the Iraqis, the Iranians, the Russians, and more frequently one another since the beginning of recorded history. Still, hearing this legacy of hatred expressed so casually over coffee was startling. Fuad had lived in America for years, exiled after his Kurdish student group had gotten into a shooting match with some Revolutionary Guards. Fuad's group had been betrayed by members of the Kurdish Popular Front, a Marxist group. SAVAMA, the Ayatollah's secret police, had hunted the group down. Fuad had escaped through Kuwait. Other members of his group hadn't been so lucky. They disappeared into Qasr prison in Tehran. They had not been heard from again. Now in his thirties, Fuad was a pleasant sort, always quick to see the good side of any situation, but Jinx knew that Fuad hid a lot of hate behind his jokes and teasing. His easygoing manner and casual dress also hid a lean, wiry body. Although not big by American standards, Fuad was surprisingly strong physically. The CIA had recruited him and taught him weapons and intelligence gathering. He was on loan from the

Agency to the Army. Fuad had no use for Marxists of any sort and felt a moral imperative to kill Iranians.

The dark liquid that Fuad had poured into Jinx's porcelain-covered steel cup was steaming, the aroma thick and inviting. Jinx tipped up the cup and took a big swig of the hot brew. Warmth spread through him, the strong coffee sweeping away the last cobwebs of sleep.

"We have far to go today, Jenkins," Fuad said as Jinx drank down his coffee, "across to that pass." Fuad pointed to a notch in the purple wall that faced them across the valley. "Ahmad's people will meet us there and escort us to his headquarters." Fuad turned, his face split by a guileless smile, "Or they will kill us and steal the weapons we carry."

"Let us hope that they will do the former," Jinx replied, mimicking the Kurd's accent. "To do the latter would be very unfortunate. For them." Jinx returned the innocent smile, then drained the last of the coffee from his cup and placed it in the pack.

Fuad laughed heartily, then began kicking out the fire.

This American is a brave one, he thought as he stamped out the last burning embers, he does not snivel like their diplomats.

The two men loaded their sleeping bags and packs on the pack mule, saddled their riding mules, and slowly made their way down the steep slope. It was after noon before they rode out onto the narrow valley that ran on either side of a tiny river. They stopped to water the animals in the cold stream.

"You ride well, Jenkins," Fuad remarked as the mules drank their fill. "Where did you learn?"

"Grew up in Texas," Jinx replied.

"Texas!" the Kurd exclaimed. "I have seen much about Texas in the movies and on the television!"

"Is that right?"

"Yes," Fuad went on excitedly. "There are still shootouts in the street and wild Indians and Mexican bandits there, yes?''

"Absolutely," Jinx replied truthfully.

"Ah!''

There was little conversation on the way up the next mountain. The steep slope required all the concentration of both men and beasts. Jinx's mule faltered near the crest, stumbled on some loose dirt, and slid off the trail. Clutching the mule and saddle for dear life, Jinx looked down the forbidding slope, seeing in his mind a vision of the pair of them, mule and man, rolling down the rocky slope. Then the mule caught himself, got his footing, and started up the final stretch of the tiny trail. Looking at the dropoff, Jinx did not see the six men who stepped out of the shade of a short tree.

"Good afternoon, my friends." The voice was soft and friendly. It scared Jinx more than the mule's stumble.

The sun was directly over the crest of the hill, behind the men, of whom nothing could be seen except their silhouettes. They were armed, the sun glinting off their AKM rifles.

Jinx recovered quickly, reining up his mule. "Good afternoon to you. You are from Ahmad?''

One of the shadows stepped forward, dropping below the sun's glare. He was medium height, about five feet eight, with dark black hair that stuck out from under a black-and-white turban. His beard was cut short. Jinx was surprised to see the traditional Kurdish headdress worn with a camo smock and crossed bandoliers.

"I am Ahmad," the man said quietly, standing at ease, his AKM cradled in his arms.

The big cheese himself, Jinx thought as he slid off his mule. What a surprise.

"I am Major Richard Jenkins, U. S. Army," Jinx said as he stepped toward the man, extending his hand. The Kurdish leader saluted instead, and Jinx, a bit embarrassed, returned it.

"You made good time," Ahmad said casually. "Did you encounter any enemies?"

Jinx started to answer, then realized that Ahmad was not speaking to him.

"None, Great Bey," Fuad answered from behind.

"Excellent," Ahmad smiled. "Then let us leave for camp." Ahmad gestured to the others standing with him. They darted back into the trees and returned with horses. Ahmad mounted a big white stallion and reined it around. The whole group started up over the crest, hardly looking back to see if Fuad and the American were still with them. Fuad fell in behind the reception party, pulling the two pack mules along. Jinx followed in the wake of the entire party.

Odd that the fellow comes out to meet me, then takes off like I don't exist, Jinx thought as he kicked the mule to spur it on, Oh, well.

"Tell me again why we are doing this alone," *Sarvan* (Captain) Kehan Homayuni said again over the intercom.

In the pilot seat behind and above the querulous gunner, *Sargord* (Major) Said Ferdowsi rolled his eyes and sighed. Kehan could be so dense sometimes.

"Because we do not wish to attract undue attention," Ferdowsi replied. "A flight would cause alarm. A single ship will not look too aggressive. The rebels will not be expecting us."

"Umm," came the response over the earphones.

"Kehan, we have the chance to catch one of the leaders of the Kurdish dogs today," Ferdowsi lectured his reluctant gunner. "We will trap them in the valley and chop them up. We will kill these puppets of the Great Satan and be back in time for dinner! Cheer up!"

In his front seat, Homayuni swung the telescopic-sight unit from left to right, watching through the sight as the chin turret, slaved to the sight unit, swung back and forth. In the chin turret, the six-barreled minigun was the only working weapon. Ammunition for the 40mm grenade launcher had run out during the war, and no more had been forthcoming. There were fourteen rockets, seven on each side.

Not a serious load of weapons, Homayuni mused, but enough to kill a bandit, I suppose. I hate these hunting trips. It is always "a report from an informer" or "our agent has confirmed". And always America behind the whole thing, the "Great Satan". Homayuni could remember the last time he had seen an American, more than a decade ago. He had been back from flight school in America only three months when the Shah fell. The Americans who taught them, who maintained their helicopters, who supplied their weapons had all fled. Since then, the war had destroyed half of the gunships, lack of parts had downed many more. This ship flew because two others were constantly cannibalized for parts.

They had wasted hours, no, days, flying around looking for mirages before. This was, without doubt, another such day. With hope, there would be no trap like the one that had claimed Mahad and Sishak two months ago. It had taken a week to even find the wreckage.

Homayuni tried his other weapons systems. Many of them were inoperable from lack of parts. The gun and the small rocket pods were still reliable.

"We are entering the valley, Kehan," the pilot said over the intercom, interrupting Homayuni's brooding. "Keep a sharp watch for men on horses." The sleek gunship dipped down, flying between the trees, skirting the western wall of the canyon.

Men on horses, Homayuni snorted, we use a hammer to kill a flea. He flipped the telescopic sight to high power and pressed his head to the scope, scanning the slopes for movement. He had been at it only a moment when he saw the first rider.

"Bandits!" Homayuni called over the intercom as he

centered the sight reticle's cross hairs on the rider and pulled the trigger under his left forefinger.

They were halfway down the far side of the ridge when the helicopter struck, an American-made Cobra gunship with Iranian markings. The helicopter must have been hiding below the trees, no one heard it until it popped up over the treetops and sped down the valley. The first burst from its 7.62mm rotary minigun raked across the trail, churning the dirt and chopping through the foliage like a flying chainsaw. One of Ahmad's men went down, horse and rider stitched with a dozen bullets. The other Kurds were off their mounts in a second, firing at the intruder with their AKs.

Jinx's mule reared up at the noise and the sudden commotion, and Jinx took the opportunity to slide down over the animal's rump, landing on his feet and running toward the pack mules, which were tugging at their leads in panic. Jinx ran up alongside the second pack mule, pulling the knife from his shoulder rig. Carefully avoiding the mule's hooves, he cut the straps that held one of the long green containers onto the mule's pack saddle. The container fell into his arms, and Jinx sprinted across the trail away from the thrashing mule.

"Got one!" Homayuni shouted as they flashed over the small band of riders. "Arming rockets!"

"I have the turret," Ferdowsi called back, flipping the switches that transferred control from the chin turret to his station.

As Homayuni threw the switches that activated the rocket pods, the pilot threw the gunship into a tight left spin, bringing the nose back around for another pass at the mounted rebels. Homayuni held tight to the left hand grip to steady himself as the nimble Cobra spun to finish off its victims.

He was lining up the men on the trail when Ferdowsi suddenly jerked the ship up, swearing and invoking Allah.

"What?" Homayuni shouted, pulling his face up from the sight, "what?"

"Missile!"

Once across the trail, Jinx flipped up the catches on the container and jerked it open. The Stinger missile lay cradled in its rack, three batteries nestled under it. Jinx pocketed one of the big batteries, hefted the missile up on his shoulder, and stepped out into the trail. The Cobra was turning around, the tip of its tail visible above the trees. Jinx pulled the battery/coolant assembly out of his pocket and screwed it into the receptacle in the bottom of the grip-stock. This done, he flipped up the sight panel on the missile's left side and pushed his face up to the sight. The Cobra was behind the trees now, but it would pop up soon.

The sound of rotors came up over the trees as Jinx pushed the actuator lever down, releasing the argon gas coolant into the missile seeker and powering up the battery. The nose of the helicopter was barely visible over the trees when the warbling tone sounded in his ear and the vibrator pad hummed on his right cheekbone, signaling a target lock. Jinx figured the range at half a kilometer. Easy. He pressed the rubber button under his left thumb to uncage the missile's seeker, centered the Cobra in the sight, lifted the nose of the launcher, and pulled the trigger. The blast from the little missile's booster motor startled him, making him flinch. When he opened his eyes, he was in the middle of a cloud of dust, leaves, and grass blown up by the back blast. Ahead, the white smoke from the missile was streaking toward the Cobra.

The helicopter pilot saw the missile and fired at the cloud of debris that marked the launch site. The dust around Jinx was suddenly alive with the angry buzzing of bullets. Jinx hardly heard them as he watched the Stinger close with the doomed gunship. The thin missile slammed into the

Cobra, exploding right behind the cockpit. The crippled chopper pitched forward and slammed into the trees below, an orange fireball marking the impact.

Jinx stood there for a minute just watching the fireball. An odd feeling spread through him, a feeling of exhilaration, power, fear, a hot flash of excitement. "Goddamn," Jinx shouted, "I got it!"

He tipped the empty launcher off his shoulder and looked at it, then looked back at the fire in the trees. Jinx laughed. What a rush, what a sensation.

"No, I said a Bud Lite!" he shouted at the flaming wreck.

He was unlatching the gripstock from the launch tube when Ahmad walked up.

"You have wasted one of my missiles," the Kurd said angrily.

Jinx looked up from his work. "I wasted an enemy gunship," he replied quietly, "with one of *MY* missiles." Jinx spoke quietly so the other Kurds would not hear him. It would not do to insult the leader in front of his men. On the other hand, it was stupid to grovel when you had all the goodies.

Ahmad stood watching as Jinx tucked the gripstock under his arm and walked back to the open green container. Jinx did not even look around as he blew the debris out of the empty case and replaced the gripstock in the box with the two remaining batteries. This done, he gathered up the container, picked up his knife, reinserted it in his shoulder rig, then stood looking at Ahmad as the other Kurds came walking up. The others were visibly impressed, both with his kill and with his coolness under fire.

Ahmad was suddenly wreathed in smiles and stepped forward, clasping Jinx on both shoulders.

"I was right to accept your services, *feringhi*, you have much to offer us," he said loudly, turning Jinx's actions into his own, "you are a fine Persian killer."

This done, Ahmad strode off, gesturing and speaking loudly to his men. Jinx stood watching the man.

Accept my services, indeed, Jinx thought, I'm supposed to be here to turn this mob of rug thugs into a fighting force, and this bozo acts like I'm hired help. Well, we'll see about that, Muhammad. You may have to come to the mountain yet.

As they rode quickly down the length of the valley, a thin finger of oily black smoke threaded its way up into the bright blue sky behind them.

The camp was a cluster of mud and straw buildings punctuated here and there with a wood-frame building. The tiny village clung to the side of a mountain, hidden in the trees that stopped halfway up the slope. The village had clearly been chosen for its defensibility. The rocky hillside was steep below the village. The single, narrow road dropped off almost vertically on the valley side with only a narrow, boulder-strewn shoulder on the mountainside. The valley itself was narrow and twisting, a tough nut to crack from either the ground or the air.

As they rode up, men and women emerged from the buildings, shouting and waving at their leader. They were dressed in the traditional Kurdish way. The men sported bright cummerbunds, and the women wore colorful scarves and belts of coins that contrasted with their otherwise drab garments. Ahmad's popularity was obvious.

All the men were armed. Most carried Soviet AKMs, but there was a smattering of German G-3s and a lone FN. The men carried the weapons casually, as if they were simply extensions of their bodies.

As the crowd gathered around the horsemen, Jinx got a better look at the Kurds. They were not Arabic at all in appearance. Their skin, though tan, was fairer than their Arab neighbors, and their noses lacked the hawk-bill hook common to Arabs.

A much prettier group then the contras, Jinx thought as he looked down at their curious faces, prettier and meaner.

Several of the men were pulling at the missile cases strapped to his pack mule. Jinx ignored them. The Stingers were hardly self-explanatory. Without his guidance, they would not be able to work them at all, much less hit anything. Right now, all he wanted was to get acquainted, gain a little trust, then make his pitch.

Hands literally pulled him from the saddle, then pounded his back, Everyone was smiling at him and rapping Kurdish at him ninety miles an hour.

"They are congratulating you on your kill, Jenkins," Fuad explained as he made his way over to Jinx's side. "News of the attack has preceded us!"

Jinx smiled back and nodded, unsure of how to respond to the praise.

"Fuad, what's the drill here?" Jinx asked as the horses were led away.

"First, we eat," Fuad answered. "Hospitality is first priority here. After that, we talk. Do not be in too big a hurry to get down to business. These folks like to work up to it slowly."

Jinx nodded. The pattern was familiar. A little wine, a little food, then down to the nut cutting.

The feast had been entertaining. The goat was tasty, the wine strong. Jinx kept a low profile, he was obviously not the guest of honor. Ahmad was the star of the show. When he spoke, the Kurds were rapt. Several times during the evening, all faces turned toward Jinx.

"What's the score, Fuad?" Jinx asked softly, leaning toward his guide.

"Your kill this afternoon impressed the hell out of Ahmad's men." Fuad downed a tiny fig and whispered back, "Ahmad is treating it pretty lightly, but your stock is strong. Bombers and helicopters have always kicked these folks' butts. Knocking them down is a big deal."

Jinx could feel the food and the fatigue starting to work on him. The air in the earthen dining hall was thick with smoke, the smell of food, and the pungent smell of unwashed bodies. It was tiring just to breathe. Jinx's eyelids felt like lead; he shook his head to wake up. The Kurds were going strong, regaling one another with tales of some sort. Fuad laughed along with the men, not bothering to translate. Jinx's eyelids had turned to anchors.

"Wake up, Jenkins!" Fuad hissed, shaking Jinx's shoulder. "They are talking about you."

Jinx was instantly awake, his heart pounding, his eyes searching the room. At the far end of the rough wood table, Ahmad was laughing.

"So, my friend, our conversation bores you?"

"Not at all, honored host," Jinx replied. "The air is thin here, it takes getting used to."

Ahmad smiled again. "So, American, what do you have to offer us?"

Jinx was wide awake now, his body flushed with a rush of adrenaline. He stood and pulled Fuad up with him to translate into Kurdish.

"I am here to help you kill your enemies," Jinx began, "for they are our enemies as well." Jinx looked around the room for any sign of agreement. There was none; he went on. "My country is at war with the Soviet Union and their bought dogs, the Iranians. Now the Russians seek to enslave all the land to the Gulf, including Kurdistan. We seek to stop them. It is as simple as that." Jinx folded his hands and waited for some response.

"We know what the Russians want, my friend," Ahmad said, laughing. "What do you want?" The Kurd's face suddenly went serious. "And what do you offer?"

"I offer missiles to kill the helicopters and jets that torment your villages," Jinx replied quietly, "and weapons to stop the tanks that thunder through your land." Around the room, there was a barely detectable lessening of tension. The Kurds knew how effective the American weapons were from the stories of Afghanistan. They wanted the same weapons. ''What I want is to join you in battle against the atheist invaders and against the Iranian dogs.''

Ahmad's face remained passive, but one or two smiles broke out around the room. One of the men turned and spoke to Ahmad. Jinx recognized him as one of the party that had picked them up. As the man spoke, Fuad translated.

''He says you showed no fear during the helicopter attack,'' Fuad said. ''He wants to learn to use the Stinger.''

Around the room, heads nodded.

''And you will teach us to use these weapons?'' Ahmad asked, stroking his short beard.

''I am only one man, Great Bey,'' Jinx answered, trying to sound humble without acting servile. ''Other Americans will come to help me instruct your people.''

''Of course!'' Ahmad taunted. ''When one foreigner comes, hundreds always follow. How many Americans will come with these new weapons, eh?''

''Twelve,'' Jinx answered quickly as the murmuring in the room began to increase, ''only twelve.''

Ahmad smiled again and looked around the room. ''Twelve men will be able to instruct us to use these weapons? A very small number for a very large task!''

''Sometimes one man can be worth much,'' Jinx answered, ''just as one Kurd is worth a hundred Russians or a thousand Persians.''

At this response, the Kurds pounded on the table and hooted.

Ahmad smiled again, his eyes never leaving Jinx's face. ''These 'teachers',' he asked slowly, ''they are Green Berets?''

Jinx nodded, ''They are, Great Bey.''

Ahmad did not reply, but Jinx could see that the man was thinking. The others in the room were nodding and talking among themselves. However exaggerated, the Special Forces reputation was widespread. Even the disaster in the Iranian desert more than a decade before had not tarnished it.

As Jinx scanned the faces in the room, one unsmiling face stood out. Omar Telebani did not look much like the photo taken by SAVAMA ten years earlier, but Jinx recognized him easily. Telebani looked like an Arab. His face was dark, not so much in color, as from expression. His hooded eyes were those of a predator. Second in command to Ahmad, Telebani did all of the dirty work. He was looking at Jinx the way a coyote looks at a poodle.

Finally, Ahmad spoke again. "We will try your weapons, American, but we must talk about your teachers." With that, he turned to one of his lieutenants and began an earnest conversation, ignoring Jinx completely. Jinx sat down slowly and reached for a piece of meat to chew on. Fuad was smiling at him.

"They are a vain lot," Fuad whispered. "You did well to compliment them. I think they like you."

Jinx nodded in reply. Vain lot, indeed, he thought, more like arrogant, ignorant, swaggering bozos. Oh, well, they weren't that different from any guerrilla army, and they were snappier dressers than most. Jinx looked at Fuad and grinned.

"Hey, guerrilla warfare is my life!"

★ 9 ★

Lieut. Arkady Lemzenko lay on his back about twenty meters from his BMD. Black smoke poured from the combat vehicle's rear hatches. The late afternoon sun was low in the western sky and shone irritably into his eyes. He could see the men from his squad lying in the dust behind the BMD. They were very still. He wrinkled his nose at the smell of burning rubber and fuel. The air was tainted by drifting streamers of black smoke. Farther to the rear, just within his limited vision, he could see more BMDs strung along the sides of the road. Most of them, too, were bleeding black smoke into the sky.

A grinding rumble behind him drew his attention. Arching his neck he slowly turned his head toward the road. A T-55 tank was slowly approaching down the gravel road. Painted sand yellow and flying the red-and-green flag of the rebel Iranians, the armored vehicles simply did not appear warlike. Green was the only proper color for machines of war.

On the tank's engine deck were clustered a knot of soldiers brandishing G-3 rifles. The machine began to edge its way slowly around his BMD. He could feel the ground vibrate. One of the soldiers, observing his interest, meekly waved his hand in greeting. Arkady lifted his own hand slightly and made an effort to return a weak half wave.

The soldier laughed and pointed Arkady out to his comrades.

Having cleared the BMD, the loyalist Iranian tank picked up speed and rumbled down the road, with its deceptive flag flapping in the breeze. Other tanks gingerly picked their way south across the rocky ground, taking pains to avoid running over any of the "dead" paratroopers. The smoke seemed even thicker now. The engineers were probably throwing more fuel-soaked tires on the fires. Their columns of dirty black smoke practically obscured the rugged mountains Arkady saw in the distance. No matter where one looked, one saw mountains in this strange country.

Arkady did not really approve of his small part in Operation Storm Front. It was all a sham, of course, for the benefit of the Americans. He did not understand the whole purpose of the deception, not that his understanding mattered to those above him. In fact, those in charge wished he knew even less because the ultimate goal of the operation was no concern of his.

This sham defeat was galling. Especially after his subunit had performed so well in the day's confused battle. His platoon's massed automatic weapons, backed by the 73mm guns and machine guns on their three BMDs, had chopped down a hundred real Iranian rebels as they charged from the ravines, screaming unintelligible words of hate.

Later the rebel prisoners had come down the road, beaten, in shock. They were guarded by paratroopers who freely used their rifle butts to herd their charges along. Many of the captives were wounded, their bodies patched with filthy blood-soaked bandages. All had the look of condemned men, moving in slow motion, staring at the ground, disoriented. He found out later they were condemned in fact as well as in appearance.

The prisoners were turned over to the loyal Iranians, themselves arrogant and boastful. Arkady's battalion commander had called all of his officers together and briefed them on the operation's next phase, passing out rough diagrams to each company describing where they would place their vehicles, how the "dead" soldiers were to be arranged, and the deception measures taken to make some vehicles appear on fire.

His unit had fought well, and Arkady thought it unfair that his proud regiment was required now to pretend it had been defeated by the Iranian rabble.

At least they were not to take part in the executions of the rebels. That was up to the loyalists. The commander further ordered that the soldiers were to be prevented from even observing the executions. The *zampolits*—(political officers)—wanted to stop all rumors and discussions of the subject.

Arkady had watched from a distance. Through his binoculars, he saw the defeated rebels herded into ravines as loyalists lined the edges. Machine guns were placed at the ends and, without ceremony, opened fire as soon as they were set-up. Soldiers on the ravines' lips shouted, cheered, and jeered while firing their own weapons and throwing grenades into the caldrons of death.

The bodies were loaded into trucks by other prisoners. The trucks moved to predetermined positions, and the bodies, now nothing more than deception aids, were dumped in clusters among rock formations and ravines. The prisoners, doing the dirty work under the watchful eye of loyalist guards, were added to the dead when their work was through. They were shot offhandedly when they completed their labors.

He turned away ill, shouting at his men to move the BMDs to their positions and set off the RDG-1 black-smoke grenades in a bucket inside the troop compartments. One man, wearing a protective mask, sat in the gunner's compartment and kept the bucket supplied with grenades. American reconnaissance aircraft, mere specks high in the sky, streaked overhead. One, a Phantom, even came screaming over at only 200 meters.

After sunset his soldiers were led from the battlefield by guides from battalion headquarters. They left their BMDs behind. Sham vehicle-recovery operations began later. While they waited for their vehicles, Arkady's men were given a hot meal, the first since they had air landed in Shiraz.

The battalion commander again called his officers together. In the morning they were to act as prisoners, Soviet prisoners of the "victorious" rebel Iranians. Then they would be trucked back to Shiraz. Some of their BMDs would be there for them to use in the operation's next phase.

Most of the officers had witnessed the executions. They were all young and inexperienced, though not the novices they had been the night before. Only a few of the battalion staff has served in Afghanistan. Almost all were Russians or other Slavics. None were from the Soviet Union's south central republics. None had a Muslim upbringing or even any exposure to such *natsmen*—a contraction for "national minorities". The commander explained that the Muslims were a self-righteous and brutal people with no respect for those not practicing their religion. He went on to say that they despised and abused nonbelievers.

"But what of what we saw this afternoon, Comrade Commander?" asked another platoon commander. "It was Muslims killing Muslims and brutally." The *zampolit* made note of the officer's name, one he had noticed before. The young officer asked too many questions and was far too serious.

"I served as an adviser to the Iraqis during the war between them and our current allies," the battalion commander responded. "Once, the Iranians forced a crossing of the Shatt-al-Arab waterway, a massive defensive complex built by the Iraqis. Almost ten thousand Iranians reached the far side. The Iraqis counterattacked and cut

off the Iranians, mostly Revolutionary Guards.'' He paused
a moment. "In three days the Iraqis killed every Iranian
that had crossed the waterway. The Iranians asked for no
mercy. They willingly died for their . . . god." His voice
trailed off as he remembered.

The *zampolit*, seeing his commander falter, immediately stood.

"The commander desires that we all be aware of the
dangers of religious fanaticism," he lectured. "These
people do not have the same values and goals as good
Soviet citizens." He swung into his practiced speech.
"They are vicious in their beliefs, having been led misguided down the path of superstition. They are different
from the materialistic capitalists but no less dangerous and
even less trustworthy!"

A quiet fart sounded from among the officers sitting
cross-legged on the rocky ground, no doubt caused by the
greasy kasha they had eaten for supper. A few of the officers chuckled.

The weary paratroopers slept in the open that night,
rolled up in their blankets on the ground. Arkady lay awake
for a long time. He could not stop seeing himself standing
on the edge of a ravine. He was firing his submachine gun
into Iranians scrambling around in panic on the blood-
drenched rocks below. Before finally falling asleep, he
saw himself in the ravine, looking up at Americans as they
peered down at him.

"What we have witnessed today, sir, is the defeat of a
Soviet airborne division!" The lieutenant colonel presented the briefing as though the corps commander was
the only individual present, even though the briefing tent
was filled to capacity with staff officers and senior NCOs.
Everyone wanted to be in on this briefing, to hear firsthand
what had happened. Rumors were rife among the XVIII
Airborne Corps' main TOC. They had practiced for this

war, but it had turned into something far different from any of the scenarios they had practiced.

"It initially developed as a classic Soviet meeting engagement," continued the colonel. He jabbed his pointer at a spot twenty kilometers north of Shiraz on the acetate-covered 1:250,000 scale map of southern Iran. "Communications intercepts indicated a well-organized Soviet operation developing. But, much to our surprise, the 27th Iranian Mech Brigade began to displace from its defensive positions east of Shiraz." He moved across the map's front as two sergeants hung up a sheet of white butcher paper profusely marked with red and orange symbols and arrows. Red tactical symbols traditionally indicated enemy forces, in this case both Soviet and loyalist Iranian. Orange had been selected to indicate another enemy, the rebel Iranians, an enemy of both sides. This three-way war was definitely different from any peacetime scenario.

The briefer stepped up to the graphic. The few light bulbs suspended from the tent's ridge pole were much too dim for everyone to see the details. "We initially thought the 27th Brigade was going to attempt an enveloping maneuver to outflank the rebel forces. Maybe that was the original intention, sir, we don't know. But the airborne regiments began to withdraw before we could determine what the 27th was attempting to accomplish." The pointer moved rapidly, like a fencer's foil.

"Due to the position of the 27th, we at first thought the Soviets were attempting to draw the rebels into a trap, that the 27th would strike into their flank and rear with other Soviet forces to be committed when needed to counter any unexpected enemy action. Their second echelon force has that assigned mission."

"But the Sovs had no second echelon, Bill," challenged the general.

"No, sir, not as such. They apparently determined the rebels were not significantly strong enough to warrant the need for a second echelon force to assume the first echelon's mission if it failed to achieve its objectives.'' The briefer stepped back as another sheet of butcher paper went up.

While this was being accomplished he continued with some additional observations. The sergeant had trouble making the tape stick. ''The Soviets employed a great deal of smoke, both artillery delivered and smoke pots. In fact, they used an inordinate amount. We feel that this was an effort to confuse the rebels. They made only limited use of tactical air support, much to their later disadvantage.''

The sheet was finally up. He stepped back up to the graphic. ''It was just after 1100 hours that we began to realize what was taking place. The 27th Brigade unexpectedly attacked the Soviets' east flank as they withdrew. The 27th undoubtedly went over to the rebels' side. The Soviets were totally unprepared for such an eventuality. The 27th rolled up the flank of the airborne regiment, whose designation we never did determine.''

''I guess that's a moot point now, Bill,'' laughed the general. The others in the tent laughed, too.

''Yes, sir, I'll skip the order of battle data.'' Unruffled, the colonel continued. ''The Iranian reserve mech brigade was finally committed as the remnants of the two airborne regiments fell back. There are some indications, from communications intercepts, that the Soviets totally panicked and began attacking the reserve brigade, which had remained loyal to the Soviets, as it attempted to cover their withdrawal. The reserve brigade was then engaged by the 27th in a well-organized flank attack. Sir, the situation became extremely confused at this point.''

Several of the audience chuckled. Everyone was feeling smug that things were going so badly for the Soviets, that they couldn't even trust their own ''allies''. Several jokes were already making the rounds.

''Sir, air recce has shown us two Soviet airborne regiments and a loyalist Iranian brigade totally destroyed.'' A captain handed the general an open folder of aerial photographs. "The three rebel brigades appear to have taken a very hard beating themselves. The third airborne regiment, defending southeast of Shiraz, and the other loyal Iranian brigade, defending to the south, have both pulled into Shiraz. The survivors of the two airborne regiments and the reserve brigade have joined them." The sergeants hung a third sheet of paper, this one depicting the current dispositions of all involved forces.

"They are hurriedly preparing a defense oriented toward the north. The three rebel brigades are digging into the hills to the north of the Soviet positions. The two original rebel brigades are mere shells of their former strength. They are now battalions, for all practical purposes. The 27th Brigade is assessed as a still-viable force." He was finished. He didn't ask the general if he had any questions; he knew there would be.

"Bill, what you're telling me is that there is an airborne regiment backed by a straight-leg infantry brigade and a bunch of whipped-ass survivors holed up in Shiraz." He stood and walked toward the map board. "Sitting on the other side of the city is a pretty good mech brigade and some more whipped-ass Iranians."

"Yes, sir."

"How far away is the main Soviet force?" the general asked earnestly.

"Almost two hundred klicks—kilometers to the northwest, sir," said someone from one of the intelligence cells.

"And how far away is the 24th Div's, eh, which brigade?"

"The First, sir," chimed in another officer. Everyone was starting to see where the general was leading. A ripple of expectation flowed through the tent.

"How heavy is it?"

"Two tank and two mech battalions, sir," responded someone from operations.

"And what else?"

"A self-propelled 155 battalion, the multiple-launch

rocket battery, and an armored cavalry troop, sir," injected another operations officer.

"The division's aviation brigade has two attack helicopter battalions, sir," chimed in another ops type. "We could even beef it up more, from the 101st attack chopper assets, and punch it in, too, sir!" Everyone was warming to the fast-developing situation.

"Harv," called the general.

"Yes, sir," answered the deputy chief of staff for operations.

"Get started on an op plan right away. Let's reinforce that brigade with aviation and get them in there fast. If we pull this off right, we can have Shiraz yet!"

"You got it, sir!"

"James," the general called for his G2.

"Sir."

"Turn the MI brigade loose on everything in the Shiraz area. I want a good picture of what we're actually facing, where it is, and any changes in their dispositions." The general looked around the eager faces of his staff. They were ready to go. "Gentlemen, it's going to be a long night for all of us. Let's do it!"

"Larry," Colonel James Larder called to his assistant as he scanned a list of his intelligence-collection assets. It was a helpful aid for managing the many and diversified collection means he had available. It was too easy to forget one.

"Yes, sir," answered the young major as he stirred sugar into his sixth styrofoam cup of coffee.

"The LRSCs—how many teams have been committed?"

The major opened a blue three-ring binder and turned to a tabbed section. "Out of thirty-three available teams from both companies, twenty-four have been committed. Two are known compromised." That was a nice way of saying that those two teams were probably all dead.

"That many?"

"Yes, sir, plus we have III Corps' company working as long-range desert groups killing tanks."

"Shit," mumbled the G2.

"Airborne to that, sir!"

"Let's put a couple of teams into the Shiraz area to get a close-up look at what's going on. This is all too strange to me," the colonel muttered.

"You, too, sir?"

"You bet, Larry. It's all starting to look too good. I want to put some eyeballs on the ground."

"I'll call the MI brigade ops ASAP, sir."

★ 10 ★

He could hear the tanks, the sound of their clanking treads borne on the cold wind that swept down from the north. With the sound, the wind brought clouds of talclike dust. The dust filled eyes, ears, throats, and weapons.

The dust hid the tanks, but it hid him as well. He hunkered down in the shallow wind-carved depression behind some scrub plants, hiding until the tanks got close. The closer they got, the better. The Muj always said to get close. When the steel monsters were close enough to touch, he and the others would spring up and fire their short-range M136 rocket launchers, more commonly known by their Swedish designation, AT4. The surprise and shock would keep the tankers' heads down while the Advanced Anti-tank Weapon System–Medium (AAWS–M) gunners went to work with their longer-range weapons. The AAWS–M, called the ass-scam by the troops, was the high-tech replacement for the Dragon missile. The AAWS–M, made by Texas Instruments, was a fire-and-forget system relying on an infrared seeker to guide the missile to its target. The old Dragon required the gunner to sit and guide the missile to the target. That also meant he would have to sit and take whatever the bad guys threw at him.

The only problem was that they would be right there

when the AAWS–Ms landed. It was a tough trade-off, but so far it was the best tactic.

BJ slid the thick tube of the AT4 forward, sliding his hand down the weapon to the firing controls. It was the replacement for the long-used LAW—Light Antitank Weapon. His fingers found the cocking lever. When he had the weapon up by his face, BJ pushed the lever forward and to the right, cocking the long firing rod. This done, he rolled the bulky fifteen-pound weapon up on his shoulder as the sound of the tanks grew louder.

To his left, Shannon Hickey was up on one knee behind a scraggly bush, cocking his launcher. The dark barrel of a T-80 suddenly appeared, spearing through the dust. Hickey was watching the lead tank, tracking it as it passed. With a little luck, they could pop these fuckers and get away clean, using the dust and the AAWS–Ms to cover their escape. Hickey let it go by, then hit it from the rear.

Watching Hickey shoot the lead tank, BJ missed the tank that ran over him. The tank was suddenly just there, its treads whirling, throwing dust ahead of it. BJ pitched the AT4 away and rolled to the left. Too late he realized that he had rolled the wrong way. Instead of rolling between the treads, he rolled right under one. The flat rubber pad on the tank's track come down on his leg, and BJ screamed, the sound lost in the roar of the turbine engine.

BJ felt himself being pushed into the soft sand. The sand gave way, then hardened. BJ's body absorbed the rest of the pressure. He felt another thick rubber pad crush his groin. The pain was sharp but not as bad as he had expected. The next tread came down on his chest. Ribs cracked, more sharp pain shot through his chest as all the air was forced out of his lungs. He gripped the tread that slowly bore down on his head, pushing vainly against it to stop its relentless fall. The rubber tread twisted his head sideways, pushing it down into the hot sand. The grinding torture in his chest was nothing compared to the pressure in his skull. His eyes seemed about to pop out. BJ lay there as the tank passed over him, suffocating him beneath the tread. The world, seen from under the tread, went red then black. The tread shook his face back and forth.

"Damn it, BJ," Hickey hissed, "shut up! Wake up! The shit's starting!"

Shannon Hickey's hand was over BJ's mouth as he woke up. Hickey was shaking his head, holding his hand over BJ's mouth. Down the hill, 500 meters away, the Soviet column sped down the road, a dozen tanks and half a dozen APCs. As the dream faded, BJ realized that he had fallen asleep on the ambush, a serious, often fatal mistake. Hickey had let him sleep, another error.

It had been cold when they arrived here before dawn. Now the sun was up and a light breeze was blowing up from the valley. It would warm up later, but right now the cool breeze, the bright sunshine, and the near-purple sky brought a flash of memory to him, a memory of football games and girls in sweaters and short skirts. He held that memory until Hickey punched his arm and pointed down the valley.

The column was just entering the kill zone, a 500-meter stretch of Highway 7 that ran from Isfahan south to Shahreza. Two hundred meters east of the highway was a dry riverbed ten feet deep. The two Humvees were hidden there. Four two-man AT4 teams were hidden in the scrub brush fifty meters west of the riverbed, between the river and the highway.

BJ and Hickey were with the AAWS–M teams hidden in the boulders 500 meters south of the kill zone. BJ only hoped that their crash training course had made them proficient gunners. The lead tank, its commander standing up in his hatch scanning the flat valley with binoculars, was closing in on the two antitank mines buried in a pothole at the near end of the kill zone.

BJ shook his head to clear the cobwebs, blinking and rubbing his eyes with the back of his hand.

"Ready, Shan?" he asked as Hickey readied the radio

detonator that would set off the decoy charges planted off to the west of the road. The decoys would divert the Soviets' attention from the real ambush, giving the AAWS–M gunners time to get their missiles on the way before they were detected.

There were four AAWS–M positions. Two at the far south end of the ambush in the rocks with BJ and Hickey, and two in the dry riverbed halfway between the rocks and the hidden Humvees. The pair in the rocks would fire first, as their missiles had the longest flight times. When their missiles were nearly to their targets, the second pair would fire. The firing of the AAWS–Ms was the signal to the AT4s to open up. Firing at close range, the AT4s would keep the tankers occupied while the AAWS–Ms reloaded. Two M60 machine guns with the AT4s and another in the rocks with BJ and Hickey would keep the supporting Soviet riflemen busy.

"Anytime, buddy," Hickey responded, his finger poised over the red firing button of the M122 radio detonator.

BJ watched as the lead tank approached the mines. He wanted it to appear that the lead tank had been hit by fire from the decoys. When the lead tank was fifty meters from the mines, BJ looked at Hickey and shouted, "Now, Shan! Blow 'em!"

Hickey pressed the red button and held it down. Two hundred meters west of the highway, the two radio receivers picked up the signal and set off the detonating cord that linked the charges. The five quarter-pound TNT blocks exploded, blasting their dirt-filled sandbags behind them in big billowing clouds. The charges were a trick designed to look like missile launchers firing. The mines in the road would simulate a rocket hit on the lead tank.

It took a second for the sound of the blasts to reach him, but when it did, the commander of the lead tank jerked his head around to the right toward the puffs of dust and spoke quickly into his troat mike, dropping back into the relative safety of his tank.

He nearly had the hatch closed when the T-80 ran over the two buried mines. The mines, linked together with detonating cord, fired twin jets of fire into the thin underbelly of the tank. The fire erupted from the open turret hatch, slamming the hatch open. The tank continued to roll for another twenty meters, then blew up, the turret popping off and landing upside down next to the highway like the shell of a dead steel turtle.

The rest of the column reacted quickly to the attack. They swung off the road toward the attackers, presenting their armored fronts to the enemy and firing quick shots at the billowing clouds of dust. The BMPs lunged forward in front of the tanks, then slowed to disgorge their infantry. The BMPs were the first to discover the mines planted in the scraggly brush along the road. Two personnel carriers ran over mines. The first was directly over the M21 when it went off, turning the cramped interior of the BMP into an oven. Its hatches flew open, but no survivors emerged. The second BMP lost a track to the mine, but its stunned occupants tumbled out the rear doors and ran from the smoking wreck. They were the first Soviets to realize the blasts were a ruse. Off to the south, they saw the back blasts from the AAWS–Ms as they fired at the now vulnerable tanks.

The AAWS–M had been a godsend to the infantry. It hadn't taken long to realize how vulnerable the old Dragon launchers were. In the forests of Europe, where their flight times were short, the Dragons had done well. Here in the desert the gunner was very exposed, easy prey for an alert tank gunner as he sat immobile, guiding his missile toward a moving Soviet tank. The huge cloud of dust the Dragon kicked up when it fired was like a sign saying, "Here I am, shoot me." The Soviets kept high explosive-fragmentation rounds loaded in their tank guns so they could quickly pop them off at any back blast cloud. Few Dragon gunners could keep their minds on the target when steel fragments were zipping around them.

Here the AAWS–M gunners held their fire until something focused the tankers' attention elsewhere, then locked their missiles on target and fired. Once locked on, the AAWS–M guided itself to the target while the gunner ducked back under cover and reloaded the command and launch unit.

As BJ watched the AAWS–Ms fly toward the exposed flanks of the nearest tanks, four more dust clouds erupted from the brush east of the road. The AT4s were firing at the backs of the tanks and the personnel carriers. Three BMPs went up in smoke as the bulbous 84mm rounds from the AT4s hit the fuel cells in the rear doors, frying the fleeing occupants. A T-80, hit in the engine, lurched to a stop and belched orange flames from the engine compartment. Its crew threw open the hatches and rolled off the burning tank.

The four AAWS–M missiles arrived on their targets with huge flashes of flame and black smoke. Three of the tanks blew up. The fourth, hit on its left track, spun to the left and stopped. Its turret slowly turned to the left, feebly seeking its attackers.

From his vantage point 500 meters away, BJ watched the ambush unfold. The tankers had been fooled, but they were wising up now, spinning their tanks in clouds of dust, searching for the real attackers. The AT4s fired again, killing two more BMPs and damaging a third. Each man in the AT4 teams carried three of the self-contained rounds. They would fire once more, then run for the riverbed where the Humvees waited to spirit them to safety. Tracers from the two M60s streaked across the highway, arcing up into the bright blue sky off the armored hides of the BMPs. The guns were raking the Soviet infantry, which sought cover behind their tanks. In the swirling dust and smoke, more than one Soviet soldier was crushed by the treads of a spinning T-80.

* * *

The first indication Sergei Gremitskikh got that anything was wrong was the dull thumps outside and the sudden screaming on the command channel.

"Back blasts! Right rear! Engage!" The company commander's voice broke through. "All subunits, engage right!"

The company was under attack from the west, the number of attackers unknown. At least the back blasts meant that there were missile crews out there. In Germany, tanks and crews died without warning, with no attacker to strike back at. Here in the desert, it was different. There was little cover for either side. The missile crews could be easily killed here, it was only a question of how many Soviet tanks they would get first.

The bastards had let them get close again. They were fighting just like the *Basmachi* had in Afghanistan, catching a column in a tight pass or using the weather, or the terrain, to get up close to the tanks.

"Right turn," Gremitskikh shouted at the driver. "Enemy right, load high-explosive fragmentation!"

"Loaded!" the gunner answered. Gremitskikh knew that there was an HE-frag round in the breech, but the drill kept everyone sharp and cut down the confusion at the beginning of a battle.

Gremitskikh clutched at his hatch lever, using it to steady himself as the tank lurched to the right. He jerked the turret control to the right, turning the long 125mm gun tube to face the attackers. The gunner's face was pressed to his sight, searching for a target. When the dust clouds were in his sight, the gunner called out, "Target, back blast!"

"Fire!" Gremitskikh shouted into his intercom.

The tank rocked under the recoil of the big gun. The whine of the automatic loader followed the sharp crack of the main gun.

"Load HE-frag!" Gremitskikh shouted to the gunner. He turned the carousel to pick up a high-explosive fragmentation round. The automatic loader snapped it up into the breach and crammed the self-contained propellant charge in behind it. Inside the turret, the air was suddenly thick with the acrid fumes still lingering in the gun breech. With the hatch shut, the temperature began to rise as well. The thought of fighting here in the summer flickered through Gremitskikh's mind. It was not a pleasant thought.

"Loaded!"

Gremitskikh was about to fire again when the command channel came alive again with an order to face about! The enemy was behind them as well.

"Driver," Gremitskikh shouted into the intercom, "face about!"

A sharp concussion shook the tank. They were hit! Inside the tank there was no fire, no explosion, but the fire lights from the engine compartment were all lit. The enemy round had hit the engine compartment!

Gremitskikh unlocked the hatch and stood up in his seat, reaching for the 12.7mm gun. The big weapon was locked in its carry position. Gremitskikh pulled the locking pin and swung the gun around. Thick, oily black smoke was pouring out of the rear deck. There were no flames, but the tank was clearly dead. Gremitskikh searched the swirling dust and the thick smoke, looking for the Americans that had killed his tank. Movement caught his eye, and he swiveled the NSV gun around to rip into the bastards.

Through his binoculars, BJ could see the tanker's face. The tanker was firing his machine gun at the scrub brush that hid the AT4 teams. BJ cringed as the stream of .51 caliber bullets ripped into the brush, incendiary rounds flashing. He searched the brush for a glimpse of his men. The stream of Soviet bullets stopped. When BJ looked back at the tank, the tanker was slumped over the side of his turret.

"Motherfucker!" Tyrone King thought as the bush a few feet away from him erupted in an explosion of dust and dirt clods. He hunched down behind the scraggly bushes that hid him from the wildly firing Soviets. Not that the bushes would stop anything, but they were all the cover he had. He heard the M60 fire a short burst, then heard a scream from Penny, the gunner. He was hit but still alive. The M60 fired again, but the bursts were short, not as persistent as before. King hefted his last AT4 and pointed it at a BMP that was emerging from behind a burning T-80. King flipped the cocking lever forward, readying the weapon, then pushed his Kevlar helmet back, wiping the hot, salty sweat from his eyes with the back of his hand. He centered the personnel carrier in the weapon's simple sights, squeezed the safety bar with his fingers, and pressed the red firing button with his right thumb. The AT4 roared, rocking King back on his rear. He did not even look to see where it went. King dropped the spent fiberglass tube and scuttled over to the machine gun position. Bob Penny, the machine gunner was hit in the head, blood running down the left side of his face. He was still firing, holding the gun one-handed by its pistol grip.

"Penny, you OK?" King barked as he slid into the shallow firing position.

The gunner slumped forward on his gun. "No, Ty, I'm hit, man," he moaned. "Fucker got me with that twelve-seven."

King pulled the gunner back into the hole and quickly looked him over. Penny had a deep crease across the top of his head. His helmet was gone, blown off his head by the bullet that should have blown his head off. His left arm was hanging useless, broken by another 12.7mm round.

"Take it easy, Penny," King told the wounded man as he turned back to man the now silent M60. As King hefted the gun up and began pumping 7.62mm rounds into the Soviets, Penny opened his field dressing pouch with his good hand and clumsily began to bandage the gory head wound that still bled like a red waterfall.

The other AT4 gunners had fired their last rounds and now threw M34 white phosphorus smoke grenades to cover their retreat. Falling back to the riverbed under the cover of the M60s, they would cover the machine gunners from the riverbed.

King fired short bursts at the shapes that darted from one Soviet vehicle to the next. Off to the right, he could see someone starting toward the riverbed. It was Murphy.

"Murphy!" King screamed as loud as he could. "Murphy! Come here, I need some help! Murphy!"

Murphy could not hear him and sprinted toward the safety of the riverbank.

"Damn it! Fuckin' deaf white boys!" King muttered to himself as he raked the column with his gun. Through the swirling white smoke to his right, he suddenly saw the reason for Murphy's quick exit. Two squads of Soviet riflemen burst through the smoke, firing at the now vacated positions. King dropped the M60 and grabbed at the four Claymore mine clackers lying on the edge of the firing position. He squeezed two at a time, hardly looking up to see which mines were detonating. As the second pair went off, King went back to the M60, jerking it around to engage the counterattack. Only half of the enemy were left standing. The Claymores had caught the Soviets in an interlocking pattern of supersonic ball bearings. The survivors were still firing, but they now sought cover. King hammered at them with the M60, firing short bursts at individuals, killing with each burst. An M203 grenade burst in front of the Soviets. The others had made it back to the riverbed.

"Come on, Penny," King hollered as he slung the M60 around his neck, "we're gettin' our asses outta here!"

He scooped up the unconscious Penny and slung the limp body over his left shoulder, leaving his right hand free to fire the gun. He ran bent over, lugging the burden of the heavy gun and his wounded buddy. Bullets whined by as he ran, but King did not stop to fight. He ran as fast as he could, his eyes locked on the lip of the riverbed.

That riverbed must be a mile away, he thought as he stumbled, a cloud of fine dust puffing out in front of him. He recovered and ran on. Why did we get so far away? Shit, we musta' been crazy! He felt like he was running in oatmeal, his legs barely moving. The bullets whipping by sounded like hornets. He saw the ravine's edge only a few feet away. He jumped.

King, the machine gun, and Penny tumbled to the bottom of the riverbed in a pile and a cloud of dust. It took a second for King to get his bearings, but there was Murphy looking down at him, his eyes wide.

"Christ, Ty, I can't believe you made it." Behind Murphy, the rest of the AT4 team were firing M4 carbines and M203 grenade launchers at the Soviet column.

"Penny's hit!" King gasped up at Murphy. "Get 'im over to the Humvee!" A stream of tracers zinged overhead.

Murphy was already pulling Penny away, tugging at the man's wounded arm.

"Easy, Murph! His arm's hit!"

"It's OK, Ty," Murphy answered, looking over at the huge black man. "Penny's dead."

The two Humvees were moving, picking up the surviving AT4 gunners. Murphy and King put Penny's body in one of the Humvees. Murphy took the M60 and told King to take the one Humvee and go on while the other stayed and kept the Soviets busy. There was no argument.

As the Humvee bounced down the riverbed, King could see Murphy and two others up on the bank, firing long bursts at the burning Soviet column.

BJ was still holding his breath when the first Humvee lurched up the riverbed. This was the tricky part, the withdrawal. The Soviets were still firing, but not in an organized fashion. The AAWS–Ms and the AT4s had taken the fight out of them. All the BMPs were on fire and more than half the tanks as well. Of the remaining tanks, only two were moving and they were firing smoke canisters, trying to get out of the kill zone. A dozen Soviet riflemen clung to the two tanks, firing wildly toward the riverbed. Clouds of black-and-white smoke drifted across the small battlefield.

The Humvees picked up the two AAWS–M teams from the riverbed and made their way quickly behind the rocks where the rest of the LRRPs waited.

"AAAOOOWWWHHH!" Murphy howled as the two Humvees skidded to a stop. "Get in, we're outta here!"

As Hickey and the remaining AAWS–M teams piled into the vehicles, BJ climbed in the lead machine and took a seat atop a Stinger missile case. In the front passenger seat, Ty King sat staring out at the narrow valley.

"King, you with us, man?" BJ asked over the roar of the engine and the clamor of the troops.

"They got Penny, BJ," King said, pointing back at the red-haired body strapped to one of the empty missile racks.

"I know, Ty. They got Thompkins, too."

King hadn't even missed the other M60 gunner. Now he turned and looked at BJ, his dark face covered with sweat, dust, and anger.

"This is some shit, BJ," the big man hissed, "some awful shit."

Two dead out of twenty, BJ thought, ten percent. It wouldn't take long to get all of them at this rate. King was right, this tank bustin' was some awful shit and sure as hell not what they were trained for.

★ 11 ★

BORRRNNK!

There is the sound again, louder this time, Ivan Tetrak thought as the BTR-80 whined and growled its way up the slope. Something is wrong with this machine.

"Driver," he yelled above the whine of the engine, "pull over and stop."

"We will catch hell for this delay," he grumbled to himself, "but better to be late than not arrive at all."

The eight-wheeled command vehicle lurched to the side of the narrow road. Behind him, the first launcher pulled to the left and came up alongside. Lieutenant Popov slid down the side window and called out, his voice lost in the engine noise. Tetrak pointed to both ears and opened the right door, stepping down into the soft dirt that lined the road. He walked around the front of the BTR. Popov met him at the corner of the vehicle.

"Trouble?" Popov shouted.

"Transmission, I think," Tetrak shouted back, "I want to look at it before it goes out completely!"

Popov nodded and turned back to his launcher. He climbed up, gesturing to the driver to pull ahead of Tetrak's BTR and shut down. Popov jumped down, and the big launcher eased forward, pulling off to the right ahead of the stricken BTR.

131

Tetrak's driver, Somov, was already under the machine, checking for damage or leaking fluid.

Tetrak walked back down the grade past the second launcher, which had pulled in behind. He looked back down the long hill.

All in all, he thought, it could be much worse. The temperature was cool but not freezing, and the night's rain had been just enough to keep down the dust without turning it to mud. If the worst happened, either launcher could probably pull the damaged BTR, as long as the grade did not get any steeper. Tetrak turned and walked back up to check on Somov's progress.

As Tetrak walked up, Somov slithered out from under the BTR. His face had a stream of red fluid across his forehead that pooled up in his right ear. He wiped at it with his sleeve, then looked up at Tetrak.

"Comrade Captain, there is a leak in the transmission case," he reported dejectedly. "I think it can be repaired, but it will take some time to fashion a patch."

Tetrak nodded and walked forward to speak with Popov.

"What are they?" Ismet Hosseini asked softly.

"Missiles, some sort of missiles," his companion, Arshak Rahman, answered.

"I know that, goat's breath," Hosseini snorted. "I do not know what type."

Rahman smiled. "Let us take them and examine them at our leisure." He eased the Dragunov SVD sniper rifle up to his shoulder. Hosseini put his hand on the long rifle.

"Wait, my friend, let them grow bored first," Hosseini cautioned. "Then they will be easy prey."

A flicker of disappointment crossed Rahman's face, but he eased the rifle down and turned to lean back against the mound of dirt that hid them from the Russians seventy meters away. Rahman rolled over on his back and pulled a piece of cheese from a pocket. He studied the cheese, nibbling at it as if he had no other concern in the world. Rahman must have felt Hosseini looking at him, because he suddenly looked up, held up the cheese, and raised his eyebrows. Hosseini nodded, and Rahman cut off half the cheese and handed it to Hosseini. The two men spent the next twenty minutes eating the cheese and watching the Russians tinker with the broken personnel carrier.

"Damn!" Somov roared again from beneath the BTR. "I need more hands under here! I cannot do this alone!"

"Safarin, Kaslov," Tetrak barked, "get under there and help him! We do not have forever to waste here." To himself, Tetrak added, and I do not wish to be stuck on this road after dark.

The two privates scrambled under the BTR to help Somov, who grumbled and swore without letup.

Rahman watched the Russians wiggle under the vehicle.

"Now they are distracted," he said softly. "Now we can take them."

Hosseini quickly counted the Russians. There were eight standing around the BTR, three underneath. Eleven Russians against the two of them. A fair enough fight. Hosseini slid forward to the top of the mound. He pushed the selector lever of his AKM down to the semiauto position and brought it to his shoulder, placing the front sight between the boot soles of one of the Russians lying under the BTR.

"After you, my friend," he said to Rahman.

Rahman took two deep breaths, his usual routine. Two deep breaths followed by ten quick shots. He peered through the four-power telescope, picking the order of his victims. When he was satisfied, he fired. His shots were spaced a half second apart, just long enough to bring the rifle down after each shot. Hosseini fired, the AKM bucking in his hands. He fired one quick shot between each set of exposed feet. Beside him, Rahman was firing steadily.

Each time the SVD boomed, a Russian fell. Even those who ran fell. Rahman did not miss.

Under the BTR, the feet of two of the mechanics were still thrashing. Hosseini fired another shot between each set of feet, then flipped up the rifle's selector to automatic and began firing short bursts at the four men who ran toward the second transporter–launcher. The middle two men fell, tripping the fourth with their bodies.

The first Russian reached the door of the launcher and was almost inside before Rahman's shot slammed him against the side of the launcher. He fell, his dead body hanging from the jacket sleeve hung up on the open door's handle.

Hosseini sighted the man who had tripped, who now rolled onto his feet, running for his life. Hosseini cut him down in mid-stride. The eleven Russians were dead. Less than a dozen seconds had passed since the first shot.

"I was wrong, Arshak," Hosseini said brightly, "the odds were not even at all."

Rahman laughed, then sat down and calmly replaced the empty magazine in his rifle with a full one. He then rolled up over the mound and put another round into each crumpled figure.

"Ismet, how many were there under the little tank?" Rahman asked.

"Three."

"I see only two now," Rahman answered, pointing.

Sure enough, there were only four feet sticking out from under the BTR.

"Allah's beard!" Hosseini swore. "One has escaped." The embarrassment showed on his face.

Rahman chuckled as he finished off the Russians he had shot. "You must finish him, Ismet."

"He will not get far," Hosseini answered casually, "shot in the manhood!"

"Russians have no manhood," Rahman laughed. "If that is where you shot, you missed him." Rahman stood and cradled his rifle in his arms. "Come on, Ismet, let us go look at our prize." The wiry little warrior stood up and casually sauntered down to the road. Hosseini followed, his rifle at the ready. There was no reason to trust Russians, even dead ones.

Rahman was already climbing around on the big launcher parked behind the smaller BTR. Hosseini walked over to the BTR and pulled the two dead Russians out by their feet, then peered underneath, looking for the missing man. He was not under the vehicle. Hosseini stood and looked around, then sighed and called to Rahman, who was now sitting in the driver's seat of the launcher.

"Arshak, I am going to find the missing one."

Rahman only waved. Hosseini carefully walked around the BTR, looking for a trail. It was easy to find, the Russian was hit, unable to walk. He was crawling, dragging his left leg. Hosseini followed the trail off the road and through the scrub trees. The Russian was strong, he had made good time. The trail led to a slight rise covered by small trees and underbrush. Hosseini dropped to a crouch. In such brush a wounded animal could strike back at its pursuers. He moved cautiously from one small tree to the next, using the thin trunks as cover. There was no sound of movement from the rise. Hosseini leaned forward and rushed the rise, planning to break through the brush and surprise the Russian. He ran, his eyes searching the brush for any sign of movement or a weapon. Reaching the top of the rise, he broke through the brush and barely caught the little tree that kept him from going over the edge.

The drop off was not deep, maybe ten meters, but deep enough to break arms and legs. As he clutched the tree, gasping for breath from the sudden rush of fear, Hosseini looked over the edge and saw the Russian on the rocks below. The Russian was still moving, but his wounded leg jutted off at an odd angle, and the bone was sticking out of his right arm through the black uniform's torn cloth.

"You should have stayed and fought like a man, Russian," Hosseini yelled down to the crippled soldier. "Now you can stay and meet the jackals!" Hosseini shouldered his AK and strolled back down to the vehicles.

Back at the vehicles, Rahman was sitting atop the BTR, dangling his feet over the front edge. He was toying with a BG-15 grenade launcher attached beneath the barrel of an AK-74.

"Ismet, I have a found you a prize!" Rahman called, standing and holding the weapon over his head. "This rifle has an extra kick. Did you find the Russian?"

"Yes, he tried to fly away but could not," Hosseini answered as he walked up to the BTR. "Give me that interesting rifle."

Rahman handed down the AK. Hosseini turned it over in his hands. "How does it work?"

"Pull the trigger and find out!" Rahman laughed. Hosseini pointed the weapon toward two Russian corpses that lay entangled next to the lead launcher. He pulled the trigger on the grenade launcher, which coughed and spat out a short grenade that lanced into the dead Russians and exploded with a bang. Shrapnel rang off the side of the launcher. One of the corpses nearby twitched and a noise escaped. The two rebels were on the man in a second.

"Ismet! Allah has sent us another prize!" Rahman shouted as he grabbed the young officer's short hair and pulled him over on his back. The Russian's eyes were wide with terror. "How is it that you are still alive?" Rahman asked earnestly. He was not used to having his victims survive. The Russian said nothing, blinking in confusion and fear. Rahman flipped the man back over to look at his back. Low on his back, a dark stain covered the khaki shirt. "Damn my eyes!" Rahman exclaimed. "Too low." The Russian's spine was cut, his legs flopping around, useless. "At least you will not run away, eh?" Rahman said to the terrified officer. "Hasan Bebehani will want to speak to you."

Rahman stood and clasped his friend by the shoulders.

His swarthy face was split by a huge smile. "Ah, Ismet, is this not a great day for the Iris Brigade? Surely we will eat lamb in heaven for taking these machines!"

Hosseini smiled back and nodded.

★ 12 ★

The next morning was cloudy. A sharp wind whipped down the valley, sending the clouds racing in twisted knots. Fuad woke Jinx from a fitful sleep.

"Come, Jenkins!" Fuad shouted happily. "Russians!"

When Jinx stumbled out the door of the tiny building a minute later, many of the Kurds were already mounted. Fuad was busily strapping the saddles on their horses, humming a toneless tune to himself.

"Russians? Where, Fuad?" Jinx asked as he dropped down on the hard, packed ground to pull tight his boot laces. "How many?"

"A motorized rifle unit, moving toward a pass east of here," Fuad replied, cinching Jinx's saddle in place. "*Inshallah*, we can intercept them. A small group of *Hamawand* are watching them."

"I thought the *Hamawand* were dead."

Fuad stopped and turned back to Jinx. "These are the *Hamawand*, Jenkins," he said patiently. "Ahmad has named his fighters after the Wolves of Kurdistan."

"I see."

Jinx's briefing on the Kurds had been confusing at best. The Kurds had fought with all their neighbors and among themselves since recorded time. Their history was filled with war, oppression, betrayal, genocide, and a stubborn-

138

ness of spirit that never failed or even wavered. The *Hamawand*, known in the region as the Wolves of Kurdistan, had terrorized their neighbors around the Bazyan Valley in western Iran for decades and had even plundered areas of Russia. In 1880 the Turks had captured some of the tribe and deported them to Tripoli. They fought their way back from Africa in six months. That Ahmad took the name of those legendary fighters told a lot about how he saw himself and his ragtag army.

Fuad was already in the saddle and had the packhorse in tow when Jinx finally got his web gear on and mounted up. His horse was nervous this morning, it could sense the tension and excitement of the riders. Jinx patted its neck and murmured, "Take it easy, babe." And to himself, "God, my ass hurts!"

The ride to the pass was a dizzying blend of narrow trails that clung perilously to steep mountain slopes and then plunged through stands of stunted, weathered trees. A dozen times, Jinx was sure that his horse was losing its footing and was about to pitch them both to their deaths on the rocky slopes. Every time, the beast managed to find its balance and lunge off after the others. It was a psychotic steeplechase in which he was merely baggage, like the three missiles strapped to the packhorse. After three hours of wild riding, the Kurds suddenly reined up near the crest of a ridge. The Kurds quickly tied their horses and disappeared through the many cracks in the rocks. Jinx and Fuad were left alone except for one man left behind to guide them through the rocks. Jinx and Fuad unstrapped the three Stinger cases and slung them over their backs. Burdened with the bulky cases, they struggled clumsily through the narrow cracks that led to the far slope of the ridge.

The column had already entered the pass, and the Soviet commander had wisely fanned out the column in the open area just past the tight bottleneck of the pass entrance. Three T-80s led the column, and they were now moving into a spearhead formation, their guns pointed outward and elevated as high as possible. Behind them, the BMPs and BTR-80s were squeezing through and fanning out, their 30mm auto cannons and 14.5mm machine guns sweeping back and forth, searching for targets along the rocky ridge.

Down the slope and 100 meters to his right, Jinx could see the Kurds' antitank section deployed. They had two old Soviet B-10 82mm recoilless guns set up on tripods and a single Milan missile launcher. The three weapons seemed pitifully weak to engage the many armored vehicles now grinding into the pass. The only other support weapons the Kurds possessed were two pairs of Soviet 82mm mortars set up just behind the ridge crest. By American standards, it was suicide to engage a mechanized infantry force with so little firepower, but the Kurds seemed eager to get on with the fight.

At least today they will have a decent antiaircraft section, Jinx thought as he popped the catches on the Stinger boxes and quickly screwed a battery/coolant unit into each launcher.

In the pass, the lead tank element was nearing the second bottleneck. Jinx could not see Ahmad but assumed he was about to spring his trap.

The lead tank was only ten meters from the rocks when the Milan launcher fired. The missile streaked down from the rocks and hit the T-80's turret just in front of the commander's hatch. The missile explosion was followed immediately by another explosion as the tank's ammunition went up, popping the turret off the tank to land overturned a few meters away.

Right behind the Milan came the two 82mm 'reckless rifles'. Their shells hit both the remaining T-80s in the flanks. One tank exploded, but the other, hit in the engine compartment, spun its turret and began pouring coaxial machine-gun fire into the ridge.

Behind the tanks, the BMPs quickly flared out, disgorging their troops. As the Soviets piled out of the personnel carriers, the crews fired back at the attackers with their 30mm cannons and machine guns. The cannons, designed to shoot at helicopters, could elevate high enough to hit the top of the ridge. Jinx watched as a Kurdish machine-gun position was peppered with projectiles from two BMPs. The Kurds died in a hail of exploding shells. When the BMPs turned their attention elsewhere, another pair of Kurds immediately ran over and, rolling the shredded bodies of their comrades out of their way, put the machine gun back in action. All along the ridge, the Kurds were pouring fire down on the trapped Soviets. The flat plain offered no cover, and the Soviet riflemen were forced to hide behind their own vehicles. Still, the Soviets were keeping good order and returning fire. Under cover of smoke, one squad after another made it to the edge of the rocks and began working its way up toward the Kurdish positions.

At the far end of the kill zone, the Soviets were busy. Rather than pulling vehicles out of the pass, the Soviet commander was pushing them in, trying to bull his way through the ambush. The lead element was getting mauled, but the follow-ons were pouring through, pushing toward the narrow gap at the near end of the pass.

The Kurds were knocking off one APC after another until a phosphorus round from a T-80 incinerated the half-dozen Kurds who were firing the recoilless guns. With their antitank weapons out, the Kurds had to rely on RPGs and the four mortars. The RPGs played hell with the thinly armored personnel carriers but were not strong enough to overcome the explosive reactive armor bricks on the tanks. The mortars were hopelessly inaccurate for antitank work, but they were keeping the riflemen busy.

For his part, Jinx was merely an observer. He sat between two huge boulders, the Stinger across his lap, watching men from both sides die.

Despite the loss of their antitank guns, the Kurds were still hammering the Russians caught in the kill zone. The

Kurds were good marksmen; Soviet riflemen were falling
like ninepins under the murderous fire. Jinx noticed one
young Kurd fighter, a boy, really, who seemed to concentrate on one Soviet at a time. He would shoot at his chosen
target until the man stopped moving, either hit or too
frightened to move. Even if the Soviets got part of their
unit through the pass, the steep slopes would prevent any
flanking move. Two good men with rifles could hold off
a dismounted company in this pass.

A cloud of smoke at the far end of the pass caught Jinx's
attention. A pair of ZSU-23-4s broke through the smoke,
their quad 23mm guns blasting away at the ridge line.
Although the ZSU had been replaced as an antiaircraft gun
by the more powerful 2S6, it was still a potent ground-
support weapon. The two ZSUs poured nearly 8,000
rounds a minute into the hillside, the high explosive-
incendiary shells ripping through the rocks like a giant
jackhammer. A dozen Kurds died in a few seconds as the
Soviet gunners found their positions. An RPG round
flashed down from the ridge and struck one ZSU on the
side of its thinly armored turret. The tracked gun lurched
to a stop as the 85mm RPG round detonated with a black
puff of smoke. The driver's hatch flew open, and the driver
scrambled out as the vehicle began to shake under the
explosions of the ammunition stored in the turret. In seconds, the entire vehicle was ablaze.

The second ZSU continued to pound the Kurds, steering
through the many wrecked vehicles in the pass. RPG rockets followed it as it made for the end of the pass. One
rocket hit a fender and for a second, the ZSU disappeared
in a cloud of black smoke. Just as quickly, it reappeared,
damaged but still moving and still firing. When it reached
the dead tank at the end of the pass, it parked, using the
smoking hulk for cover.

Even with the hammering of ZSU and the 30mm guns
of the few remaining BMPs, the Kurds were still holding
their own. Jinx looked at his watch. The ambush had been

going on for nearly ten minutes now. That was more than enough time for a Soviet commander to get an artillery-fire-support mission laid on. The self-propelled 122mm guns could have rounds on the way by now.

"Fuad!" Jinx yelled above the din, "come over here and get down in the rocks. It's artillery time!"

Fuad laughed. He crouched and put both hands over his head, grimacing in mock fear. Jinx laughed back.

These silly bastards aren't afraid of anything, Jinx thought as he watched Fuad's antics.

Fuad's eyes suddenly darted toward the dark-blue sky as if he could see shells falling. "Helicopters!" the suddenly excited Kurd shouted as he scrambled down between the boulders and slid down to the wide crack in the rocks where Jinx sat tending the Stinger.

Jinx slung the missile over his shoulder and crawled on all fours up to the mouth of the crack where the other two Stingers were cached. He peered around the rock just as the four Mi-28 Havocs cleared the ridge at the end of the kill zone. They swept down the ridge line, raking the Kurds with 30mm cannon fire and 57mm rockets that flashed from their stubby wings in clusters.

Halfway down the ridge, a small group of Kurds began to fire RPGs at the flying tank killers. The unguided rockets were little threat to the Havocs, which simply zigged and zagged to avoid them, while firing quick bursts at RPG gunners. As Jinx watched, a burst of 30mm shells stitched the rocks above the RPG teams. Three of the Kurds fell, ripped by steel from the exploding shells. Two others abandoned the position for the safety of a rock crevice below them. One tenacious figure remained to fire at the attacking gunships. As one of the Havocs lined up for a shot, the lone gunner fired the RPG, then calmly reached down for another round and stuffed it down the barrel of the launcher. The helicopter, faced with a head shot, jerked quickly to the side. The Kurd fired again as the chopper slewed around. Incredibly, the rocket hit the Havoc's tail section, severing the tail rotor. The sleek gunship spun to the right and slammed into the rock face of the ridge. It exploded, sending burning fuel and twisted wreckage cascading down the steep slope.

The other Havocs quickly spread out to nail the RPG gunner, coming in a wide angle. The gunner was unfazed, calmly reloading the single-shot launcher.

As the Havocs lined up on the gunner, Jinx scurried out in the open, got up on one knee, and hefted the launcher up on his shoulder. He thumbed down the actuator lever to release the coolant gas to the seeker head, then popped up the sight bar, centered the nearest Havoc in the sight, and uncaged the missile's seeker head. The tone warbled in his ear immediately. Jinx jerked the launcher up, super elevating it, and pulled the trigger. The missile exploded from the tube and sped off toward the doomed Havoc. Jinx was busy opening another missile case when the attack helicopter exploded and fell onto the sharp rocks.

The other two Havocs had not seen the launch, but now quickly wheeled around to seek out the source of their newest trouble, ignoring the RPG for the moment.

All that was left to mark the launch was a small cloud of dust kicked up by the booster motor, but that was enough to mark the spot. The two Mi-28s wheeled again and sped in toward Jinx's position.

In the rocks, Jinx screwed a battery/coolant unit into one of the two remaining Stingers. He snapped up the sight bar, thumbed down the actuator lever, and hefted the launcher to his shoulder. Crouching against the rocks he quickly looked around the edge of the rocks. The Havocs were on line now, coming in fast. Jinx pivoted around the corner of the rocks, lined up the chopper on the right, and uncaged the missile seeker. Again the tone was immediate. Jinx held down the trigger, waiting for the booster motor to fire. As he fired, he could see the flame and smoke sparkling around the Havoc's rocket tubes. The booster motor fired, kicking up a large cloud of dust that filled the crevice. As the missile sped off, Jinx jumped back around the rocks and flattened himself behind the empty missile case.

"INNNCOMMMINNGG!" Jinx screamed at Fuad as the 57mm rockets slammed into the little clearing next to the crevice. The rocks roared and shook under the hammer blows of the rocket warheads. Fire and whistling metal filled the crevice, the sharp bits of steel splanging off the hard surfaces and ricocheting around furiously. Jinx felt a hot knife stab into his back high on his right shoulder.

"Jenkins!" Fuad yelled. "Are you alive?"

"Mostly!" Jinx yelled back as he peered cautiously up over the empty Stinger case. The case was riddled with tiny holes along one side.

"Here, my friend," Fuad yelled again as he crawled over the other packing cases with the remaining Stinger in his hands, "kill the last one!"

There was nothing Jinx wanted to do less than stick his head around the corner of the rocks again.

I can't look like a coward to these people, Jinx thought, looking at Fuad's excited face, but it's hard to remember that when every cell in your body is screaming, "Run away!"

Jinx took the launcher and, taking a deep breath, pivoted around the rocks again. He expected to see a Havoc hovering next to the slope, waiting to puree him with its cannon. Instead, all he saw was a dark speck screaming away down the pass. The burning wreckage of the three less-fortunate Havocs sent thin pillars of oily black smoke into the bright-blue sky. Jinx was still staring at the retreating helicopter when he heard the missile's coolant unit expire. Unthinking, he unscrewed the dead unit and tossed it into the rocks.

Below, the battle was still raging. The Kurds were slowly but surely kicking the Russians' butts. Caught in the bowl of the pass, they could not pass but would not retreat. A sense of wild exhilaration began to build in Jinx, a feeling he had not had since Vietnam. It was a feeling of power, the sure and certain knowledge that you were the baddest motherfucker in the valley. Jinx threw his head back and whooped. Christ, this felt good!

Below him, the lone RPG gunner that had faced the helicopters was leisurely popping off one personnel carrier after another with his RPG. A couple of his comrades had returned and were screwing green rocket motors onto the RPG warheads as fast as the gunner used them up.

Jinx scurried back down the crevice to watch the show again from there. He had just gotten back into his seat when the ridge began to rumble and huge gouts of rock and dirt erupted from the ridge. Artillery was pounding the Kurds' positions, plowing the mountainside like some harrow from hell. Smoke shells mixed with high explosives covered the Kurds' positions with thick, gray smoke.

The Kurds were no strangers to artillery. They hunkered down the cracks between the rocks and kept firing. In the rocks, only a direct hit posed any real danger, though the blast effects were devastating. The Kurds were dispersed enough to ride out the shelling. The Soviets were using the barrage to cover another thrust into the pass. The blasted tank that blocked the mouth of the pass had been pushed aside, and now the column was racing through. The Soviet commander was kissing off a battalion to keep on his timetable.

At the far end of the pass, a dismounted Soviet company was climbing the steep slope, trying to flank the Kurds and roll up the ambush.

"Fuad, I think we're fucked!" Jinx shouted above the din of the barrage. "Let's move it!" He slung the Stinger over his shoulder.

Fuad was wide-eyed, flinching with each detonation, but he quickly scrambled over and followed Jinx through the crevice back to where the horses were tied on the reverse slope. The shells were now falling behind them. The crevice from which they had fought the helicopters was now covered by black smoke.

Jinx could hear Fuad praying aloud as they made their way up through the rocks. Jinx suddenly had a mental image of shredded dead horses tied to splinted trees.

"Our Lady of Still-living Horseflesh," Jinx whispered to himself, "be with us today. Amen."

The rest of the Kurds had already pulled back and mounted up before Jinx and Fuad found their way back through the rocks to the sheltered spot where the horses were tied. Most of the others were already spurring their horses down the steep slope, fleeing the whistling death that continued to shake the front slope of the ridge.

Fuad was in the saddle at once, agitated and eager to be on his way. He untied the packhorse's rein from his saddle and turned to Jinx,

"Hurry, my friend!"

"Go!" Jinx called back as he fought to get a foot in the stirrup. "Go on!" The missile on his back hindered him as he tried to get up into the saddle.

Fuad did not need further encouragement. He spurred his horse and wheeled off down the ridge after the others.

Jinx's horse, excited by the noise and the sudden activity, was skittish and reluctant to let Jinx on board. The two did a circling equine pas de deux as Jinx angrily maligned the beast's ancestry. Once in the saddle, Jinx turned the horse and reached over for the packhorse's reins. The animal did not seem to want to run with the others, and Jinx did not want to leave it to be turned into dog food by the Soviet shells. It took two tries to catch the reins.

As he was tying the packhorse to his saddle, he caught movement out of the corner of his eyes. Two figures were hobbling through the rocks, one supporting the other. Jinx recognized the fearless RPG gunner. He was helping a wounded Kurd.

"Here!" Jinx shouted to the two figures. As they made their way down, Jinx spurred his horse up the slope to meet them. The wounded Kurd had a dark stain on the front of his shirt that matched the dark red of his cummerbund. The gunner boosted the wounded man up behind Jinx, then pulled the packsaddle off the packhorse, leapt up on its bare back, and kicked it in the flanks. The packhorse, finally motivated, sped off down the slope.

The wounded man was leaning heavily on Jinx, holding him around the waist, the long missile tube between them. Jinx guided the horse slowly down the slope, not wanting to shake up the wounded man more than necessary. The ride back to the village would be hard enough without hurting him now.

At the base of the slope, Fuad and the gunner were waiting. Fuad fell in behind Jinx and the wounded Kurd; the gunner took the point and acted as their guide.

The ride back was much slower than the pell-mell rush getting there had been. It was dark by the time the four stragglers reached the village. It was not a happy place. The Kurds had suffered big time. They had killed a lot of Russians, but there were far more Russians than there were Kurds.

The sound of moaning and soft crying hung in the night air. Dozens of the Kurds were wounded. There was no doctor to tend to their wounds, only the women, who bandaged the ripped flesh and comforted the wounded until death released them from their pain.

A pair of SF medics would be gifts from Allah to these people, Jinx thought. So would some serious antitank and antiaircraft weapons, better commo, you name it. In one way, the Kurds reminded Jinx of the contras. They had lots of heart and guts but very little else. The Soviets were heartless, but they had guts and they had all the firepower in the world to back them up.

The gunner was reaching up to help the wounded man off his back. Jinx gripped the man's shoulder and lowered him into the gunner's waiting arms. The wounded man's weight was too much. He and the gunner fell in a pile, and Jinx had to rein his horse to keep it from stepping on the fallen pair.

A group of women from one of the huts rushed out and carried the wounded Kurd off to the makeshift hospital. The gunner rose and, shaking the dust off, pulled loose the red turban that covered both head and face. A long shock of thick, sandy-blond hair cascaded from the turban. Jinx stared down into the most beautiful gray-green eyes he had ever seen.

"Thank you for saving Malot," the woman said in English, dusting out the red fabric of the turban, "and thank you for shooting the helicopters. I believe that I owe you my life."

For a second, Jinx could not find his voice. He had been impressed by the gunner's courage in the battle, now he was stunned by her beauty.

"Uh, sure," he stammered, "no problem. Anytime."

She smiled and turned away, walking toward the makeshift hospital.

"Say," Jinx called after her, "I'm Richard Jenkins. Who are you?"

She turned and looked at him, a slightly shocked look on her face. "I am Fatima Ahmad. You may call me Tina."

"Ahmad?" Jinx answered. "You are . . ."

"The Great Bey's sister, yes."

Jinx nodded. "It is a pleasure to meet the sister of the Bey."

She stepped closer to his horse and spoke softly. "American, it is not polite to call out to strange women on the street. I have lived in the West, in Europe, and do not mind, but others here follow the old customs. Try to be more polite."

Jinx flushed with embarrassment. "Sorry. I forgot myself."

"That is all right, I will remember you," she answered quietly, then turned and walked away.

Jinx whistled softly between his teeth. What a hot number in this unlikely place! She was right, though. He would have to watch his manners here. A social faux pas here could result in the loss of your gonads!

That night, the camp was quiet except for the occasional groaning of the wounded and the low crying of women. The Kurds had lost more than their men in the fight, they had lost much of their spirit. They had expected easy victory and gotten bitter losses instead. Now they sat around their small fires muttering and shaking their heads.

Fuad disappeared from the hut an hour after dark, saying that he would return for breakfast. Jinx let him go. He wanted to keep a low profile for a day, then hit up Ahmad with his plans. Jinx unrolled the quilted poncho liner onto the rough bed and dug the tiny airline pillow out of the bottom of his pack. He fell asleep rehearsing the little speech he would give the Kurd chief.

Jinx started awake. Someone was in the room. He reached over his head for the pistol. A cool hand covered his mouth as Tina Ahmad's soft voice whispered in his ear, "Shh, American, be quiet!"

Jinx felt the long, slim body slide in next to him in the rough bed. The cool fingers now ran along his cheek to the back of his head as soft lips grazed his eyes and settled on his mouth. Long hair cascaded over his face and shoulders.

Tina's mouth was hot on his, and her tiny tongue ran back and forth across his lips. For a second, Jinx resisted. Making it with the leader's sister could seriously compromise any mission. Basic SF training said this was not a good idea!

His resistance lasted less than a second as the little head took command from the big head and kicked Jinx's hormones into high gear.

He slid the 9mm pistol back under the small pillow, thumbing the safety catch on.

Tina's hand was slipping down his stomach, her nails teasing a path toward his groin. Jinx put an arm around her back and pulled her closer, flattening her small, firm breasts against his chest. She hooked one leg over his and strained against him as she fumbled with the drawstring of his sweatpants.

Their tongues fought as they twisted and pulled, fumbling with the clothes that now seemed to bind them. Tina broke from the rough kiss with a little gasp, then whispered in Jinx's ear.

"I owe you my life and Malot's as well," she whispered hoarsely, biting his ear and plunging her tongue deep into it. Jinx stiffened and squirmed all over as her tongue explored his ear, driving him crazy with the sensation. He twisted away and twined his hand in her thick hair, pulling her face back to his.

She had undone the drawstring, and now her hand plunged down into the sweatpants, her hand seizing his rigid erection, making it swell and stiffen even more. She pulled it roughly, then stroked it lightly with her fingertips before pulling it again. Jinx gasped into her mouth, and she stuck her tongue down his throat.

The sudden onslaught of sensation made Jinx's head reel. Somewhere in the back of his mind, a voice kept yelling to watch out, to keep his guard up, but the rest of his body was busy keeping something else up, and finally the little voice was drowned out by the gasping and moaning.

It was obvious that Tina had not spent all her time in Austria with her nose buried in a book. Right now her nose was buried in his pubic hair, and her tongue was running a taste test on his testicles.

He pulled her head up. "Here," he murmured, trying to put his swollen organ into her mouth. She pulled herself up onto his chest with both hands, her face touching his.

"Please be quiet, I am running this blow job," she

whispered into his face, kissed him light, then slid back down onto his outstretched legs.

Might as well lie back and let this lady have her own way, Jinx thought. She knows what she's doing. The tiny voice of watchfulness piped up again, screaming for caution. Jinx grabbed the little voice, slammed it into a mental closet, and locked it.

Later, she slid her fingers behind his head and wrapped her leg around his, pulling his closer. Their tongues teased and swirled as they clutched and pulled at each other. Jinx's recently deflated organ began an amazing comeback.

"Ummm!" Tina murmured. She rolled on her back and pulled Jinx over on her, guiding him inside her. Jinx needed no encouragement. He buried himself in her and rocked up and down, grinding their groins together. Tina pulled her legs up and crossed them over Jinx's back, her heels locked together over his butt, gently spurring him on each upstroke. Her short nails raked his back, leaving red streaks in an ever-widening pattern. They rocked this way for a while, speaking only in gasps and groans. Finally Tina took his face in her hands.

"Oh, Jenkins, you are big in me!" she whispered, then added, "you are also breaking my legs. Here . . . "

As Jinx rolled off her and lay panting next to her she reached for her shirt and slipped it on.

"You going somewhere?" Jinx asked softly. She nodded and stood up.

"Hang on a second," Jinx whispered, taking her hand and pulling her back down on the narrow bed. "It's your turn."

He guided her down onto the bed and kissed his way down her shirt, over her still-damp navel and into the wet tangle of curls below. Tina started to object, but changed her mind.

* * *

Jinx wiped his sopping face on the poncho liner and slid up to her, gently pulling the pillow away and kissing her gently. She responded slowly, languidly, stretching and sighing, then pulled away.

"Thank you, that was nice."

"My pleasure, for sure," he answered. "What . . ."

She put her fingers to his lips and shook her head.

"I must go," she whispered. She slipped into the rest of her clothes and, as quietly as she had come in, let herself out. Jinx flopped back on his sleeping bag, tired and suddenly sleepy. He found his little pillow on the floor and tucked it under his head.

Too bizarre, he thought, this whole deal is just too bizarre. But at least I'm not as old as I feel.

Omar Telebani watched as the woman slipped out of the American's hut and quickly slipped back up the dark street to her quarters. He had heard them inside the hut, the sounds of their fornication plain. She was Ahmad's sister, but she was a harlot, a harlot who slept with foreigners and unbelievers. He would not speak of this to Ahmad, not yet, at any rate.

Tina eased herself between the covers of her bed. So that is what an American is like, she mused warmly. Full of surprises and more active than other men she had experienced. The big American had been the first man she had been with since Sayid had left her in Moscow. Others had since approached her, but she had shunned them all. A brief pain made her shudder—remembering. Do not do this to yourself, she pleaded! Do not think of him. He had a duty to perform, just as you do, and no less dangerous. He did it for our people, just as I do. She remembered her last briefing.

"Tinya," the GRU major at the 1st Southern Front's intelligence post had said, "you have served your people's cause well. Though you failed to neutralize the Iranian rebel, General Mossadegh, your mission achieved one of its goals.''

Tina looked down at the floor in shame. She had failed, the murderous bastard still lived. The deep sense of failure she felt was not for her people's cause or that of the Russians, but for Sayid. Mossaddegh's people had murdered him.

''You have showed the rebels the wrath of the Kurdish peoples,'' the major continued, ''and that they face many enemies from all sides and that their own cause is doomed to failure.''

She looked up, her eyes tearing up. ''Comrade, I wish only to serve my people. I—I failed to destroy one who is a threat to my people. I want another chance to kill the dog!'' she snapped. Her small fists were clenched. She trembled in rage.

The GRU officer was startled by the young woman's outburst, even though he had been forewarned of her fire. This was the perfect opportunity to make his move.

''Yes, I understand, and you will have that chance.'' He looked at her firmly. ''But not now. In the future.''

She started to speak, to stand, a savage anger flooding through her. ''I want . . .''

''In the future, Tinya, but not now.''

She fell into a stormy silence, glaring at him.

''We want you to go back to your people first. There is a task we wish accomplished and one that will be most difficult for you.''

Bewilderment clouded in her eyes.

''Your brother, he is fighting us.''

She stared at him, still confused. ''Yes, I know, but . . .''

''It is all right, Tinya, we understand. But you must talk to him. He will only hurt your people more and undo everything you and Sayid have tried to accomplish. We want you to go home, Tinya.''

★ 13 ★

Tommy Allard stretched and tipped his head back, rolling it from side to side to work out the soreness. The mission had been uneventful so far, just routine intercepts between Soviet units. Some Soviet commander had run into a *Basmachi* force of some sort that he claimed were equipped with Stinger missiles, but that had been the only interesting message intercepted.

His net, the Iranian Army and the Iranian rebel forces, had been all but silent on his last two flights. He had scanned and monitored the entire duration of the aircraft's almost six-hour endurance on both. He stretched his arms down and behind him, arching his back in the seat, which was bolted to the floor in front of his console. He was in mid-stretch when the scanner locked onto a transmission and began to record it. He fine-tuned his intercept transceiver to the transmission. It was in Farsi, in the clear, no encryption. Probably a rebel radio. They seemed to have no code equipment.

Allard, the American-born son of an American father and an Iranian mother, spoke Farsi like a native, even though he had never set foot in Iran. His father had been an aircraft maintenance specialist, working for the Shah's Air Force when he had met Tommy's mother. They both had to flee Iran when the Ayatollah returned. At home,

Tommy's mother had insisted on teaching the boy Farsi. That language skill had been his ticket to Army radio intercept school. Now he orbited just outside the combat zone in an RC-12H Improved Guardrail, a twin engine electronic-surveillance plane, the Army's version of a Beechcraft Super King Air.

The voice on the radio was excited, rattling on about the capture of some kind of big missile—no, missiles. The message was acknowledged with just as much excitement. When the message ended, Allard noted the transmission on his log and went back to stretching, working out the kinks as the scanner began to search the frequencies again. In twenty minutes, the Guardrail would dump all its intercepted messages in a long data burst back to the monitoring station in Saudi Arabia. Allard had no idea what a stir his brief interception would cause.

★ 14 ★

Jinx waited a day before speaking to Ahmad. He wanted to let the hurt of the battle sink in on the young Kurd before he made his pitch for a Special Forces team. He also wanted to check the rumor mill to see if his indiscretion with Tina had made the rounds. One of the principal precepts Special Forces taught was simply not to mess with the local women, regardless of who made the pass. More than one mission had been shot down by a misplaced dick. Fuad had not mentioned it, and if anyone knew the village gossip, he would. He had seen her only once, and then she had made no sign of recognition.

The anguished faces of the new widows and the freshly turned ground of the graves were the only reminders of the failed ambush. As Jinx walked up the dusty street, the men of the village were bustling around, bragging to one another about their exploits and cleaning their weapons, already talking about the next fight.

The meeting began as all did, "In the name of God . . ." In the tiny frame building that functioned as his headquarters, Ahmad listened distractedly to Jinx's proposal as he outlined the benefits to be gained from the Green Beret advisers. Ahmad cut him off halfway through his spiel.

"No, Jenkins, we do not wish to have any Americans," Ahmad said flatly. "We welcome the new weapons but

157

not American soldiers.'' The Kurd leaned back against the
rickety table, steadying it with his hands.

"May I ask why?" Jinx asked impatiently. "The Green
Berets can teach your men much about fighting the Soviets.''

"My men have been fighting the Russians for two hundred years,'' Ahmad replied, a touch of amusement in his
voice. "We do not need instruction in that. We wish no
foreigners in our ranks, Jenkins. Foreigners are always the
same. First they advise, then they lead, then they domi-
nate. Foreign domination is what we seek to overthrow.
That is the heart of our nationalist policy.''

"Many revolutions have profited from foreign aid and
leadership,'' Jinx answered back. "Our American revolution was aided by the French."

Ahmad stared at Jinx for a moment, then smiled. "Allah, save me from the French! They are the people who
harbored that insane Khomeini!''

Jinx looked down at his feet and stifled a grin. Ahmad
felt the same way about the French that Jinx did. It had
been a poor choice of examples.

"There are many other examples," Jinx went on, trying
to recover, "Look what we did for the *Mujahideen* in Afghanistan!" He made a point not to mention the contras.
"A revolution that has no outside support cannot survive.
Your own history is proof of that."

"That is true, Jenkins," Ahmad retorted as he stepped
back around the table and sat on the padded chair. "But
our history is full of foreign promises that went unfulfilled,
of support that never came." Ahmad stared at Jinx, his
dark eyes filled with visions of wrongs long past and still
owing. "We are the *Hamawand*, Jenkins, do you know
that name? We are the Wolves of Kurdistan. We do not
beg for what we want, we take it from the unbelievers and
the treacherous dogs that live around us. Our grandfathers
took what they wanted from the Russians armed with
lances.''

You take it from anyone you can beat the shit out of, even other tribes, Jinx thought as Ahmad launched into his history lesson.

Ahmad went on. He was rolling now, pacing back and forth behind his little desk, telling this *feringi* about the glory of the Kurds. "We have ruled these mountains since the time before Alexander. Our tribes are descended from the Medes, Jenkins. We are not Arabs or Persians!" Ahmad's tone made Persian sound like some sort of intestinal ailment. "We are a race apart. A race whose history has been written in fire!"

Written in the blood of innocents, Jinx thought as he sat smiling, a rapt pupil. The bullies on the block.

"Over and over, we have been betrayed by outsiders. Like Barzani," Ahmad explained, his hands held out before him. "The British promised him much, but when they got what they wanted . . ." Ahmad slammed his fist into his open palm. Ahmad's face took on the look of a patient teacher working with a moron.

Jinx was trying to look like a man receiving enlightenment, when he really felt like the floor of a stable. Ahmad was happily glossing over the less-savory aspects of Kurdish history. There was no mention of the Armenian holocaust, the constant depredations against other Kurdish tribes, or the frequent sellouts and betrayals that make up the history of the Kurds. Mustafa Barzoni, for whom this mission was named, was the best known of the Kurdish rebels of the past.

"We must seize destiny by the throat, Jenkins!" Ahmad concluded.

Jinx stood and walked over to the tiny window, turning his back on Ahmad. "Destiny is about to seize you by the balls, Ahmad," Jinx said flatly, "and throw you off one of these mountains, you and the *Hamawand* with you." He turned around to face the affronted leader. "These aren't the same Russians your grandfathers whipped with their lances. These are the guys who kicked the hell out

of NATO a few months ago. These are the guys who used
to stack up Afghan villagers like cordwood and set them
on fire with gasoline. I watched your 'Wolves' in action
the other day. They have guts but no firepower and not
much skill to use the firepower they have. They got their
butts kicked and didn't even slow that goddamned armored
column down, much less stop it.''

''We killed hundreds of Russians!'' Ahmad retorted
hotly.

''Right.'' Jinx shot back, ''I got news for you. I'll bet
that Soviet regimental commander described his casualties
as light. I'd describe your losses as heavy. The Soviet
commander kissed off that battalion simply because his
commander told him to keep moving!''

''That is why I will not permit any foreigners in our
army! Send all the missiles and medicines you wish. We
will use them against our common enemies. Do not send
us any soldiers. We do not want them. And do not blaspheme the name of God, even your own!''

Jinx stared at the Kurdish leader. The man was not going to give in on this one. Better to try another time. ''I
will request more Stinger missiles and medical supplies.
Perhaps in time we can speak again about the Green Berets.''

''Perhaps,'' Ahmad replied, ''but do not embrace any
hope on this matter.''

Jinx nodded and left the building. This guy was a tough
nut to crack. Maybe if he got his ass kicked again he
would come around, but Jinx doubted it. For now, missiles and medicine would be all he would accept.

Fuck it, Jinx thought, if he uses our stuff to kill Soviets,
that's enough for now.

As Jinx walked back to his hut, Tina Ahmad fell in
beside him. Not a good idea, he thought.

''Let me guess,'' she cooed. ''My brother has turned
down your offer of American aid.''

''Not aid,'' Jinx replied, glancing at her, ''just Americans. He wants the weapons but not any advisers. Do you think you should be seen with me?'' he quickly added.

''No way, Green Beret?'' she asked, her voice filled with mocking laughter.

''That's about it,'' Jinx snorted.

''And what will you do now?'' she asked as they walked up to the door of Jinx's hut.

''Ask for more Stingers and whatever else we can get,'' Jinx answered. ''The SF'll still be there if he changes his mind.''

''He won't,'' Tina said. She looked back over her shoulder as Ahmad and two of his lieutenants emerged from the headquarters. ''He is a stubborn man.'' She looked back at Jinx. There was something in her gray-green eyes that Jinx could not decipher. ''Are you stubborn, Jenkins?''

''When I have to be,'' Jinx answered.

''Good.''

With that she turned and walked away. Jinx stood a moment to watch the motion of her hips as she walked off, then ducked into his dark hut.

★ 15 ★

The next few days were spent training the Kurds on the weapons the Americans were sending. In addition to the Stingers, Jinx had an AT4 "tracer trainer" with him. It simulated the real antitank launcher and used cheap 9mm tracer ammo for target practice. He hoped to have at least some of the Kurds up to speed on the weapon by the time a supply of the real ones arrived. It was too bad they hadn't had any of the throwaway tank busters when they had taken on the Soviet column.

The Kurds were natural soldiers and learned quickly. After all, they had been conditioned since childhood. The only glitch in the training came when Fuad translated for him as he demonstrated the subcaliber training device for the AT4 launcher.

Jinx had gone through his dog and pony show with the weapon, firing the training cartridge at a rock. The tracer had hit the rock dead center. He was surprised to see the Kurds looking mystified.

It turned out that Fuad had not made it clear that they would use a training device rather than the actual rounds. They were very skeptical that a 9mm tracer bullet could defeat Soviet tanks and could not understand why such a large weapon was needed to fire a pistol bullet. After Fuad got that straightened out, things had gone better.

The Stinger classes had gone very well, too. The Kurds were eager to learn about the missiles that would kill Soviet and Iranian fighters. Half a day's instruction with the spent launcher had the Kurds boasting about their missile skill, seemingly eager to take on an Iranian Cobra or a Soviet Su-25 Frogfoot. Ahmad was still adamant about foreign advisers, but at least the Kurds were learning some new skills from him.

After two days of tactical practice with the AT4 simulator, his students were ready to fire the real thing. Jinx had planned to set up a simple range in the small box canyon near the village, but when he made this announcement to his class, they immediately began shouting in Kurdish, shaking their rifles and gesturing.

"Okay, Fuad, what did I do now?" Jinx asked.

Fuad was laughing and nodding vigorously at the unruly class.

"They say that they will not waste such shells on stones," Fuad explained. "They want to kill Russians, not rocks."

"Do they have some specific Russians in mind?"

Fuad rattled off a string of Kurdish at the crowd, which argued briefly among themselves, then spat out an answer.

"Oh, yes," Fuad translated, "the road to Bakhtaran is always crowded with tanks and trucks. They wish to practice on some of the Soviet travelers there."

Jinx stood for a moment looking over his unruly students. A more ruthless, uncivilized bunch of cutthroats would be hard to find, he thought. The Vietnam-born Cambodians came to mind, but, no, not even those natural mercenaries. Still it could be worse; they could be on the other side.

"Tell them that I would be pleased to watch them kill more Russians, Fuad," Jinx said quietly. "We'll whip up a plan this morning and try to hit a convoy tonight or tomorrow morning."

When Fuad translated Jinx's reply, the class responded

with loud whoops and a few short bursts fired into the dark-blue sky. The entire class then promptly walked off back toward the village.

"What a bunch of crazy bastards," Jinx said to himself.

Fuad turned and faced his American partner. "Do not be so quick to judge them, Jenkins. These men have fought the Russians, the Iranians, the Iraqis, and the Turks for generations, for hundreds of years. Sometimes they have had weapons, machine guns, and artillery. Sometimes they have had only rifles and pistols. Before that they had only lances and swords. They know how to fight, how to kill, how to die." Fuad looked out over the steep valley below them, a sad, distant look on his face. He sighed. "I'm afraid that all my people understand is war. What we cannot seem to grasp is peace."

Jinx stood quietly for a second, then clapped Fuad on the back.

"Come on, my friend," he said, "let's go figure a way for them to do what they do best and maybe even come out of it in one piece."

Fuad nodded and the two men walked back down to the village behind their happy class.

Senior Private Pyotr Churbanov felt the vehicle slip to one side. He jerked his head up, jerked his eyes open, and pulled the BMP-2 back onto the road, bouncing over a large hole in the pavement and jostling his human cargo in the rear of the BMP. Loud cursing erupted from the troop compartment, and an empty ration tin sailed past his head, banging off the vision block and rattling around underfoot.

Churbanov turned and yelled, "Sorry!" to the seven riflemen in the back of the BMP.

In the turret behind Churbanov, Estekov, the gunner, kicked the driver's seat and barked an insult. Estekov, an Afghanistan veteran, always cursed in Afghan. That was fine with Churbanov, who did not speak Afghan. Next to

Estekov, Sergeant Kolbin, the BMP's commander, slept like the dead. Even the jolt and Estekov's outburst had not awakened him.

Churbanov shook his head, trying to drive the cobwebs out. It was not the first time he had fallen asleep on this trip but the worst. He rubbed his puffy eyes with his fist, driving his hand against his eyes, attempting to lock them open. The heat from the vehicle's heater and the engine's steady hum had a hypnotic effect on him. He prayed they would stop soon so he could get out of the cramped personnel carrier and walk around. Maybe he could get some feeling back in his butt then. At least he was still alive, a claim many soldiers of his motorized rifle battalion could not make. The attack yesterday had killed dozens of soldiers and destroyed all of the battalion's attached tanks.

They had never seen the attackers, nor fired a shot in return. All at once, the lead tank had exploded, followed a second later by one of the 2S6 guns. After that, another vehicle had gone up each second until nearly twenty were destroyed. As suddenly as the fire had started, it stopped. There had been only one stray round and it hit behind a personnel carrier and riddled the fuel tank with holes. The men inside had been lucky to get out alive. One of the officers said the attackers had been helicopters.

Churbanov could hardly believe that the attack had been only yesterday. It seemed like a year ago. Now he was exhausted.

The radio crackled, bringing Sergeant Kolbin instantly back to life in the small turret. Churbanov could not hear all the message but heard Kolbin answer, "Exactly so!"

Kolbin stretched and leaned down to Churbanov.

"We are pulling off for a break in a kilometer or so. Watch the lead." Kolbin stretched again. "A long trip, eh, Estekov?"

"Just so, Comrade Sergeant," the gunner answered, "just so!"

The radio barked again, and Kolbin answered. He

tapped Churbanov's seat with his foot. "Here." Churbanov eased the BMP off the pavement onto the road's wide shoulder.

"Turn it off," Kolbin yawned. "We will refuel here."

"Finally," Churbanov sighed as he flipped off the ignition switches.

"Fuad, this is stupid," Jinx hissed. "If these guys have any air support or artillery on call, we're a bunch of fucked puppies!"

Fuad looked over and smiled. "*Inshallah*, they will have none."

"*Inshallah!*" Jinx muttered. *Inshallah*—if God wills— was the catchall word that covered the unexpected. It usually was invoked when there had been no planning or common sense. It had another meaning, a cross between "we'll get to it later" and "who cares?" It was like mañana, only without the urgency.

The ambush site was a pile of boulders on a small rise about 100 meters from the paved road that ran toward Bakhtaran. There was good cover from small arms fire, but not much from tank guns and none from air attack or artillery.

Good thing we don't have too many AT4s, Jinx thought. We can't stay here long enough to get caught.

Each two-man team had four launchers, for a total of twenty launchers. The teams were spread out the length of the boulder field, about sixty meters altogether. The teams had rehearsed all afternoon and moved to the ambush site after dark. The plan was to hit the first Soviet or Iranian convoy that came by around sunup. With hope, the Kurds would have the sun to their backs, making it harder for their victims to shoot back. After all the launchers were expended, the Kurds would pull back through the network of deep ravines that ran away from the ambush site, using them to cover their withdrawal.

Jinx had managed to get them a little fire support in the

form of Hosain Aykut's two captured 82mm mortars. Aykut's squad would fire their mortars on Jinx's flare, their white phosphorus rounds aimed at the rock pile. If there was a Soviet counterattack or pursuit, the mortars would discourage them.

It was a simple, little plan, the sort that can go so wrong so quickly. The sky behind them was a pale pink when the sound of motors first reached them. Fuad heard it first and jabbed Jinx with his elbow.

"Listen!"

The sound of diesel engines and the whirring clank of tracks grew louder. The Kurds all scrunched down in the rocks waiting for the shots that would kick off the ambush. A few minutes later, a squat 2S6 antiaircraft gun appeared, followed by a host of other tracked vehicles. Jinx focused his Steiner binoculars on the column.

"Looks like BMPs," he said softly to Fuad, "no tanks, thank God."

Jinx reached down into his cargo pocket and pulled out the small West German H&K flare gun. He idly wondered if the plant was still in operation. He checked it for flares and placed it in a small crack in the rocks. It would signal the end of the ambush with a yellow flare. This done, he pulled the AT4 launcher into place and readied it for firing by pushing forward on the cocking handle and rotating it over to the right. He then slid back the plastic sight covers, allowing the sights to spring up. Finally, Jinx pulled the safety pin out of the launcher's base and eased it up over his shoulder. Next to him, Fuad was going through the same drill. The Kurds were, Jinx hoped, going through the same steps where they hid in the boulders.

Jinx waited until Fuad was ready, then took a last look at the kill zone. As he slipped his head up over the rocks, Jinx heard the engine noise change pitch. He watched as the column slowed, pulled to the side, and stopped. The troops in the personnel carriers clambered out even before the engines whined to a halt.

"Oh, shit!" Jinx exclaimed. "Don't shoot, Fuad!"

The 2S6 was stopped on the roadside, its crew climbing down over the 30mm guns and the SA-19 missile launcher boxes on the sides. The infantrymen emerging from the BMPS were not rushing into skirmish lines but standing and stretching, lounging against the sides of the personnel carriers as they lit smokes and relieved themselves on the side of the road. On the pavement, two fuel tankers pulled up and began filling the vehicles. The 2S6 was the first customer at the head of the column.

"Fuad, we may just get lucky this morning." Jinx watched as the tanker fed fuel to the 2S6, the thick hose twitching as it pumped diesel fuel into the nearly empty fuel tanks.

Jinx slid the launcher up over the rocks and centered the fuel tanker next to the 2S6 gun in his sight. He wanted to knock the four-barreled 30mm gun out first. It had too much firepower and could dig them out of the rocks with ease. He pushed the safety bar forward with his fingers and pressed the red button with his thumb. The launcher roared, the muzzle flash bright in the predawn gloom. The round arched over to the big fuel tanker and hit the rear of the tank. The fueler disappeared in a huge ball of black-fringed orange fire that swallowed up the 2S6 as well.

The fueler's explosion set off the ambush. The Kurds opened fire on the BMPs, blasting the personnel carriers and ripping the troops standing nearby with shrapnel. They scrambled about looking for cover. One BMP after another shook and belched fire from its hatches. The second fueler went up in flames, too, incinerating the BMP next to it and a dozen luckless troops too near it to escape the ball of burning fuel.

Jinx could hear the whoops of the Kurds on either side of him over the roar of their launchers. The Kurds were operating in two-man teams. One would fire his two launchers and then use his rifle to cover his partner as the second man fired.

* * *

Pyotr Churbanov had just begun to drain his swollen bladder when he saw the flash from the rocks off to the east. The boom of the back blast reached him just in time to get lost in the roar of the exploding fueler. Churbanov stood there for a split second, mouth open, organ in hand, as the huge fireball from the exploding fueler leapt up into the still-dark sky. Churbanov lurched into motion, the warm urine streaming down his leg, soaking his coveralls as he ran for the personnel carrier.

"Estekov!" he screamed, "shoot! Shoot right over there, in the rocks!"

Estekov was already lunging through the open rear door of the BMP, heading for the turret. Churbanov was right behind him, scrambling into the driver's seat, switching the 300-horsepower diesel engine back to life. As the starter turned over, Churbanov felt the BMP's turret spin, its 30mm gun firing on high rate, pouring 550 rounds per minute into the hidden attackers. Churbanov felt the engine catch just as a bright hell erupted inside the BMP, and then the world went suddenly black.

In thirty seconds, most of the launchers had been fired. On the road, burning fuel from the tank trucks flowed like a river of fire. A few of the BMPs were unscathed. Their 30mm guns searched the rocks for their ambushers. Jinx watched as one of the Kurds stood to fire his launcher and was cut in half by the big shells from a BMP. From the far end of the column, a wire-guided AT-5 missile flashed off the turret of a BMP and streaked into the north end of the rock pile, exploding just above one of the AT4 teams. The Soviets were getting their act together, it was time to boogie.

"Come on, Fuad, let's cheek it!" Jinx pulled the little flare gun out of the crack in the rocks and fired it high over the kill zone. The little yellow flare looked like a shooting star above the black smoke that billowed up from the burning vehicles.

Jinx pocketed the little flare gun and followed Fuad as he slid down the backside of the rock. Several of the Kurds were already running for the safety of the ravine. As Jinx reached the ravine, he turned and took up a firing position to cover the other ambushers as they ran for the gully. By the time the first mortar round landed, the whole class was accounted for. Three of the Kurds had been killed, another two wounded. Behind them, the short mortar barrage continued as they ran for the cover of the mountains four klicks away. An expensive FTX, Jinx thought as he followed his obstreperous class, but a hell of a live-fire exercise!

Churbanov woke up and screamed. The last thing he remembered was running for the BMP as shells rained on the column. He thrashed around for a second, searching for wounds. There were none. Churbanov twisted in his seat to see the rest of the BMP. Smoke drifted down from the turret. Estekov's legs hung limp from his seat in the turret. Black flash burns streaked the metal walls below the turret. Light streamed in through the open hatches. Aside from a faint crackling sound there was only silence. The ambush was over. The air stank of burning fuel and burned meat. Churbanov pulled himself out of his seat and crawled back through the BMP. He checked Estekov in the turret. A thin shaft of light speared in through the small ragged hole in the armor. The HEAT round had flash burned right through the turret armor and then blown a ragged hole through Estekov's face, the rest of his body peppered by fragments. Churbanov looked away and gagged as the smell of charred flesh and bone filled his nostrils.

He dropped back out of the turret and stumbled out the back of the BMP. Outside there was worse carnage. Dead riflemen lay in piles near their smoking carriers. For fifty meters on either side of the road, there were huge burned patches that still smoldered and a few small pools of still-burning diesel. The smell of burned diesel made him gag again, and Churbanov had to lean on the BMP to steady himself. The metal was still warm to the touch. He gagged again, then vomited against the side of the BMP, retching until there was nothing left in his stomach to heave.

Omar Telebani stood in the door of the headquarters and watched the ragtag group dismount their horses. Ahmad was down among the fighters, congratulating the bragging men and comforting the women whose men had not returned. Telebani ignored all that, he was only interested in the American. This one was like all other *feringi* who came to help the Kurds. His father and his grandfather had both fought for foreigners who promised much but gave little. The Turks, the British, now the Americans.

He remembered his grandfather's stories of the Turks' promises during the Armenian revolt. The Kurds had killed the Armenians for the Turks, then had been crushed themselves. How they could have believed the Turks at all baffled Telebani. The truth was not in Turks.

The British were no better. They hinted at recognition for Barzani's republic but forgot their promises when their oil was threatened. Cowards! Honor and courage were unknown to the *feringi*. Perhaps their Christian god forbade honor. At least this American had courage. He smiled, remembering the Iranians' constant harping about the Great Satan, America. *Marg bar Amrika!*—Death to America! No wonder the Persian pigs hated the Americans. Compared with the Americans, the Iranians were revealed as spineless dogs.

He had not attended the university as Ahmad had. Telebani's education was the Koran and the stories told by his elders. He cared not at all for the elegant political theories of the others. Those theories were only dreams, fantasies for the powerless. Telebani understood the true nature of politics. The Kurds were surrounded by Arabs and Persians, the two most oppressive races on Earth. As long as these oppressors lived, the Kurds would never know peace. It was that simple. His hope was that the Americans and the Russians would annihilate the Persians and the Arabs as they fought one another. Only then could the Kurds be free.

He hated the way the men fawned over this American, but if they could profit from him, so be it. In time, the American would either run away, as the others had, or die in another foolhardy fight like this one. It hardly mattered either way.

Dawn was lighting the mountaintops as Telebani stretched and went inside to find some coffee.

Jinx slept until noon, then spent the rest of the day talking to the fighters about the ambush. The Kurds were excited about the new weapons. No one seemed to care that they had lost men in the fight.

That night, Fuad disappeared again, vague about his destination. Tina slipped into Jinx's hut an hour later.

"I thought I might see you tonight," Jinx whispered as she slipped her arms around him and kissed his neck and chest. "Have you got Fuad in your pocket, too?"

"No," she murmured, biting his ear and pushing his back toward the bed, "he has an eye for one of the women in the village. She is a widow and happy to help me in this matter."

"I see."

She pulled off her jacket and tugged the long tails of her shirt out of the fatigue pants, pulling the shirt off over her head. In the dim candlelight, her skin seemed to glow. Her breasts jiggled back and forth as she jerked the bootlaces out and pulled each boot and sock off. Jinx sat on the edge of the bunk, pulling off his cotton shirt and hanging it on a little peg in the wall over the bed.

"You are so slow!" Tina said softly as she tugged at

his belt. She had her pants off and now knelt naked, pulling the rough pants off Jinx's legs. She stood and tossed the pants on the floor.

Jinx pulled her close and buried his face in her soft stomach, kissing and nuzzling his way down her belly to the softness of her sex. She held his shoulders and stood with her feet apart as Jinx followed his tongue on a search-and-stimulate mission. Tina moaned and swayed for a few moments as Jinx snuffled around in her crotch, then pushed him backward onto the bed and lay on top of him, kissing him deeply as she writhed around on him.

Finally she broke the kiss and began nibbling her way down his belly, her hand stroking his stiffening erection.

"Tina, we need to talk," Jinx said, his voice strained and cracking.

"You talk, I'll listen," she murmured as her lips closed in on their rigid target.

"No, I mean, this is serious," Jinx protested. "What we're doing could have serious—oh, God!"

Jinx's fit of conscience terminated when Tina slid her lips down the length of his swollen shaft in a disappearing act that would have made the Great Copperfield proud, much less Linda Lovelace. He strained and shook as she tongued, teased, and generally tried to swallow his organ. She made two slow trips up and down his cock, then pulled it out of her mouth with an audible pop.

"I thought you wanted to talk," she whispered.

"About what?" he groaned.

Tina smiled and stood, pushing Jinx's legs up onto the bed. She straddled him and slipped him slowly up into her, settling down onto his hips, pulling him up into her with muscles that felt like a wet fist.

Jinx tried to remember why this was a bad idea, failed, and gave it up completely. Tina was rocking back and forth, pulling and squeezing him inside her, trembling and clutching him with her hands. Both of them began breathing in ragged gasps. For her part, Tina alternated between lying down on Jinx and giving him a series of mouth-to-mouth tonsillectomies and sitting upright, rocking back and forth while he kneaded her breasts and tugged her taut nipples.

She suddenly picked up the pace and began slamming her hips into him, her body becoming slick with sweat. It felt like she would pull his organ out by the roots as she slammed harder and harder into him, finally gasping as every muscle in her strong body seemed to spasm into tetanus.

She's either coming big time or having a heart attack, Jinx thought as he held on for dear life, and she's too young for heart trouble.

She collapsed onto his chest as her spasms became shorter and she began breathing again. Finally she opened her eyes and kissed him gently between gasps.

"Ohhh . . ." she moaned.

"Jesus H. Christ!" Jinx whispered.

"Do not blaspheme," she scolded, then smiled. "If you blaspheme, heretic, I will have to punish you—again."

Jinx turned his head and kissed her still-damp face. "Teach me the meaning of respect!" he whispered solemnly.

An hour later, Jinx was much more respectful, as well as spent, drained, used up, and wasted. They lay there on the narrow bunk, their bodies curled against each other like a pair of spoons as Tina smoked a cigarette.

"Those things are bad for your health," he said, blowing away the cigarette smoke that curled up over her bare shoulder.

She chuckled and twisted her head, blowing smoke at him. "They are the least of my worries! They can only kill me slowly."

"True," he answered, then took a more serious tone. "Tina, you realize that our . . . relationship . . . could cause us both serious trouble."

'You mean my brother might kill you for fucking me?"

"That, too, but I was thinking more about my mission here in general and about your, eh, reputation with your people."

"I have no reputation and no concern for the opinion of my people." She sat up and put her back against the shirt hanging over the bed. "I share no values with these people, Jenkins. My only concern is our struggle. No one doubts my reputation there." She took a last puff of the cigarette and snubbed it out against the packed dirt wall. "Do you not wish to see me again?" she asked bluntly.

"I didn't say that," Jinx said, sitting up to face her. "I am just concerned about both of us."

"Do not be concerned for me," she snapped, standing and pulling her clothes back on. "I do not wish or need your concern."

"Tina," Jinx began, then stopped and swung his legs over the edge of the bed, watching her as she jerked on her boots and tied the laces around them in a knot to speed the process.

When she was dressed, Tina sat next to him on the bed.

"Jenkins, you are the only man I can have sex with here, do you understand?"

He shook his head. "I would think they would be lined up outside your door."

"They would be, but none will approach the sister of the Great Bey. Well, almost none," she added, remembering Omar Telebani's loathsome attempt. "You are the only man here who does not serve Ahmad. Besides, you saved my life."

"I'm not complaining, but a simple thank-you would have sufficed for that," he whispered, searching her eyes for another reason.

"Yes," she said, thumping his chest softly with her fist, "a thank-you note."

"You're welcome," he smiled. He kissed her lightly on the shoulder. "Come again."

"I will," she giggled, "if you are lucky—and respectful!"

"I hear, and I obey!" he said solemnly.

She stared into his face for a second, then stood and pulled on her jacket. "I doubt that very much," she said, then kissed him quickly on the lips and bolted out the door, leaving Jinx sitting naked on the edge of the bed, wondering how he got himself into such situations.

Back in her hut, Tina felt her way through the door, reaching out cautiously for the table at the foot of her bed. She found the little candle on the table and lit it, shielding the tiny frame until it burned brightly enough to shed a bit of light in the dark room.

She felt a motion behind her and spun just as the hand slapped her hard across the face. Instincts bred by her training snapped into motion, and she was barely able to stop before she killed her brother. He had not seen the thin-bladed knife.

"Slut!" Ahmad hissed at her. "Harlot! You shame our family! Would you destroy all my work? Have you forgotten your faith?"

Ahmad's eyes were bright, even in the dark room. He was more than angry, he was barely in control of himself.

Tina stepped back and leaned against the small table, gripping it with both hands to keep from stabbing her brother.

"I know you have been with the American!" Ahmad sneered. "I expect no less from him, he is a *feringi*, an unbeliever. But you, Fatima! What happened to you in the land of the *feringi*? You are a Muslim woman!" His voice took on a pleading tone. "You are also my sister! How can you treat me with so little respect?"

"Respect?" she shot back. "What respect have you shown me? Since my return, you have ignored me! The *Hamawand* show me more respect than you do! At least they respect my skills in combat—you do no even acknowledge that!"

Her stinging words seemed to take a little of the wind out of his sails. "You are a woman, you are not supposed to be a warrior," he answered lamely.

"Yes, I see," she taunted, crossing the room to lean against the far wall, putting some distance between them in case he felt the urge to slap her again. "I am supposed to stay home wrapped in huge dresses and belts of coins, content to bear one child after another for some illiterate goatherder."

Exasperation flashed across Ahmad's face. "You are supposed to behave like a Muslim woman, like a Kurdish woman!" He stepped toward her, then stopped and threw up his hands in frustration. "I have worked my whole life here to lead our people on a *jihad* against the rats that surround us. I have prayed to God every day to help me, to show me the way to do His will and lead our people to their destiny. You come home and humiliate me in front of the men who believe in me! How can you do this?"

She searched for the right words to answer him. She knew his history as well. When their parents had been killed, she had gone to Austria. Tadjii, as she had always known her brother, had stayed with relatives near Bakhtaran.

He had avoided the Iranian draft and fought instead with an outlawed Kurdish political group that preyed on both sides. It was during the last years of the Gulf War that Tadjii had emerged as a natural leader and a Kurdish zealot. His reestablishment of the *Hamawand* as a fighting force had given him a status that few had attained since Mustafa Barzani had rallied the Kurds in the Sixties.

"Ahmad, I know that you have spent your life fighting for our people," she said, rubbing the slap mark that still glowed on her neck and face. "I have, too. You have been here, fighting with bullets, but I was also fighting, with words. Kurds died in Europe, too." She sat on her bed and untied her boots. "I sought out the American because he is a good man, even if he is a *feringi*." She kicked off the boots and curled her feet up under her on the bed. "Besides, he is hardly the only one to make indecent advances, some of your own *wolves* have done as much," she lied. Only one of the wolves had done so.

"Who?" Ahmad blurted. Tina gave him a look that said "do not ask."

Frustrated and angry, Ahmad put his fists on either side of his head and grimaced, making a low, feral sound. Tina sat on her bed, impassive. After a moment of grinding his head between his fists, Ahmad spun and left her room. Tina sat for a moment, half expecting her brother to storm back in, but he did not. She stood and pulled off the rest of her clothes, then stepped over to the small basin to wash herself.

Ah, Great Bey, you are no king in your own house, Telebani chucked to himself as he watched Ahmad storm out. That she-devil has bested you. Perhaps she should be the Great Bey.

When Ahmad disappeared into his quarters, Telebani watched for a few more minutes to see if his leader reappeared. When he didn't, Telebani slipped out of the shadows. She had not named him to her brother. Perhaps after the American and his friend were dead, he would try again with her.

"Okay, I got good news and bad news," Captain Schultz started.

"Fuck you, sir, I got some news for you, too," BJ snarled. "You wouldn't have brought us back here just for good news, so give us the bad news first."

Do other commanding officers have to put up with NCOs who say "fuck you, sir"? Schultz wondered. Probably.

"The good news is that you are not in the tank-busting business anymore." Smiles broke out all over the room.

"Thank you, sir," BJ said. "Now what's the bad news?"

"You're back in the nuke-busting business again."

A chorus of expletives rippled through the room.

"Sir, I thought we were in a nuclear stand down," Sterling interrupted. "What about the cease-fire?"

"The cease-fire is what this is about, Norm," Schultz explained. "It seems that a bunch of rebel Iranians have managed to steal a couple of the Soviets' SCUD missiles and launchers. They are believed to be nuclear tipped." Groaning broke out all over.

"Let me guess," BJ asked, "they want us to find them."

"Roger that."

"Roger this!" a voice from the back of the room muttered. Schultz looked in the voice's direction and saw Parker's radio operator, Armstrong, holding his hand up and rapidly wiggling his fingers.

"Wonderful!" BJ exclaimed. "What a treat! Tell me, is our yuppie friend from that lab here to give us another brilliant lecture?"

Schultz smiled at the memory of Brian Hagerty, the nuclear-weapons specialist who had briefed the teams on the Special Atomic Demolition Munition back in Germany.

"No," he chuckled, "all you have to do is destroy the launchers. Maybe the warheads will take care of themselves."

"Hey, I don't know about that," Sterling said. "I hear the Iranians have heat-seeking stealth cruise camels that could deliver those babies."

"Naw, Norm. They deliver only chemical weapons— their breath and camel farts!" Hickey chimed in.

"Okay, calm down," Schultz said, trying to regain control. He began to drone on with the usual mission briefing. It was unusual because Schultz never presented briefings himself, leaving them instead to the O&I Section.

One of the operations sergeants handed BJ, Hickey, and Parker a black isolation packet. Each NCO pulled out two

computer printouts. The first was an operations order
(OPORD) of sorts. The other was the aviation annex. The
LRRPs were used to highly detailed OPORDS—mission
packets several pages in length, accompanied by numerous
annexes and packets filled with maps, requisition forms,
and mission-planning materials.

The three NCOs looked at one another with misgiving
as they realized the sparseness of the mission information.

"Uh, sir," BJ injected, interrupting Schultz in mid-
sentence.

Schultz broke off from the weather forecast and glared
at his platoon sergeant. The CO was on edge already, and
these assholes were not making it any easier. "What?" he
snapped at BJ.

"A goddamn leg rifle squad gets more info than this to
go check out a crossroads a klick away!" grumbled BJ.
"We're goin' in to look for these nuclear missiles and we
aren't given shit! What's the deal—sir?"

Schultz looked at him levelly. "The deal is, Sergeant
Kirkley, that we've got no info or time! You little shits
have got a mission assignment and I expect you to fucking
do it!" Schultz was hot now. "All I've ever heard from
you assholes is how flexible LRRPs have to be! Well,
mister, it's time to put your money where your mouth is!"
He crossed his arms and glared at the silent soldiers, his
face tight with rage.

BJ looked round at his little band and slowly rose to his
feet. "What the captain meant to say was that he knows
we're the only people who can successfully accomplish
this mission and he has complete faith in our ability to do
so." BJ sat down, his expression still serious.

Fuck me sideways, thought Schultz, how do you follow
that? "Yeah—damn straight! Now here's the deal, guys,
we don't have any more info than what's in your hands.
We're going to have to play it by ear. But we're not putting you out on the ground blind. You're going to link up
with some Kurd freedom fighters."

Parker raised his hand. "Any of those guys speak English, sir?"

"There's an SF officer with them, and he needs some backup. We want some U.S. personnel on the ground to take control of those missiles. We'll either get some real horsepower in to reinforce you so we can bring the missiles out or, failing that, we'll order you to destroy them in place."

It was BJ's turn to raise his hand. "What if these Kurds don't want to give up the missiles, sir?" BJ asked, recalling what he had learned about freedom fighters motivated by ethnic persecution, nationalism, or religion back in his Special Forces days. True, these freedom fighters fought for freedom of religion, freedom of speech, freedom of self-determination, or freedom to fornicate in the streets before sunset on odd-numbered days, but all they usually wanted was the freedom to settle some old scores with whatever other ethnic, national, or religious faction currently controlled the government. Superior firepower was a means to achieve that desire.

"That's an unknown, BJ, but be prepared for that eventuality," responded Schultz.

"How about something to blow these babies with, sir?" asked Saul Moser, raising his hand.

Schultz had never heard so many "sirs" before. Maybe his little fit had accomplished something after all. Looking at it from a realistic standpoint, he doubted it would last much longer than this briefing. "Yes, indeed. You'll be taking in some thermite grenades, detcord, and C-4."

"Remember, BJ," Ty King solemnly cautioned, "nobody carrying detcord or C-4 should carry any blasting caps!"

"Yeah, thanks, King," said BJ, looking up from the OPORD. "Important safety tip. You can carry the caps."

BJ looked back at Schultz. "Basically, sir, we're going to link up with Kurds and find the missing missiles. After that we're left to our own devices, so to speak." It was not a question but a statement. His expression was un-readable.

"Exactly," said Schultz quietly.

"Well, hell, sir. No big deal," BJ quipped, lifting his hands in a no-sweat gesture. "You've picked the right man for the job. I mean, after all, I saved Fort Hood from total destruction and the world from nuclear Armageddon in Germany. I think I can handle this little assignment! No sweat, sir!"

"And he's modest, too," Hickey added brightly.

"Indeed," responded Schultz, a tentative smile cracking his face.

Schultz turned back to the briefing chart and began droning on about the station time the unescorted C-130 would pick them up.

BJ sat looking out the tent's open flap at a pair of thin contrails that etched a tiny white line across the sky, headed north. F-16s, probably.

Nukes. Fuckin' nukes! BJ thought as the two streaks thinned and diffused in the too-blue sky. I never even saw a nuke before the war, now they're turning up in my breakfast. Fuck me running.

"Sergeant Parker." Schultz motioned for the team leader to join him as the two teams filed from the briefing tent.

Parker momentarily stared at him as though he were a panhandler accosting him outside a convenience store. "Sir?"

Schultz momentarily felt like an outcast. It occurred to him that there was still a very real class distinction between officers and NCOs, one the latter wished to maintain. He shut the thought out. "What was Armstrong's finger wiggling all about?"

"He's a radio operator, sir."

"Yes?" Schultz encouraged.

"Well, sir, he gave you the bird—in digital data burst."

* * *

"Come on, Fuad, it is time to make contact with the SFOB." Jinx slipped the notebook back into the black nylon pouch and slipped it inside his shirt. The notebook had both his communications schedule and a set of code phrases. Jinx hefted the AN/PSC-3 radio onto his shoulder while Fuad gathered up the operating systems. They walked down the slope of the mountain until they reached a small, flat spot, then began setting up the radio.

The AN/PSC-3 was the Army's satellite communication radio. Linked to the communications satellites that circled the earth, it provided secure, long-range communications. Since the transmission from the radio was beamed directly at the satellite, it was almost impossible to intercept.

As Jinx set up the antenna, unfolding its four thin metal strips that always reminded Jinx of old venetian blind pieces, Fuad unfolded the solar panels that provided power to the system. The solar panels saved the few radio batteries for night transmissions.

A group of the village children had followed them down to their transmission site and now sat on the slope above them, watching with the exaggerated seriousness of children as the strange foreigner set up his odd machines. The first few times he had set up the radio, a few of the Kurdish soldiers had come to watch, too. Omar Telebani had even come a couple of times but had tired of the process when he found that most of the transmissions were routine communication checks and contained no sinister messages. Now only the children tagged along.

Once the radio was set up, Jinx connected the Special-Operations Improved Crypto System (SOICS), the successor to the old DMDG—Digital Message Device Group. He called up his previously stored message and transmitted it in a quarter-second burst, repeating the burst twice at thirty-second intervals. A minute later, a long burst came back via the satellite. Jinx saved it in the system, acknowledged receipt of the message, and logged off. With the message saved in the system's memory, he and Fuad gathered up their gear and returned to the hut to decode the message and record a reply, if necessary.

Back in the hut, Jinx sat on his rough bunk with the SOICS device on his lap. Essentially a palm-top computer, the SOICS weighed less than two pounds and replaced all the one-time pads and conventional cryptographic equipment of the past. Jinx called up the message he had received and ran the program to decipher the message. After a second, the message came up in plain text. As Jinx scanned the text, his expression changed, growing darker and darker.

"Oh, fuck, Fuad," he moaned.

"What is it, Jenkins?" Fuad asked, suddenly concerned.

"A few days ago, our friends the Islamic rebels captured two Soviet missile launchers and made off with them intact."

"Excellent!" Fuad beamed. "Perhaps they will use them on the previous owners!"

"Let's hope not," Jinx answered. "The missiles are nuclear tipped. If the rebels manage to arm them and fire them at anybody, the nuclear moratorium could collapse. If that happens, everybody in Iran could get a taste of nukes like the Germans did."

Memories of the devastation caused by the small number of atomics used in the European war flashed through Jinx's mind. Even though both sides had fired their nukes at military targets, the collateral damage had killed thousands of civilians on both sides. It was a horror that no one wanted repeated but neither side would tolerate unchallenged.

"Oh, my," Fuad said gravely. "It would appear that the excrement has fallen into the air conditioner!"

Jinx laughed, wondering where the Kurd had picked up that expression. "Indeed, Fuad, and now it's landed on us as well. Since they were taken north of our zone of operation, we have been ordered to look for the two launchers. Our intelligence people believe that they have been moved into this area. They want us to find the launchers and destroy them before the rebels can use them on either side.''

Jinx folded the SOICS unit and stored it with the radio. The only bright spot in the message had been the sign off. It decrypted ''your sweetheart''. Jenna had added it to the code groups.

Thanks a lot, babe, Jinx thought as he packed up the radio and slid it under his bed.

''Jenkins, the Americans cannot order the Kurds to do anything.''

''I realize that, Fuad. I will have to persuade Ahmad to do it.''

''How will you do that?''

''By using the military adviser's traditional means of persuasion: flattery and blackmail.''

★ 16 ★

Well, at least he's still alive, Jenna thought as she watched the message come up on the SOICS. His last message had been the request for more weapons the day after the action that the S2 had told her about. She had been scared sick for him after the S2 described the satellite photos of the battle. She knew he had been in it, the burning helicopters were the proof of that.

As she walked back across the compound from the commo complex. Jenna wondered what was in the message they had sent Jinx. She had hoped it was a recall, but that was unlikely. The Soviets were pushing hard now; any help Jinx's partisans could give would be welcome. For the first time since this crazy war had started, Jenna felt stupid. It was stupid to be here in this worthless country fighting the stupid Russians. And for what? Oil? Let 'em have it.

Oh, God, she thought, I know this feeling. I hoped I would never feel it again, but here it is. Shit. This was the worst time to fall for someone, especially a rolling stone like Richard Jenkins! Everyone called him Jinx. Perfect! That's what I need, another jinx! Jenna took a deep breath, hoping to clear Major Jenkins from her mind. She succeeded in filling her lungs with diesel exhaust from a passing deuce-and-a-half. She coughed all the way back to the TOC. As she walked in, she overheard Colonel Taylor talking to Captain Haskell.

"If they fire one of those suckers, this whole place will be ground zero!"

"What things?" she asked, walking around her little desk and blowing the dust off the papers anchored on the desktop by empty 30mm shell cases.

"One of those SCUD missiles your boyfriend is looking for," Haskell answered.

"Which boyfriend are you referring to?" she asked as if there were legions.

"Jenkins," Taylor answered. "He and his band of rag heads are out looking for a couple of stolen nuclear missiles. That's what that message was this morning."

Jenna sat down quickly. The pit of her stomach felt awful, and her head seemed to be buzzing a little.

"I hope he finds 'em!" Taylor went on. "If he doesn't, this little show could be over before it gets started good. This isn't Germany. A few nukes here isn't going to gross out everybody back home like they did in Europe. Hell, a lot of folks have wanted to nuke Iran for years."

"That's okay with me," Haskell answered, "as long as I'm not here when it happens."

Oh, God, Jenna thought, why me? Taylor noticed her miserable look.

"It's okay," he soothed, "we're sending him some help. He wanted an A-team, but all we've got are some LRRP teams. They'll help him out."

"These for you, hotshot?"

BJ looked up from his rucksack to see Spec. 4 Jennie Cormack squinting in the sunlight from behind the wheel of a quarter-ton truck. Stacked in the back were a pile of MC1-1/B steerable parachutes. The trailer held reserves, weapons containers, and other air items.

"Yeah, I guess so, Jennie."

"How about roundin' up some help, BJ?" asked an-

other Spec. 4, Debbie Halberstadt, as she swung out of
the jeep's passenger seat. Jennie and Debbie, the self-
styled "Jumping Bimbos of Company G," were the only
two women in the unit. Only the small Parachute Rigging
Section was authorized females. Though good parachute
packers, they were a mild pain in the butt for the Headquarters Platoon as they, or rather the Army, required separate quarters and latrine facilities for females. The guys
minded their manners around them. The Army was serious
about equal opportunity and sexual harassment, although
both of the women had dated some Company members.

"Hey, it's my favorite riggers!" exclaimed Hickey as
he emerged from the headquarters.

"They don't like to be called riggers," said Ty King,
following Hickey out the door. "They want respect. Call
them rigros!"

"Gee, thanks, King Kong," gushed Jennie. "How
about puttin' your back where your mouth is and unloadin'
this shit? I mean, I like the feel of nylon on my skin, but
they're your chutes after all."

"Where you guys goin', BJ?" asked Debbie.

"You know I can't tell you that."

"I'm goin' crazy," Hickey said. "Wanna go along?"

"Get real, man!"

"This ain't reality, babe, this is war," Hickey said
gravely.

The chutes were quickly unloaded amid mild sniping. The
women knew the men were tense from preinsertion jitters,
and they made an effort to lighten things up. The air items
were stacked on a tarp and covered to protect them from the
sun. No smoking was permitted near them, even pinholes
from cigarette sparks could damage the nylon.

Everyone except Staff Sergeant Randell had pitched in.
Randell, the supply sergeant, stayed in the supply tent until the riggers were gone, claiming he needed to inventory
the batteries for use for communications, night vision, and
other equipment.

"Damn," he announced after the women were gone, "I hate that fucking slut!"

"Well, Randy," asserted Hickey, "maybe you should never have dated Debbie."

"You've got some room to talk, troop," Randell shot back. "I seem to recall that when your wife asked if you were faithful to her in Germany, you said, 'Yeah, frequently.' "

"Hey, what was it like, Randy?" asked Hickey. "She fix you dinner and everything in that trailer she was renting in Killeen?" Debbie and Randell had gone together for some time while the unit was at Ft. Hood. Hickey had difficulty believing the stories he had heard before. He couldn't picture Debbie being housewifey.

"Well," drawled Randell, "I won't say she couldn't cook, but for breakfast once, we had creamed chipped beef on Pop-Tarts. Strawberry, as I recall."

"Yuk!" chorused the LRRPs.

"They're coming whether you like it or not," Jinx said flatly. He leaned back in the rickety chair and crossed his arms. Flattery had already failed, now he would try blackmail.

Ahmad leapt to his feet and slammed his palm onto the desktop. "I will not permit it!" Ahmad railed. "We have already spoken about this!"

"That was before your Iranian friends upped the ante."

Ahmad's eyes bulged at the thought. "Our friends!" he shouted. "We have fought the Persians for ten centuries! We . . ."

"Save it, Ahmad," Jinx interrupted. "Either we find the missile launchers or you don't get any more goodies. It's as simple as that." Jinx didn't add that if the war went nuclear again, the Kurdish homelands would look like an asphalt parking lot.

Ahmad fumed and muttered dire imprecations under his breath, none of which Jinx understood. After pacing for a minute, Ahmad turned and jabbed a finger at Jinx.

"They will not lead my men!" he barked. "They will not fight with my units! They will live by themselves and eat their own rations." A look passed over the Kurd's face. "They will not annoy our women!"

Jinx fought hard to keep a straight face. He hoped the new rules were not retroactive. "Agreed. They will function only as scouts, acting as your eyes and ears."

"We need no eyes and ears, we have our own."

Jinx said nothing, letting the young Kurd vent his anger. Jinx knew that the shouting was carrying out into the street so the other Kurds could hear Ahmad's objections.

Ahmad sat down heavily behind his desk. "When are these larks to arrive?"

"LRRPs, not larks," Jinx corrected. "They will be here at midnight tonight."

"How? By helicopter?" Ahmad asked, draping one leg over the arm of his chair.

"Parachute. They'll be bringing some goodies with them. Night vision, laser designators, more antitank stuff."

Ahmad nodded, his eyes focused on the far corner of the ceiling.

"Great Bey," Jinx said softly, slipping back into his placating mode, "the Russian missiles must be found. If the Iranian pigs use those weapons on either side, all hell will break loose again."

Ahmad stood and stepped around his desk, heading for the door. "It is always the way. When foreigners come, hell always follows."

He motioned that the interview was over. Jinx just sat looking at him for a moment, then stood and walked slowly toward the door.

"American," Ahmad called as Jinx opened the door, "this one time only. Do you understand? After we find these weapons, the other Americans will leave."

"As you wish, Great Bey," Jinx replied, then stepped outside.

Ahmad walked back around and sat at his desk.

These Americans, he thought as he idly moved around the few items on his desk, they are worse than the British! They descend on you like locusts and expect you to do whatever they wish. They are the worst sort of unbelievers! Except maybe the Russians. At least the Americans will leave your god alone. For just a moment, Ahmad felt the weight of the superpower struggle squeeze him, felt their terrible indifference to the fate of his struggle. He slammed those thoughts out of his mind.

The Kurds had always fought all comers, he remembered, they always would. The words of his teacher, Ibrahim Mahmud, came to his mind. The Kurds have no friends, the old man had told him. Ahmad smiled, remembering the many afternoons he had spent sitting in a sunny meadow with the old man, listening to stories of the Kurds' struggle against the treachery of the world. Mahmud had been old, his age a mystery even to him. When asked about it, he would always shrug and answer, "I cannot remember when I was not alive!"

He remembered the old man's sayings, his cryptic proverbs. When Ahmad had been a child, the sayings were only confusing. Now their meanings were clearer. Now the old man's wisdom was a guide. Ahmad felt a lump in his throat as he thought of the old man's fate. Iraqi poison gas had killed him. The Iraqis had used it on them during the long Gulf War. Wisdom and experience were no match for gas. The old man had understood the treachery of the world, but that wisdom had not been enough to save him. Ahmad heard his blood begin to pound in his ears. The skin on his face suddenly felt hot, hot with rage, with hatred, with grief. He fought to control the rage, to harness it. Slowly the pounding in his ears quieted and his face lost its red color, returning to its normal ruddy brown.

Only power could protect you from the world, he thought, power.

★ 17 ★

The C-130 was late. Ahmad was still irritated, but he wasn't pitching any fit about the delay. If they didn't show up at all, it would be all right with him. At 0040 hours, the radio crackled for a second. "Mustafa, this is Bad Karma. Designate."

Jinx motioned to Fuad, who began switching on the tiny infrared lights that marked the narrow drop zone. Ten minutes later, the dark shape of the Combat Talon swept by 500-feet overhead. Ten large cargo bundles followed by a dozen airborne soldiers tumbled out of the dark plane.

Jinx was struck again by the image of a huge, prehistoric bird giving birth in flight, her tiny offspring plunging to the end of their twisting yellow umbilical cords, ripping free, their silken wings blossoming to lower them to Earth. He had once shared this image with another officer and had been told to cut back on his medication.

In seconds, the men were all on the ground, gathering up their billowing chutes. The big transport was gone, the drone of its engines lost in the mountains. Ahmad's men were bringing in the bundles. As the Americans made their way to the center of the valley, Jinx recognized the tall figure who was rounding up his little flock.

"Hi, guy," Jinx said as the Americans walked up,

"welcome to B. F. Kurdistan." Even in the dark, Jinx could see BJ's face light up.

"What it is, bro," BJ answered as he shook Jinx's hand, then hugged Jinx, thumping him on the back. Behind BJ, the rest of the LRRPs were moving off the drop zone.

"So, what fresh hell are we into here?" BJ asked as they shouldered their rucksacks and supplies and made their way through the thin stand of trees that bordered the valley.

"The same," Jinx answered, laughing, "only different."

Ahmad's men loaded the pack mules with the new supplies and took off with them toward the village, leaving Jinx and the other Americans behind.

"What the fuck, Jinx?" BJ asked as the Kurds rode off into the darkness. "Do we get to walk or what?"

"Our hosts are not too thrilled with this mission. You guys are about as welcome as skunks at a garden party."

"Fuck 'em if they can't take a joke," Hickey said, shouldering past. "We ain't exactly thrilled to be here either."

"I'm afraid my guys aren't too keen on looking for nukes," BJ apologized.

The understatement of the century, Jinx thought. At least one of the three LRRP teams had been on the ADM mission in Germany. Jinx assumed that some of them had been on the receiving end of nukes in Europe. He didn't blame them for being hinky about this gig.

"At least this time, we don't have to lay hands on the damn things," a voice remarked in the dark. "We just have to locate 'em, then let the Kurds knock 'em out or call in the Air Force." Jinx gave BJ a look and made a low humming noise.

"I hope it will be that simple," Jinx answered, "but I doubt that it will be." Fuad stepped out of the trees, motioning them over. In the trees, a dozen horses and several mules were tethered.

"Lighter guys, double up," BJ instructed his teams. "This is all the transport we got."

The LRRPs used the mules to carry their heavy rucksacks and mounted the horses. Several had little or no experience with horses and suffered some low catcalls, "And you call yourself a Texan, cowboy!"

"This is fucking wonderful," Mitch Pius complained. "Horses against Hinds. Wonderful."

"At least we're not stuck with Shank's mare!" Hickey laughed back as he spurred the horse and cantered off with Saul Moser holding on behind.

"Who's Shank?" Pius asked as the others followed.

"So tell me what you know about all this," Jinx said after the men had stashed their gear. "The message I received was pretty sketchy."

"Well, the SIGINT boys picked up a couple of Iranian rebel radio transmissions that said the rags had captured a couple of SCUDs with nuke warheads," BJ explained. "Naturally, everybody upstairs went nuts, and the next thing we knew, we got jerked off our tank busting and here we are."

"So who are these guys that have the SCUDs?" Jinx asked.

"G2 says they're a splinter group of the Iranian Army that feels like the government sold them out to the Russians. These guys are hard-line Khomeini types, real fundamentalists. Call themselves The Path. They hate us and the Russians and their own people, too. Mostly they hate everybody who's not as fanatical as them."

"Sorta like Baptists," Hickey chimed in.

"White Southern Baptists," King added.

"I get the picture," Jinx chuckled. "What else?"

"Well, G2 got a quick fix on the radio, but not a real tight fix. They know the launchers were captured in this area, but they aren't sure where they are now. They want us to look for them, along with your guys here. If we find them, we knock them out. If we can't knock them out, we call back for support. The mission is to knock out the launchers, whatever it takes, before the rags pop 'em on either side.''

''Any idea what the Russians are doing?''

''Nothing, but I suspect they're after the things just like we are.''

''Interesting. Somehow it seems like we're doing Ivan's work for him.''

''That's what I think, too. I think we ought to let the Russians get their own shit back!'' Hickey injected. ''They wouldn't help us get any of our stuff back.''

''We aren't helping them get it back, Shan,'' BJ corrected his sergeant, ''we're supposed to blow them up. We're more likely to take the hit from the damn things than the Russians.''

Jinx smiled and butted in, ''We are the Great Satan, remember? The Soviets are merely the Lesser Satan.''

''I think Satan thought up this whole fuckin' thing,'' King said, making everyone laugh.

''You may be right,'' Jinx answered. ''Sounds hellish to me.''

''We didn't know if you had any maps here,'' BJ went on, ''so we brought a couple.'' He pulled the detailed maps out of a plastic case in his rucksack and spread them out on the cot. ''I never saw so many contour lines before. This place is just straight up and down.''

''Easy to hide large vehicles in,'' Jinx answered, ''but the terrain also helps narrow it down to where they can be hidden. They can't drive on these mountain trails.''

''Yeah. Anyway, we divided up the area into three recon zones. We will start tomorrow morning on our patrols. You got any orders for us?''

''Not really. We'll coordinate with the Kurds tomorrow. Don't expect them to be too helpful. Their main man, Mohammad Ahmad, is not happy you're here.''

''What did we do to him?'' Hickey asked, confused.

"Nothing. I had to push you guys down his throat. Now he's madder than a Russian jump master with a planeload of quitters. You guys can't have any contact with his people at all, especially with the women. With hope, you won't be here long enough to get in trouble. Just keep clear of the Kurds as much as you can."

"No prob, we won't be around here much anyway."

"Okay, why don't you guys get some sleep, we'll talk to the Great Bey in the morning. BJ, come on with me, I want to talk to you some more." The two friends left the other Americans and walked out of the hut into the dark woods.

No one had to tell the LRRPs twice. They were flaked out on the floor and were sound asleep in minutes.

"You look good, BJ. A little R and R did you good."

"A little sleep, you mean. You look like a rug merchant," BJ laughed softly. "Where did you get that outfit?"

"Wait until you see your hosts in the daylight. They dress just like this, only more so," Jinx snorted. "Don't underestimate them, though. They're hard, ruthless mothers who'll slit your throat in a heartbeat. They're good fighters, and they don't take shit off anybody. Tell your guys to keep a very low profile around them. Don't even look at their women either. They're serious trouble."

The tone in Jinx's voice got BJ's attention. "Sounds like you have firsthand knowledge in that area."

Jinx let a low moan serve as his answer. BJ just chuckled.

"Did you get home after we pulled out?"

"Yeah, I did," Jinx answered, glad to change the subject. "I got back to Houston for a couple of days. Saw my mom. She was worried sick. Shit, who isn't? Paid another year's rent on my storage locker."

The two men stood silent for a moment, listening to the wind sighing through the trees. Neither one wanted to talk about home. In Europe, there hadn't been time to get homesick. Here, it was different, and both men felt the pain of separation from everything familiar.

"How long you think this war will last?" BJ asked quietly.

"Who knows. I don't think either side has enough ammo to keep it up long, but that doesn't mean it'll end. There were long stretches in World War II where not much happened."

"Yeah."

The two men stood silent for another minute, then Jinx turned back for the hut.

"Come on, we both need to get a little rest. It'll be busy tomorrow."

"Roger that," BJ answered as he turned and followed his old friend.

"Do you not see, Great Bey?" Telebani said. "The Russian missiles can make us a nation!"

"Two missiles do not make a nation, Omar," Ahmad chuckled. "Two missiles make only a target."

"Two nuclear missiles can change the outcome of a war," Telebani went on, "if the other side fears their use." He turned a chair around and sat facing his chief. "The superpowers used their nuclear weapons as a threat for years. Neither side would attack for fear of retaliation. So can we use the missiles to intimidate the Iranians and the Iraqis! The Soviets and the Americans have sworn not to use atomic weapons. We can secure our nation with these weapons!"

Ahmad leaned back in his chair and stared at his second in command. There was much in his arguments, but there was also incredible danger. His Kurdish heart warmed at the thought of the missiles. Power, real power, lived with them. The power to destroy a city, to wipe out a division, to make the other tribes cower. No Kurd could ignore such power. What of the danger? There was only danger in store for his people anyway. Danger was the entire history of the Kurds. With the two missiles, he would be the danger the others needed to worry about. The thought warmed him. He had heard that power was an aphrodisiac. If that was true, the missiles were like two warm hands running up his thighs. A thought broke into the sexual fantasy like a hangnail on a caressing finger.

"And what of the Americans?" Ahmad asked.

"War is dangerous," Telebani smiled like a wolf watching a wounded sheep. "If they are killed by the worthless Iranian fanatics, well, too bad. Strike now!" he urged pounding his fist onto the tabletop.

Ahmad was silent for a moment, watching the dust motes that had been stirred up by the Telebani's fist. He tipped his head back and sat with his hands pressed together, almost as if in prayer, pressing the tips of his fingers together. Finally, he stood and exhaled heavily.

"Omar, perhaps these missiles were sent by Allah. We will take them from the Persian swine and use them as the vanguard of the Kurdish people's nuclear forces. Make whatever plans are necessary to secure them."

"And the Americans, Great Bey?" Telebani asked.

Ahmad merely smiled and walked out of the room. Telebani watched his commander walk out of the building, then sat down and began to make a list of things to do. The first item on his list was death for the Americans.

Outside, Ahmad stared up at the night sky.

Nuclear power. He rubbed the sides of his head with his fingertips. Allah's wisdom sometimes took strange forms. This annoying American was the unwitting tool of Allah's will. He would deliver the power Ahmad wanted so desperately.

"*Allahu Akhbar!*" Ahmad whispered softly. He raised up his eyes and held his hands up in supplication. "*Allahu Akhbar!*" he shouted, God is truly great!

"BJ, I want you to meet with Ahmad's number two man to coordinate the patrols."

"On the way." BJ slipped the carbine back together and joined Jinx outside. They walked up the dusty street toward Ahmad's headquarters.

"So, who's this number two man?" BJ asked.

"Omar Telebani is his name," Jinx answered. "I don't know much about him except he's a mean motherfucker and no friend of anybody's, except maybe Ahmad. Don't expect him to be too agreeable."

"Roger that, I'll be cool," BJ reassured him. "Are you going to sit in?"

"Nope, I have a class to give. Fuad'll be your translator."

As they approached the door, Fuad stepped out.

"There you are. Please come in. Mr. Telebani is impatient."

"Here I am," BJ said brightly. He turned to Jinx. "See you later, infiltrator."

Jinx laughed and walked off down the road.

Inside, Omar Telebani was clearly agitated. He sat tapping his middle finger on the rough tabletop. A small but quite elaborate tea set on a hammered copper tray sat in the center of the table.

"Morning," BJ said, extending his hand, "sorry if I'm late."

Fuad translated for the Kurd, who barked back at Fuad.

"Mr. Telebani says never mind, now you may begin."

"Fine," BJ replied. He took the map of the region out of the cargo pocket of his BDU pants and spread it on the table, carefully moving the tea service to one side. Fuad nervously picked up the enameled pitcher and bowls and placed them safely in the corner of the room.

"Okay, Mr. Telebani," BJ began, "here are the sectors we will be patrolling in." BJ explained which team would patrol where and gave a quick overview of the LRRP's timetable. Fuad translated, asking questions for Telebani and translating the answers. When BJ finished his briefing,

Telebani rattled off a long string of Kurdish, and Fuad translated it in English.

"Mr. Telebani says that you will take one of his people with each team when you go out to patrol. This person will relay any information to him and stay in communication with the camp."

"Anything else?" BJ asked, keeping all emotion out of his voice.

Fuad looked very uncomfortable as he answered. "He says that you are all under the command of the Great Bey, Mohammad Ahmad, and you will follow all his orders."

BJ just looked at the Kurd for a moment. Telebani was a mean-looking bastard, but no more than the average pissed off Marine gunny sergeant. BJ knew that if he knuckled under to any of this, he and his teams would be kowtowing from then on.

"Tell Mr. Telebani that we thank him for the offer of assistance, but my teams are used to working by themselves and do not wish to risk the lives of his men in such a dangerous pursuit."

Fuad began to translate, but BJ interrupted. "Tell him also that my men and I are under the command of the United States Army and obey the orders of our superior officers. Tell him we will be happy to cooperate with his men, so long as that cooperation does not violate our orders. Tell him we serve our president just as he serves his bey."

Fuad looked like he had been hit in the ass by a sour apple, but he translated BJ's speech to the waiting Kurd. Telebani's reaction was immediate. He slammed the table with his palm, barking directly at BJ in Kurdish.

Rave on, fucker, BJ thought as the Kurd gestured and ranted, I've been chewed on by bigger dogs than you. At the end of the short tirade, Fuad nervously translated.

"Mr. Telebani says that is unacceptable, that you cannot go out without an escort."

BJ leaned forward and rested his knuckles on the table. "Tell him we spent weeks behind the Soviet lines in Germany without an escort. We will be just fine."

"That is not what he means, Sergeant," Fuad corrected BJ. "He means that he will not allow you to operate independently."

"I know that's what he means,' BJ replied, sitting down. "I just don't want to acknowledge it."

Fuad translated again and Telebani shook his head and waved his hand. The two men went back and forth, each holding his position, with Fuad nervously translating each exchange. Finally, Telebani muttered an oath and waved his hand again, this time to signify that the meeting was over.

As he got up to leave, BJ had Fuad translate one more little speech. "Tell Mr. Telebani that we are fighting the same enemies and that the enemies of his enemies are his friends. We will work together to find these missiles and to kill the Soviet invaders of his country."

Once again, Telebani barked out in Kurdish. Fuad turned to BJ.

"Mr. Telebani says that any foreigner in Kurdistan is his enemy."

BJ just smiled and left with Fuad following along in tow.

Later, Jinx returned to the LRRP hut from his weapons class.

"So, how'd it go with Telebani?"

"Like shit," BJ answered. "I don't like that guy, Jinx. He has eyes like a pair of ball bearings. I've seen hammerhead sharks that had more charm than that asshole. A real bogus dude."

"What was the problem?" Jinx asked as he leaned against the wall.

"He wanted to run our missions and have one of his boys along with each team. I told him that wasn't how we did business."

Jinx looked pained but not surprised. "How did you leave it?"

"Just the way we started it, except I'm not waiting to send out my teams. They're going out tonight."

"Fine," Jinx answered, "I'll take care of any flak that comes along. The main thing is to find those damn launchers, not to placate our so-called friends."

"A-fuckin-firmative."

★ 18 ★

"There," Hickey hissed, "see?"

Even with the binoculars, BJ could hardly make out the figure crouched in the rocks. The man was watching the road. He could see down it for miles into the flat plain. Several miles away, beyond the horizon, a column was moving. Both the trail watcher and the two Americans could see the dust cloud that marked the column's progress.

The trail watcher was so intent on the column that he had not seen BJ and Hickey as they slipped through the rocks across the narrow pass.

The watcher slipped back into the rocks. It was very hard to spot him now. BJ kept the binoculars on him. Hickey's hand on his shoulder startled him.

"He's got a visitor. To the right about fifty meters."

BJ swung the glasses over to the right. Making his way through a crevice in the rocks was another man. BJ could see the khaki uniform and the blood-red band around the man's left arm.

"Bingo!"

There was no way to follow the men back to their camp. The rocks were too exposed. The men would be there again to watch the road. BJ and Hickey slipped back over the ridge and started toward the Kurdish village.

* * *

Ahmad feigned disinterest as he listened to the Americans' report. In reality, he was very interested in their story. Telebani was right, these missiles were a gift from Allah. They would be the weapons that forced the great powers to recognize Kurdistan as an independent state. They were his personal ticket to power.

"Anyway, we know the direction he was coming from," BJ explained as he pointed to the spot on the map where they had watched the two rebel Iranians. "If we snatch the one here, out of sight of the other, we can switch uniforms and bag both of them." Beside him, Hickey nodded in concurrence.

Jinx looked over at Ahmad, who nodded his head like a patient father humoring his infants.

"I recommend that we effect this capture as soon as possible, Great Bey," Jinx said, his voice a model of humility. "These watchers could give us the location of the launchers, and if not that, then at least the location of other rebels."

"Indeed," Ahmad replied. "We shall send a group to capture them."

"Great," BJ began, "we can lead them back to . . ."

"It is not necessary to lead any men," Ahmad interrupted. "They can find the spot with ease. You may continue to search for other locations where the missile launchers may be hidden." With that, he stood, leaning forward on his small desk. "Thank you for your presentation. Good day."

BJ stood, openmouthed at their abrupt dismissal. Jinx kept his face a blank and stood. "Thank you for taking the time to hear us." He got BJ by the arm and led him out onto the street.

"Excuse me!" BJ growled. "I thought we had some exciting news, but it looks like we bored the big cheese!"

"I don't think so," Jinx answered as he steered Hickey and BJ down the street toward his hut. "I think he was plenty interested. If he hadn't been, he wouldn't have said anything about sending his men to look for the two rags. He just didn't want you two to think he was impressed.''

The sun had just dropped behind the mountains, and the street was gloomy and dark, even though the sky over the mountains was still bright, the high, thin clouds tinged with pink and orange.

"This place reminds me of Boulder," Hickey said as they walked up to the hut.

Both BJ and Jinx turned and stared at him.

"Not this hut, I mean," Hickey stammered. "I mean this valley. The way the clouds look after the sun drops."

Jinx and BJ looked at Hickey for a second, then at each other.

"Altitude sickness," BJ said quickly.

"Definitely," Jinx concurred. The two men turned and entered the hut, leaving Hickey outside to commune with the spirit of Colorado.

A little after eleven o'clock that night, the Kurds returned with the two captured Iranians. Both captives were blindfolded, their hands ties and arms bound over thick poles that ran across their backs and inside their elbows. One of the Iranians was bleeding from a wound on his right shoulder, stumbling as he walked. From the heavy stain on his sleeve, it looked like he had lost a lot of blood on the trip back to the Kurds' camp. The two men were herded into Ahmad's headquarters.

"That didn't take long," BJ observed.

"These guys can work fast when they feel like it," Jinx answered. "You got any cigarettes?"

"Huh uh. Maybe one of my guys does. Since when do you smoke?" BJ asked.

"They help cover the smell sometimes," Jinx said quietly. He turned back into the hut and emerged a moment later with two cigarettes and a tiny Bic lighter.

"I'm going to see what those two fellows have to say for themselves. I'll be back. You guys stay here and keep alert."

"Roger," BJ said to Jinx's back as he walked up the dark street to Ahmad's headquarters.

Inside the tiny room, the two Iranians were already tied to two sturdy wooden chairs, facing each other. Their blindfolds and gags had been removed. The wounded man was drinking water from a cup that Omar Telebani held to his lips. Telebani gave the man a tiny sip, then pulled the cup away. He asked the wounded man a question. The man shook his head no. Telebani asked it again, and again the Iranian shook his head. Telebani walked around behind the man and stood with his hands on the wounded man's shoulders. He patted the man gently, then dug his fingers into the man's wound, twisting and gouging the bleeding flesh. The Iranian struggled against his bonds, trying to get away from the pain. Abruptly, Telebani stopped and leaned down close to the man's ear. He asked his question again, and this time the man gasped out an answer.

Telebani looked up as Jinx stepped into the room. "There is no Geneva convention here, American. There are only questions and answers."

Jinx only nodded in reply. This was not the first interrogation he had watched. They were mostly the same: sweat, fear, blood, and answers.

Telebani pulled a chair over next to the other Iranian, who sat rigidly in his chair, his eyes wide with fear. Telebani turned the chair around and straddled it. For a moment, he sat just looking at his victim. Sweat began to run down the Iranian's face. His eyes darted around the room, looking for—what? Telebani pulled a knife from his belt, a thick-bladed hunting knife. He ran the point of the knife gently down the Iranian's face, making a thin blood trail, then leaned back and began to clean his nails with the tip of the blade. He quietly asked a question. The man nodded yes. He asked another question, and the man shook his head no, rapidly jabbering in Farsi. Telebani nodded and cleaned another fingernail. He asked another question, and this time the Iranian said nothing. He asked it again, and the man shook his head no.

Telebani just sat for a moment, cleaned another nail, then stood and stepped over to the wounded man. He grabbed the man's right index finger and stretched it over the end of the chair arm, pressed the knife blade down over the middle joint of the man's finger and slowly forced the blade through the joint, cutting off half the finger. The wounded man gasped, then screamed. The room was suddenly filled with the smell of sour sweat and another smell, a smell that left a coppery taste in the mouth. Jinx knew that smell. It was fear. He took one of the cigarettes out of his pocket and reached for the lighter, then stopped and put the smoke away. Better to see how long this lasted.

The wounded man was thrashing in his chair, the ropes digging into him as he tried to stand. A huge Kurd slammed the chair back down on the floor. The man strained against his bonds once more then slumped forward, his breath coming in ragged gasps.

The other captive was staring at his comrade, his eyes dilated with fear. Telebani walked back over and straddled the chair again. He opened the Iranian's shirt pocket and tucked the severed finger into it, then asked his question once more. The Iranian jerked his eyes over, staring at Telebani's expressionless face. His eyes darted back to his wounded comrade, then back to Telebani. He stammered, a torrent of words tumbling from his dry lips. His tone was that of beseeching, begging.

Telebani just looked at the man, shrugged, stood up, and walked back over to the wounded man. Again he pulled a finger out straight and this time cut the entire second finger from the writhing man. The big Kurd could hardly hold the amputee in his chair as the rough blade amputated another finger. The man screamed, rattled off a long string of Farsi, tried to spit at Telebani, but choked instead and collapsed back in his chair. Blood from the severed fingers ran all over the arm of the chair and dripped onto the floor.

Telebani stepped back over and tucked the second severed finger into the other Iranian's shirt pocket. The man's eyes looked down at the red stains that soaked through his shirt pocket and gagged.

Again Telebani asked his question. Tears ran down the man's face as he answered. Telebani patted him on the arm and walked over to Jinx.

"The wounded man is a sergeant in the rebels," Telebani explained. "The other man is his lieutenant. He confirms that they do have the missiles."

Jinx only nodded. Telebani went into the other room and came back with a cup of tea. He walked back over to the chair and sat down again, speaking softly to the terrified lieutenant, who stared at him with horror.

The interrogation went on for another two hours. Jinx lit his first cigarette after the next finger was cut off. The smoke helped cover the smell of blood that had mingled with the other odors into an olfactory miasma, a charnel house smell. A prickly heat spread down Jinx's back. No matter how often you watched one of these sessions, it never got any easier.

Four fingers and a thumb later, the Iranian sergeant began to talk, convinced that his lieutenant was going to let the Kurds cut him to bits. He babbled on for ten minutes before he passed out.

Telebani walked over as Jinx reached for his second cigarette.

"May I?" he asked, pointing at the Marlboro. Jinx handed it to him. Telebani was flushed, his breathing shallow and rapid. A primitive smile played across his face. Jinx lit the cigarette, and Telebani took a long drag.

"The sergeant was quite helpful," Telebani said, blowing the smoke out in a thin stream. "When he awakens, we will get more details. His friend will tell us more, too."

"They know where the missiles are?" Jinx asked.

"Oh, indeed. Now we will find out how many defenders there are and what weapons they possess."

Jinx nodded. The wounded man was coming around now. Telebani took a last drag on the cigarette, then knocked the fire from the end of it, and placed the remainder in his own shirt pocket. He stretched, took a deep breath, and went back to work.

Jinx stayed another half hour, then walked back to his hut. Telebani, engrossed in his work, never saw Jinx leave the room.

"Okay, let's run through it once more," BJ said. They had already been through the procedures half a dozen times, but he wanted them to be instinctive. If the shit hit the fan, he didn't want to rely on memory alone.

"Right before you move out," Parker led off, "we move to Point Alpha and hole up there."

"Every hour," Armstrong took up the litany, "we spend the first fifteen minutes monitoring 55.5."

Moser took over from Armstrong. "If we hear, 'Red Raider', we abort and call for evac."

"If we hear 'Golden Harvest'," Littlejohn finished, "we return to the Kurd village, set up observation, and wait for you to get back."

BJ looked over to Randell's team. "And if you don't show up with the Kurds, we call an Arc Light strike on the fuckers and evac."

"BJ, this whole thing makes me nervous," Parker butted in. "These guys don't have any reason to do this our way. They're way too easygoin' about the whole deal. I don't trust 'em!"

The others nodded. BJ knew that part of the problem was that his people were used to working by themselves or with a small, tight-knit group. The Kurds were tight knit, but the LRRPs were not part of their group. This exclusion bred mistrust.

"I know, guys," BJ answered, "I don't like it much either, but it's not our show. Major Jenkins is running this one, and he's a good man. Anyway, that's why I'm leaving you behind, so we don't all get caught in one place if these folks turn on us.''

The other LRRPs looked at him with raised eyebrows and skeptical expressions but said nothing. They had their orders.

''Okay, then, Team 22, saddle up,'' BJ said as he stood and shouldered his ruck. ''Teams 23 and 25, get ready.''

When Hickey, King, and Paterson had their gear on, the four men went outside to join Jinx. There was much commotion as the Kurds loaded their horses and readied themselves for the ride to the caverns. The Americans went unnoticed by all except Telebani. He watched the four Americans talking to Jenkins.

It would be better to have all of them along, he thought to himself, but not essential. They could deal with the others when they returned. Perhaps even engage in a little sport . . .

Ahmad's voice interrupted his musings.

''Come my Wolves! We go to kill Persians!'' Ahmad shouted. ''We will soon have the power to bend all before us, to drive the foreigners out of our lands, to proclaim a republic!''

This declaration was met with loud affirmation. The *Hamawand* were eager to get on with the fight.

Telebani looked over their faces. Not one in ten of these cares a whit about a republic, he thought, they only care about raiding and plundering, the same thing their fathers and father's fathers cared about. But, what matter, he told himself, a revolution always needs more fighters than thinkers. The column had already started out of the village. The Americans were up behind Ahmad and his slut sister. Telebani mounted his horse and spurred it up to the center of the column behind the Americans. This would be an exciting night. Telebani whistled a tuneless song through his teeth. The column set off just as the sun rose above a notch in the mountains, throwing a golden spotlight on the band of riders.

★ 19 ★

The rectangular cursor flashed down the amber screen halting on "Mr. and Mrs. Rodney Harrison, 2418 Rosehill Rd., Lenexa, KS 80226". He tapped a key marked RE-PLACE and resumed typing. The names and address were quickly changed to "Mrs. Robert Bradford, 136 Northern Blvd., Flushing, NY 11354". The cursor moved again. "Dear Mr. and Mrs. Harrison" changed to "Dear Nancy". Selected words were changed, "your son" became "your husband". "Second Lieutenant Harrison" changed to "Staff Sergeant Bradford".

The cursor moved through the final sentence: "Your husband will be greatly missed but long remembered by the 4th Battalion, 75th Ranger Regiment". He looked again at his signature block: SAMUEL K. FULNER, MAJ., IN, Commander.

Leaning back in the gray chair Major Samuel K. Fulner muttered, "Is it *Commander* or *Acting Commander*? What the hell, leave it, Commander'll look better to the moms and dads."

He commanded the portable computer to SAVE and then PRINT. Laying the lap keyboard on the desk as the built-in printer clattered, he stood, bumping the folding chair away with the back of his legs.

Only twelve more condolence letters to go. At least he

didn't have to write each one. Thank the big ranger in the sky for the miracle of computers! How the hell did they ever get around to fighting World War II, he wondered, picking up the half-full coffee cup.

"Shit!" It was cold again. He set the cup on the rickety folding desk, then picked it up and tossed the cold contents out the side of the tent.

An olive-drab Humvee was slowing on the road at the turnoff to the makeshift camp. It covered the quarter mile quickly and came to a stop outside the compound's gate. The driver was looking at a paper and then up at the crude unit sign. The driver stopped a passing Ranger, who pointed at the battalion's headquarters tent. He seemed to be pointing directly at Fulner.

"I have a bad feeling about this," Fulner growled as the vehicle pulled up in front of his tent. He shut down the portable computer and refilled his coffee cup.

"Sergeant Major!" he barked into the adjoining office. "Get the Two and the Three up here ASAP!"

"They're on the way, sir. I seen him comin', too," droned Command Sergeant Major Croton.

Sometimes he wondered why he even bothered giving orders with Croton around. The hard-nosed sergeant major always seemed to be two steps ahead of him. All he had to do was sign the papers that Croton stacked on his desk.

"I got a bad feelin' about this!" he muttered. He felt a chill come over him as he remembered their introduction to the Southwest Asian Theater.

The 4th of the 75th Rangers had deployed to Iran on the fourth day of the American operation. Staging out of Ft. Benning's Lawson Army Air Field, they had crossed the Atlantic and chuted up over the Mediterranean. There had been no intermediate staging base, just a very rushed parachute operation straight into the combat zone. Instead of days to prepare, they had only hours. The twenty-minute warning had come as they crossed the Gulf from Saudi Arabia. The air-movement plan was almost a repeat of the

REFORGER battalion exercises conducted before the war. They had even used an old 1st Battalion operation order as a basis for their own. The planning and preparation time had been much shorter, though.

The Soviets had suckered the Americans to commit a reinforced mechanized brigade in an effort to take Shiraz after an apparent Soviet defeat by rebel Iranians. The Soviet 104th Airborne Division was fully capable and, reinforced by loyal Iranians, was waiting for the Americans. In effect it had been a massive ambush. The U.S. brigade had been badly mauled and had fallen back to hasty defensive positions. Other follow-on mechanized forces had created a huge traffic jam as the retreating units pulled back. They, too, attempted to deploy into some semblance of a defense. The terrain was rugged, the road network almost nonexistent. A defense of sorts was established, but the front was not broad enough. A handful of mechanized units were forced to secure the flanks. And now the Soviets were rolling through southern Iran with heavily reinforced motorized rifle divisions, their regiments of tracked BMP-2s and eight-wheeled BTR-80s churning across the rugged desert behind massive rolling artillery and multiple rocket-launcher barrages. The regiments' tank battalions followed the BTRs on the roads, speeding toward the Zagros Mountains and beyond them, the Gulf.

The Soviets ignored their exposed flanks and barreled through to their initial objectives. The lead division's attached tank regiment followed on two routes, keeping to the roads until its battalions were called forward to help the tank battalions of the motorized-rifle regiments overrun the few American units encountered.

That tank regiment had to be stopped before it could drive into the American defense's shallow rear, if the first echelon motorized-rifle regiments broke through. The Rangers drew the job of stopping it.

The 4th Battalion jumped in just before dawn. Company A was to cover the battalion's flank to the west. Companies B and C would establish a series of platoon-size antiarmor ambushes on the roads. The companies left their Swedish-made M3 84mm recoilless rifles back. Each Ranger company had three Dragon missile systems, mostly stripped from the 197th Infantry Brigade at Ft. Benning. Each of the companies' nine squads now had one, and the AT section had three. Some of the Rangers had only a one-day familiarization course with the weapon. Door bundles of extra missiles and AT4 rockets were rigged. One of the battalion's C-141s would low-drop pallets with more Dragon missiles and ammunition.

No attack helicopters were available, but a squadron of A-10s had been moved to a forward, and greatly exposed, airfield. They would launch ten sorties in the first hour of engagement with the Soviet regiment. Four more sorties were being held back for on-call launch while the others rearmed and refueled. The only other fire support were the two diminutive 60mm mortars in each company. Even with a direct hit the mortars had virtually no effect on a tank, so the mortars would just provide screening smoke with their white phosphorus rounds.

The ten-minute warning had come southwest of Bandar 'Abbās. Two F-4D Wild Weasels, escorting four F/A-16s, went in first to jam air defense radars and kill surface-to-air missiles. The six C-141s carrying the three Ranger companies came in over the drop zone, flying in trail from the west. On each pass, half the troops on each aircraft barreled out the doors. The rangers jumped at 500-feet without reserve parachutes, just as they had done almost ten years before on Grenada and in Panama more recently.

Fifteen minutes after the first sticks of Rangers hit the ground, the Starlifters made their racetrack turnaround and came in again, this time at 600-feet in an attempt to throw off SAM acquisition. The Wild Weasels made their runs jamming on every band. Just as a Weasel launched a Shrike antiradiation missile at an air-defense radar north of the town, a surface-to-air missile hit the second C-141. The missile hit the port side inboard engine, tearing off the engine mounting and ripping the wing off with it. The twisting wing still had its own lift and folded upward before tearing loose. It sheared off the plane's vertical stabilizer. The remaining fuel in the wing tanks billowed into a massive fireball as the huge transport slowly rolled onto its port side.

Though poised in the doors, not a single Ranger made it out. Fulner never thought he would see a Ranger cry, but he saw many weeping unashamedly on that day. They stopped the tanks with a vengeance. Whenever their courage faltered, all they had to do was look south at the black column of smoke still hanging in the sky.

Finally out of antitank weapons, the platoons evaded to the pick-up zone where, only an hour later, they were extracted by Navy CH-53 helicopters under the cover of F/A-16 strikes that took a further toll on the remainder of the tank regiment. There had been no Soviet pursuit.

They lost more Rangers on their second operation. Again they had only hours to prepare for an extremely complex mission. Coinciding with XVIII Airborne Corps' counterattack, each of the battalion's three understrength companies was targeted on the three Soviet regimental artillery groups, or RAGs, of a motorized-rifle division. The Soviet division had just passed through a devastated first-echelon motorized-rifle division and was continuing the former's mission. Corps wanted to blunt the division's attack before it gained momentum. By staging simultaneous raids on the artillery battalions, the Rangers would hamper the Soviet division's fire support.

The Ranger companies were infiltrated by Blackhawks while AH-64 Apache attack helicopters executed a diversionary attack on what was thought to be the division's forward detachment. All were inserted without major problems, but finding the artillery battalions turned into a nightmare. Once on the ground, the companies splintered into platoons, each assigned one or two batteries to attack. Only a few batteries were found in the calculated positions. Some had displaced after a sunset, a common practice. Night was when the Soviets resupplied and changed position.

Many platoons stumbled into material support units and convoys. A few were unfortunate enough to tangle with tank and motorized-rifle units moving to new positions.

The raid, while inflicting little damage on the Soviet artillery, did create a great deal of confusion. As always in this sort of operation, the enemy feared there were more intruders than there actually were. Many Soviet units overreacted and, instead of moving to their assigned positions, set up a defense in place. More than a few Soviet soldiers were mistakenly shot by their comrades. Dawn found almost a third of the division's sixteen motorized-rifle and tank battalions far from their assigned attack positions.

The Ranger operation delayed the resumption of the attack and allowed III Corps to push the Soviet division and its southern neighbor back a few klicks. Fulner realized that their efforts had not been wasted, they had scored a tactical victory, but it had hurt the battalion badly, again. He was now the commander. Battle losses on both operations had reduced the battalion to two companies. Company B had suffered the worst from the crash of the C-141. Further losses on the ground that day and during the second operation had reduced it even further. The fifty surviving Rangers were reassigned to Companies A and C, but even this failed to bring them up to strength. Only eight replacements had arrived. Any kind of infantryman was suddenly a critical commodity. It was the same old problem that had plagued the Rangers in the Second World War, Korea, and Vietnam: No effective system existed to rapidly provide qualified replacements. The units were forced to train their own replacements in the combat zone. The tempo and intensity of this war did not permit enough time to do that.

As Fulner ruminated, Sergeant Major Croton came in with the tan U.S. Government Messenger Envelope and laid it on the desk without making eye contact. Sighing, Fulner picked it up and unwound the securing string. In it were half a dozen sheets of teletyped paper and a small envelope.

The envelope contained another operations order. This one called for the Rangers to link up with a Long-range Surveillance team in the enemy rear area and attack a regimental headquarters.

So there it was. The shortest and about the most simplistic ops order Fulner had ever seen. The ops boys at Corps must have their hands full and, peering at his watch as he quickly calculated, ten hours and twelve minutes to get it all together before the trucks picked them up. A quick look at Annex A, the intelligence overlay covered with small red rectangles depicting enemy units. It looked almost like a repeat of the second operation. What would they really find on the ground? There was one good point, there was a LRS team on the ground, apparently moving around. He didn't know anything about them, except they were "weekend warriors".

The S2 and S3 came in with inquisitive expressions. "Croton, have the company COs here in thirty minutes."

"I already called them, sir. They'll be here in twenty."

★ 20 ★

"This is too easy. Only a squad to guard these babies?"
Hickey shifted his M4 carbine, a shortened version of the
M16A2 rifle, and peered again through the small fold-up
binoculars, searching for more guards. The Iranians were
dug into the rocks on either side of the cave entrance.
Sandbags filled the spaces between the rocks, creating natural bunkers. A log-and-barbed-wire obstacle blocked the
entrance to the cave itself.

Above the entrance, another small bunker clung to the
rock face. There were no other defenses in sight.

"No shit," King echoed. "This is way too easy."

"It is easy because the Persians are pigs," Ahmad said
blithly. "They are stupid by nature."

"Even pigs are smarter than this," Hickey shot back.
"This looks like a trap to me."

"Me, too," Paterson added, joining the list of doubters.

"Guys, this is not Germany," Jinx said, trying to calm
the restive Americans. "These guys are not the Soviets."

"Thank God for small favors," Hickey muttered.

The interior of the cave was dark. BJ pulled the AN/
VIS-6 night-vision scope from his rucksack and used it to
look into the cave's interior.

"See anything?" Jinx asked.

"Nada," BJ answered, "it looks like the cave makes a turn to the right. All I see is rock wall."

"See any heavy stuff?" Hickey asked.

"Nope," BJ answered, lowering the scope, "just rock."

"We go then," Ahmad said firmly. He turned to Telebani and motioned with his hand. Telebani nodded and slipped down from the crest.

"We'll give you fire support," Jinx said as Ahmad turned back.

"And let us do the dying for you, of course," Ahmad said dryly.

"Of course," Jinx answered, his voice as flat and expressionless as possible. Ahmad slipped back down the rocks to join his assault team.

"What's eating him?" BJ asked as the turbaned figure disappeared into the rocks.

"I don't know. He changed his mind about this deal, but now he's acting like he's got a cob up his butt again."

"All these rags are like that," Paterson pitched in. "They all have the ass about something all the time."

Jinx didn't answer. Something was up with Ahmad, but he didn't know what. The flash of an RPG round on the bunker above the cave interrupted his musings.

The LRRPs had their AT4s in action, too. Two rounds slammed into the bunker on the right of the entrance, covering it in smoke. The back blasts from the AT4s filled the rock crevice with smoke that choked Jinx. He slid down the slope, feeling around for something to cover his nose and mouth. As he pulled up the field dressing he used as a bandanna, he could see BJ sighting his launcher on the remaining bunker. BJ pushed the button, the launcher roared, and a hail of dust and rocks pelted down on Jinx.

"Goddamn it," he yelled as he scrambled back up to the crest to rejoin the others. Their launchers expended, the LRRPs were pumping three-shot bursts into the bunkers, covering the force of Kurds who were assaulting the entrance.

From inside the tunnel there were muzzle flashes as the Iranians rushed to defend the cave entrance. From their position above, BJ and the LRRPs fired 40mm grenades over the heads of the attacking Kurds into the tunnel, firing at the flashes. The front rank of Kurds fell, but the others pushed through into the cave. Their fierce screams mixed with the screams of their victims as they swept into the cave.

"Come on," Jinx yelled over the firing, "let's go!" He and the LRRPs slid down the rocks and joined the trail elements of the assault. Behind them, other Kurds fanned out in front of the cave, occupying the bunkers and throwing out the shattered bodies of the Iranian defenders.

Inside the cave, there was still heavy firing, but the Kurds were clearly in control. The cave was really a chain of caves connected by a gravel road that twisted its way into the mountain. The firing was coming from a tunnel that led off to the right. Ricochets whined out of the tunnel and sparked off the walls. One hit just over Paterson's head.

"Shit!" he yelled as he dove to the floor. "Incoming!"

"This way!" BJ shouted. He pulled the LRRPs over to the right side of the main tunnel, moving toward the sound of the firing. They crouched near the tunnel entrance. Jinx dropped down flat and peeked around into the tunnel. The Kurds were plastered along both walls of the tunnel, firing down farther into another room. Fire teams were rushing the room under cover fire from the others. A team on one side would rush in while the Kurds on the other side of the tunnel fired. A grenade bounced into the tunnel and exploded in a small black puff. Two Kurds twitched and dropped to their knees as the fragments tore into them. The others ignored the wounded men and kept up their fire.

"Whadda you see?" BJ asked, leaning over Jinx.

"Not much," Jinx answered. "The Kurds are pushing 'em back into another room. No launchers yet."

A shout followed by a flurry of firing erupted from the tunnel, and the noise suddenly changed. The firing was not as loud; the Kurds had penetrated into the next room.

"Come on," Jinx said back over his shoulder, "let's keep up!"

He scrambled to his feet and slipped around the corner into the tunnel. The other Americans followed, watching the walls of the tunnel for any stay-behind defenders. Ahead, the firing stopped.

The Iranian voices were close. Heshim held her back with his arm as he slowly peered around the rock, looking for the source of the excited conversation. His head instantly snapped back. Leaning close he whispered into her ear.

"A crack in the rocks," he hissed. "There are half a dozen of the dogs guarding." Mohammad, guarding their rear, looked around. Heshim gestured to him with six fingers. Mohammad nodded, took one more look down the tunnel, and stood, turning next to Tina. Heshim looked at the two of them, then peeked around the corner again, slid his hand down to his weapon, and jumped around the corner. Before Tina and Mohammad could even clear the rocks, Heshim was firing his AKM. Tina was greeted by the sight of two Iranians bouncing off the dark rocks twenty meters away, their khaki uniforms blotched with high-velocity wounds. Behind the two martyrs-in-the-making, other rebel guards struggled to get a shot at their attackers. Tina fired her AKR from the hip, walking the burst into the wide crevice in the rocks. Behind her, Mohammad was firing, too. The Iranians looked like some macabre circus clown act, falling over one another, flying up against the rocks, doubling over, and falling on their heads. Heshim finished off the first two and lined up another. Tina's burst hit the man, but from behind him a gun barrel came up and fired a long burst. Heshim was slammed backward, took two faltering steps, and fell forward. Tina only glimpsed him out of the corner of her eye as Mohammad screamed and jumped in front of her, pouring fire into the crevice. In a second, his AKS-74 was empty. Mohammad dropped his rifle and reached in his belt for the Soviet RGD-5. He pulled the pin on the grenade and let the spoon off, then threw the grenade as hard as he could high into the crevice. Tina continued to fire as the grenade arched into the rocks, then threw herself back behind the rocks. The blast echoed down the corridor. Tina jerked the empty magazine out of her AKSU-74 and fumbled with a full one. It seemed to take years to get the new magazine in place, but no shots came from the crevice. She wheeled around the rocks into a kneeling position. The crevice was filled with smoke and silence, save for a faint moaning sound. Mohammad, lying prone on the gravel, crawled forward to check Heshim. He rolled the big man over and felt for a pulse in his neck. After a second he looked back at Tina and shook his head, then stood and inserted a new magazine in his weapon. He walked up to the crevice and used the barrel of his rifle to poke the lifeless defenders. One by one, he pulled the dead Iranians out of the rocks and made his way into the crevice. Tina heard another moan and a shot. The moaning stopped. Tina slowly walked up to the crevice, her weapon still pointing inside.

"Heshim was wrong," Mohammad said as he stepped out of the crevice, "there were eight of them in there."

"What is this?" Tina asked as Mohammad began stripping the dead of their weapons.

"An air shaft, perhaps," Mohammad replied. "There is light coming in from above."

Tina stepped over the two dead rebels in the crevice and looked up. High up in the rocks, a shaft of sunlight lit the wall of the crevice. It was hard to judge the distance, but the hole in the mountain seemed large enough for a man to escape from the caverns through it.

As Tina slipped down out of the crevice, Mohammad was turning over another of the dead, rifling his pockets. "You know, I . . ."

He never finished. Tina pulled the short rifle to her shoulder and fired twice. The first shot hit Mohammad just above his pistol belt, pitching him forward. Her second shot hit him above the left eye and took a large piece of his skull with it when it exited his head. She turned and dragged the remaining two dead Iranians out of the crevice and left them all in front of it, soaking the gravel with their blood.

She crawled to the top of the crevice and peeked quickly out the hole at the top. The crevice opened onto a steep, bare rock slope on the back side of the ridge. Fifty meters below, the scraggly forest began again. It was an excellent escape route.

She reached down into the leg pocket of her trousers and pulled out the small transmitter unit. She flipped the covered switch to 'ON' and wedged the transmitter into the rocks. Its signal would bring the Soviet troops.

One thing was obvious, the godless bastards were winning. The corridor was littered with bodies. As he reloaded his SVD rifle with another ten-round magazine, Rahman watched the Kurd bastard lying only a few meters in front of him, the blood from his belly wound soaking through the bright-blue cummerbund under his battle jacket, turning it an ugly black. The man had looked so surprised when Rahman shot him.

"Rahman!" Ismet Hosseini shouted. "Come now!"

Rahman scuttled backward, watching the corridor for more of the Russians. Rahman had stayed up to cover the others' withdrawal to the next room. Now they covered him. He was nearly at the entrance to the room when the next wave of Kurds burst into the corridor and opened fire. Rahman spun and dived into the room as slugs whined off the rocks all around. As he rolled to his feet, a grenade

went off outside the room. Two of the faithful dropped
like stones. Rahman felt a burning in his right thigh. He
did not have to look to know that shrapnel had hit him. It
did not matter. He crawled over the bodies of the two new
martyrs and slid his rifle barrel around the corner to join
the others in repulsing the accursed Kurds. There was no
shortage of targets. Rahman dropped one of the bastards,
then lined up another. He was so intent on his target that
he did not notice the long, thin snout of the RPG as it slid
around a rock and fired. The rocket was halfway to the
door of the room when its motor fired. Rahman heard a
noise that was part rocket blast, part scream and mostly
detonation as the RPG slammed into the wall behind them.
The concussion slammed the soles of Rahman's feet and
stabbed his eardrums with a pain that felt like two knitting
needles. As he tried to get his rifle back up, two bodies
fell on him from above, killed by fragments from the RPG.
Their weight pinned Rahman to the floor. He struggled to
crawl backward. When that failed, he rolled over on his
back to move the two dead.

"Aaahh!" he cried as Ismet's ruined face stared at him
from above. A large fragment of the RPG's warhead had
hit Hosseini in the side of his head, shattering his skull
and gouging out his right eye.

It was suddenly hard to breathe. Rahman struggled
harder to free himself, staring at his dead friend. Above
him, the others were still fighting, keeping the Kurds at
bay.

No, he thought, no, not like this, not trapped like a
hare. He pushed with all his might, and Ismet and the
other corpse slid off him. He freed his rifle and crawled
back from the door. They were losing. The Kurds were
after their prize and soon would get it.

His leg was throbbing now. The room seemed very light
and so did he. The sounds of the fight were quieter now,
although everyone was firing as fast as they could.

The Russian, thought Rahman, they will want the Russian. He told us the missile's secrets, he will tell them, too. Rahman turned and walked slowly toward the back of the room where the Russian, what was left of him, lay on the floor near the launchers. Hasan Bebehani was a master. He had broken the man's body and spirit but not killed him. The man had talked like a magpie! Now he would be silent. Rahman had taken only a few steps when the Kurds rushed the entrance and burst into the room.

Rahman turned, the fire in his leg dropping him to one knee. He brought the SVD up and fired. One of the attackers spun as Rahman's bullet tore into him. Rahman did not have time to fire again. A stream of slugs from an AKM stitched across his body, flinging Rahman down like a bundle of soiled wash.

The sounds of combat woke Ivan Tetrak. The sounds were far off, dreamlike. As he strained to hear them better, the pain returned, crumpling his damaged body into a ball, pushing the air out of his lungs. He gasped, the memory of his torture returning after the sweet release of unconsciousness. He had no idea how long it had been since his capture. In the cavern, it was always light. The physical abuse, followed by periods of unconsciousness, had destroyed his sense of time as well as his body.

The sounds were closer now, and the Iranian bastards were moving around in the cavern. Using his one remaining hand, Tetrak painfully twisted his body to see toward the entrance to the huge stone room.

A group of the Iranians were clustered around the entrance, firing down the long tunnel. Ricochets whined around the cavern, the tracers making red and green zigzags around the room.

I hope that one of those stray slugs hits me, he thought, and puts an end to this. There was no way to get out of here alive, he knew that. Better yet, if a tracer set off the fuel in one of the missiles, none of these bastards would get out alive. That thought cheered him.

The Iranians were losing the fight. Several of those clustered around the entrance lay dead. One of the defenders—the man who had captured him?—walked slowly back toward him. The man carried his rifle in his left hand, his right arm hanging useless.

Like mine, which your friend twisted out of the socket, Tetrak thought. Come kill me, *badmachi*, I welcome it.

The Iranian was still halfway across the room when a flurry of explosions shook the room. Bits of steel whined and whipped through the air, pinging off the launcher. A sliver hit Tetrak's cheek. He winced but felt no pain. His body already hurt as much as it could hurt. All he felt from the fresh wound was the warmth of his blood as it ran down his cheek and wet his parched lips. He licked the blood, it tasted salty sweet. He was thankful for anything to drink, even his own blood. The would-be executioner was on his knees, firing at a group that had burst around the corner. The newcomers were killing the remaining Iranians like dogs, the booming of their rifles reverberating through the stone cavern. Tetrak could not see the killers clearly, but they were not in Soviet uniforms.

His executioner pitched backward, hit by a burst of AK fire. Tetrak was not happy to see the man fall. Death would have meant release. Now he merely had new captors who would want the same information from him. This time he would give it to them quickly. There was little left of him to torture, but these brigands might find a new way.

The shooting stopped. A few of the Iranian bastards surrendered and were led off. Two of the newcomers stood looking at the launchers for a moment, laughed, and clapped each other on the back, then walked toward him. Tetrak twisted his head up to see them better through his remaining eye. He could see their checkered turbans and the bright clothes around their waists. They were not Iranians. Who knew what they were? It did not matter. They would ask him how to fire the missiles; he would give them the answers.

"Looks like the rags have thrown in the towel," Hickey said.

"So to speak," BJ answered as they approached the entrance to the room ahead. Inside the room, single shots marked the demise of the Iranian wounded. The five Americans checked the entrance, then stepped into the room.

The cave room was long, a hundred meters or so. Inside it, dead Iranians were scattered all over. The Kurds had done a thorough job. Now they were busily searching the bodies of the Iranians, taking anything that looked valuable. At the far end of the room, the two SCUD launchers were parked, the fronts of their transporters pointed toward the entrance. There were bullet holes in the windshields, but otherwise the launchers were undamaged. Ahmad and Telebani were standing between the launchers, talking to a Kurd who stood atop the launcher on the left.

"BJ, send your message and leave your people outside," Jinx said softly. "Take Fuad with you. I don't want all of us in one place with these guys."

"Roger," BJ answered. He nodded to Hickey and Paterson, who turned and trotted back toward the outside entrance. King remained behind, his M249 machine gun cradled in his big arms. BJ checked the magazine in his M4 and checked the grenade launcher under the barrel for a live round. This done, the three Americans walked down to the launchers where Ahmad and Telebani were laughing.

"Good work, Great Bey," Jinx said as they walked up to the two men. The launchers were larger than Jinx had expected. They looked appropriately sinister for nuclear weapons.

"Indeed," Ahmad said, smiling, "we are lucky. The Persian dogs were about to blow them up." He pointed to the missile on one of the launchers. The soldier was gently pulling off blocks of explosives from the body of the mis-

sile. A cut length of fuse dangled from the charges. On
the ground below, an American M60 fuse lighter and
burned length of fuse lay smoking next to the body of a
dead Iranian.

"My sergeant cut the fuse after killing the man who lit
it," Ahmad continued. "It would have been unfortunate
to lose them."

"Too bad you'll have to lose them anyway," Jinx answered. "They have to go, that was the deal."

The two Kurds turned and smiled at the Americans.

"No, my Yankee friend," Telebani sneered, "that was
your deal. Our deal is to possess these weapons, to use
them as we see fit."

Jinx glanced over his shoulder. A group of Kurds had
moved in behind, their rifles leveled at the Americans'
backs.

"Yo' mama!" King exhaled softly. That pretty much
said it all.

"It is quite simple, my friend," Telebani beamed. "The
Russian missiles will force the powers, great and small,
to take heed of us. For centuries, we have been pawns and
playthings of the nations around us. We have fought and
died by the thousands for a homeland of our own. Now
we will have it!" He and two guards stood over the group
of bound Americans, gloating and arrogant. The American
prisoners had been moved to a small chamber off one of
the branch corridors. Now they lay on the stone floor in a
heap, their wrists and ankles tied with nylon cord that
threatened to cut off the circulation if they moved around
too much. Fuad was not with them. He had been rounded
up with BJ's people as they tried to get back outside to
transmit their message. When he had learned of Ahmad's
treachery, Fuad had complained loudly. Omar Telebani
had shot the man as casually as most people stepped on a
bug. The last they had seen of Fuad was his body being
piled up with the dead Iranians.

"What you'll have if you use one of them is a shitstorm like you've never heard of before," Jinx replied, pulling his legs up under him so he could sit up a little.

"Shitstorm!" Telebani laughed. "I like that. Shit-storm." Telebani turned and translated for the other guards, who chuckled.

"Laugh it up, Bud," BJ barked.

"Omar," Jinx interrupted before BJ could get himself beat up, "the reason your people do not have a homeland is that they have cut one another's throats for centuries. You've sold out all your potential allies and murdered your neighbors for money. The reason the Kurds have no friends is that they refuse to be a friend to anyone. You and the Afghans can never quit fighting one another long enough to fight anyone else."

"Do not tell me our history, American!"

"I will tell you your history," Jinx insisted. "You helped the Turks kill the Armenians back in 1915, you sold out Barzani in the Sixties, you fought on both sides in the Gulf War."

"Lies!" Telebani barked. "You know nothing of our struggle!"

"Okay, let me tell you *our* history, then. We invented the atomic bomb in 1945 and blasted two Japanese cities to hell right then. We fired them on the Russians in Germany this year and killed a little more than a million of them and a few thousand of our German allies. Americans love nuclear weapons! Right now, there is a nuclear truce in place. If you set off those missiles and break that truce, the U.S. will turn your precious mountains into a big glass brick, Omar. What the Americans don't fry, the Russians will. The last thing they want is a bunch of nuclear crazies in their backyard. They'll burn this whole region, plow it under, and salt it so nothing will grow here. Your Kurdish homeland will be the graveyard of the Kurdish race. The Kurds will be a dim memory, a footnote in the history books!"

Telebani's expression stopped Jinx's litany. The Kurd's face was dark as a thundercloud. Hatred flashed in his eyes. The man was shaking with fury.

"I will cut out your tongue," he hissed in Jinx's face. Telebani stood and slowly pulled out the knife in his belt. The air in the room suddenly seemed thicker.

"Now you will . . ."

A thunder clap shook the cave. Dust billowed in from the cave's front entrance. The rattle of small arms was punctuated by the loud thumping of heavy weapons. Telebani glanced back over his shoulder, then looked down at his captives.

"I will be back, American, we will finish this later." He turned and ran from the room. The two Kurd guards remained, their attention directed toward the noise of combat.

★ 21 ★

Aleksei Bodnya looked at the cave's entrance and surrounding area in an abstract way. His experienced eyes saw only three things of immediate interest. First was the small security force guarding the entrance. They seemed to be none too alert, casually sitting or standing about the cave's mouth. They were well armed but not dressed like soldiers. Partisans! he thought with scorn. His unit was used to dealing swiftly with their kind. They were oblivious to his force's presence. Second, there had been recent fighting around the entrance. The sandbagged defensive positions were shattered and scarred. Uniformed bodies were strewn about the area, some were dramatically draped over the sandbags. His third observation was the most important, the terrain. His force had ample cover which to deploy weapons in support of his attack, but there was no cover or concealment for the attack force. They would have to destroy the guards at once. None could be permitted to gain the protection of the cave.

Bodnya lowered his binoculars and slid down behind the rock outcropping. Mopping sweat from his forehead with his field cap, he looked at his three company commanders. "We now possess a rare luxury, comrades," he mused.

"More forces than the mission calls for?" observed Senior Lieutenant Dubovik, the 4th Company commander.

231

"A wishful thought, Comrade Lieutenant," said Bodnya.

"Such as no aircraft," offered Captain Yurasov, the 1st Company commander and a veteran of the Summer Harvest operation in Texas.

"Exactly," said Bodnya. "Now what do you think our problem is?" glancing about the eager young faces. He enjoyed placing his officers in these little classroomlike situations. Study the problem, analyze it coldly, and develop a workable solution. It also served to calm everyone down. "What do you see as our present problems?" he again asked the small group.

"While we possess more than sufficient forces to defeat the enemy grouping," muttered Lieutenant Dubovik, "we are able to employ only a small portion due to the limitations posed by the terrain. A very small enemy force would be able to defeat, or at least neutralize, whatever force we were able to deploy on such a small frontage." Dubovik looked around the group for approval. The young officer had proved himself many times but still sought acceptance from the more experienced company commanders.

One of his few faults, thought Bodnya. "Yes, one can pour only so much water through a funnel. What tactical considerations does this terrain restriction impose on us?" Bodnya asked, picking up a pebble and absently tossing it from hand to hand.

"We are unable to employ any of the three principal forms of attack," said Captain Yurasov as he sketched arrow-pointed lines in the dust with his fighting knife. Looking up, he said, "We are restricted to a frontal attack, Comrade Commander."

"And how do we ensure that this least-desirable form of attack will have the maximum opportunity for success?" Bodnya asked, still tossing the pebble back and forth.

"Overwhelming firepower," injected Captain Shepelev, who had so far remained silent through the exchange.

Bodnya nodded slowly. He had expected no other solution from his most aggressive of commanders. "And how should we organize our attack force?" questioned Bodnya.

Dubovik had drawn his knees up under his chin and wrapped his arms around them. "A small select main assault subunit . . ."

"Heavily armed," injected Shepelev.

"Supported by?"

"The bulk of the force from overwatching positions . . ." began Yurasov.

"Supported by overwhelming firepower," finished Shepelev.

"Exactly!" replied Bodnya as he pulled a notepad from his trousers pocket. He looked around the group of officers as he quickly formulated his plan, his mind prowling. Defeating cave defenses had been developed to an art in Afghanistan. For once, he possessed more than ample forces. He might as well take advantage of the situation. Security of the main force was the prime concern.

"I order," his commanders' pens were poised, "Comrade Yurasov, 1st Company is responsible for securing this zone and preventing penetration by external forces. Comrade Dubovik will select sufficient soldiers to form a platoon-size assault group to penetrate the cave's entrance."

The officers all realized that that meant the young officer was to personally lead the assault group. "Comrade Shepelev will organize the fire-support group to be composed of his 2nd Company and the remainder of the 4th Company. On command, the 4th Company will reinforce the assault group and exploit the penetration. Once penetration is gained 2nd Company will prevent the escape of any enemy from the cave as well as secure the immediate vicinity of the entrance. I will initially remain with the fire-support group and accompany the 4th Company reinforcement group." Bodnya looked at his East German watch.

''The assault will be launched in thirty minutes, comrades. Report the progress of your preparations in twenty.''

He turned and slid himself back up to his observation position as the three officers departed to institute their assignments.

Another most unusual assignment, Bodnya thought. He had been told little, though that was not unusual in itself. But what he had been told made the mission unusual. His unit was on alert, subunits clustered in the shade of the big Mi-17 transport helicopters when a staff car arrived. Its passenger, a deputy of the army chief of reconnaissance had simply said, ''We suspect that this may be the location of two SS-1 missiles and launcher transporters captured by rebel Iranians. An agent has signaled us, and a radio beacon marking the location has been intercepted. You will attempt to recover the agent, but your primary mission is to capture or destroy the missiles.''

''It is done, Command Colonel'' was his only response.

Captain Shepelev had hurriedly ordered one of his platoon leaders to assemble all available snipers and the 2nd Company's best light-machine gunners. These dozen soldiers were positioned among the rocks and each assigned a specific enemy guard as a target. The other supporting weapons, from both 2nd and 4th Companies, were sited by the other platoon leaders. He quickly drew up a fire plan that specified the sequence of fire of specific weapons. He was still jotting it down when he reported his progress to Bodnya. A quick conversation with a nervous Lieutenant Dubovik followed to coordinate the lifting of supporting fires when his assault group attacked. He had wanted to give a word of encouragement, but there was no time.

Shepelev looked at the sniper lying beside him, the best in the company. The sniper's SVD rifle was unwaveringly aimed at the enemy partisan sitting closest to the cave's entrance. He glanced back over his shoulder at Bodnya, who was sitting with his back against a boulder below the ridge line. The man was a study in composure. Shepelev knew it was an attitude contrived to steady his subordinates, but it was infectious to those around him. Shepelev swore that the commander's radio operator, leaning against the same boulder, was asleep, though he knew this would not be tolerated. The battalion commander casually looked at his watch and nodded to Shepelev.

The second hand crept around Shepelev's watch. Four seconds from the minute hand, he softly said to the sniper, "Stand by." He raised his binoculars. "Fire!"

The Dragunov rifle cracked, its muzzle blast followed immediately by the rattle of RPKS-74 machine guns spitting out short bursts, their noise punctuated by more sharp cracks from other SVD rifles. Some of the enemy guards simply crumbled to the ground in slow motion. Others spun like tops, slammed into the rocks, and then bounced across the ground by machine gun bursts. Then it was silent for a moment. The darkened mouth of the cave lit up with a sparkle of of return fire from the remaining enemy posted inside. Shepelev had calculated for this response. Rather than immediately sending a barrage of devastating fire into the cave, he gave the enemy the opportunity to react naturally and expose themselves as they attempted to retaliate with return fire. This was their final act in life as a dozen RPG-16 and RPG-22 rockets detonated on the cave's inside wall, turning the entrance into the gates of hell with searing high-explosive flashes and shredding shrapnel. Following in the rockets' vapor trails were slower 40mm grenades fired from rifle-mounted BG-15 grenade launchers.

Long streams of tracers now lanced into the cave's mouth, creating a kaleidoscope of flashes and ricocheting tracers as they bounced off the walls. A second volley of RPG rockets boomed out, blasting into the sandbagged positions around the cave's entrance, scattering them even

more. The positions appeared to be unoccupied, but Shepelev had decided to take no chances. Clouds of dust billowed down the rock wall's face, obscuring the entrance.
Machine gun tracers continued to zip into the cave. The
grenadiers used them as an aiming point to fire a final
barrage of 40mm grenades. This final display of high explosives signaled two actions.

The machine gunners shifted their fire from the entrance
to the hillside, not so much to suppress any enemy that
might be concealed there, but simply for noise effect to
keep any bold surviving defenders in the cave from exposing themselves to fire at the assault group.

The second action was a signal to the figures who now
darted from among the boulders on their side of the small
canyon. The assault group rushed forward at a crouch.
Two groups of men, each composed of two squads, jogged
across the intervening ground, their weapons ready but not
firing. The tan clouds of dust, reinforced by dirty gray
smoke from the high explosives, concealed their movement. Disappearing into the dust and smoke, Shepelev
knew they were not yet entering the cave, but each sub-
group clustered on either side of its entrance. With an
exaggerated gesture he signaled all supporting fires to
cease. Several deep booms reverberated from the cave-
demolition charges and grenades, intended to stun and kill.

There was more movement among the rocks at the
ridge's base as a reinforcement platoon from 4th Company
moved into the assault group's former position. Shepelev,
engrossed in the action, felt movement beside him as Bodnya wriggled into position.

"The assault group has penetrated the cave, Comrade
Commander," whispered Shepelev. There was no need to
whisper, just a habit among the Spetsnaz. "There is not
much to see now."

Short bursts of automatic weapons fire competed with
one another, interspersed with the muffled bangs of grenades. The assault group was now inside. A single tracer

emerged from the dust cloud and arched into the rocks as its tracer element separated from the bullet, deformed from ricocheting off the stone walls. A cluster of red flares burst from the dust, slowly curving as they bounced into the rocks. The reinforcing platoon rushed across the canyon and disappeared into the dust.

Bodnya slapped Shepelev on the back and rose without a word. Shepelev, now in command of the forces outside the cave, watched the battalion commander thread his way down the ridge side and join up with the last reinforcing platoon.

★ 22 ★

Larry Cohen, Team 14's leader, wiggled his rear end one more time, attempting to mold the inflatable pad to a better shape. He and Gomez, one of his scouts, had been in position for almost two hours. Insulating pad or not, his butt was cold. Once more he scanned the edges of the clearing with his night-vision goggles (NVGs). There was no movement.

"I ain't looking forward to this shit, man," Gomez muttered.

"What's wrong, you still got a grudge against Rangers?" Gomez had had a mild run-in with some off-duty Rangers during the last REFORGER, a not uncommon occurrence for Gomez.

"Nah, that's not it. It's that 'fix bayonets and charge attitude'. They feed 'em Kevlar pills so they think they're bulletproof!"

"Well, mind your manners and keep your mouth shut when and if they get here," counseled Cohen. "This gig is too strange to begin with, and I don't need no fistfights in the rally point!"

Cohen had his own bad feelings about this mission. Everything had been fine, considering where they were, until half the Soviet Army used their observation site as a parking lot. When he and Gomez had first reconned the area

238

for a suitable site, they found one of those little quandaries that so often befuddle LRRPs. The vegetation on the north side of the highway was sparce and laced with a network of one-lane dirt roads and trails, not a good place for an OP. The south side was perfect: dense underbrush, a rarity in Iran, and no roads or trails. There was just one problem. The ground to the north was slightly elevated, giving an excellent view of the highway. The ground to the south was lower and offered little visibility of the highway. The team was forced to set up their OP on the north side.

The night before, right after sunset, several reconnaissance BMPs and light trucks had crawled into the area. Troops dismounted and began walking through the area with flashlights. At first, the recon team thought they had somehow been spotted during the day. But soon the night-vision goggles revealed marker signs being hammered in and small colored lights attached to trees. It was apparent that this was a unit advance party selecting unit positions. Cohen got his team out fast, returning the OP to its natural appearance.

Once well out of the area, they reported the situation. An hour later they received instructions to observe the Soviet unit's arrival, recon the area, and report all subunit locations. Cohen and Gomez moved into the area from the east. Albert, the assistant patrol leader, and Manning came in from the north. Chappel, the radio operator, manned the ORP. At 2100 hours, scores of vehicles began to rumble into the area, taking up positions on both sides of the highway.

They were all over the place, dozens of them. They did not stop coming in until just after midnight. After hours of thundering armored vehicle engines and clanking, whining tracks, it grew eerily quiet. The two recon elements were back in the ORP by 0100 hours.

"They're like fleas on a fuckin' dog!" snorted Albert. "We had them comin' in behind us all over the place. Those colored marker lights were everywhere."

"Yeah, but we're going back. They want locations for everything. I think they're planning a big-time air strike and want detailed targeting info. Identify the types of vehicles in each group. Try to plot their coordinates as close as you can. I know that's almost impossible at night, so give an azimuth and distance from a landmark on your map. And don't write on your damned map this time, Manning! Use overlay paper, okay?"

"Gotcha!"

"Okay, we're going into the same areas we came from since we know the ground. If you hear firing, get the fuck out of Dodge and back here. If one of us gets caught they'll put out patrols and double security. No way we'd be able to do anything more. Once you're back here, wait half an hour and go to the rally point. Report what info you have. If it goes all right, come back here when you're finished or at 0600, whichever comes first. I want to report what we've got and get away from here."

They quickly planned their moves and took off. It became a long night of crawling on hands and knees, dodging sentries, and peering at vehicle silhouettes with NVGs. Gomez had a big mouth, but the guy moved like a ghost and could almost see in the dark. They pulled it off and reported the results. It took two data bursts to send all the information.

Later that morning they received new instructions. Keep the unit under surveillance, report any major changes, locate and recon a helicopter landing zone, and prepare to brief and guide a Ranger battalion to the Soviet assembly area.

"Motherfuckers are tryin' to put us in the middle of a shootin' war!" exclaimed Gomez.

"No shit, you Mexican Dumb Dick!" growled Manning. "Where the fuck you think we are? Back in the fucking Sam Houston National Forest?"

"Hey, fuck you, gringo asshole!"

"Cool it, you two!" snapped Cohen. "Take a break under a poncho liner and make up."

"Don't get us started, boss. Besides, Dumb Dick here probably couldn't get it up. I know I can't. I'm too damned tired."

"Okay, we got a lot to do. Albert, take Manning and Chappel back to the area, set up a hasty OP where you can see any major movements, and send Chappel back here so he can show us where you are. If there're any major changes, send Manning back here so it can be transmitted. Dumb Dick and I are going to check out the LZ."

At least we don't have to take part in the raid, Cohen thought. Poor saps. He really could not picture a bunch of gung ho Rangers armed with only rifles and machine guns kicking too much ass on several dozen tanks and fighting vehicles.

Gomez nudged him out of his thoughts. "Listen, man!"

Both men strained their ears. Cohen cupped his hands behind his. Sure enough, he could hear a faint, but deep, thumping sound. He quickly grabbed his strobe light, making certain the infrared filter was in place. He punched the on switch and waited for the nearly inaudible whine as it powered up. Ping! Pointing at the treetops on the clearing's far side, he flashed the invisible light.

Two awkward black shapes appeared just above the treetops. Amid swirling clouds of sand and dead leaves, the two MH-47Es settled to the ground, looking like giant science-fiction insects pouncing on something to eat. Stooped-over troops ran out the backs, and the big choppers lifted off seconds later. Two more came in immediately to replace them. This continued until eight choppers had landed and disgorged their human cargos. Cohen was amazed that they had made it in, eight big choppers this far behind the lines!

They had been briefed last year on the MH-47E, a special-operations version of the venerable CH-47 Chinook. Cohen's experience with the earlier cargo models had been far from impressive. Company G had been supported by them on training exercises in Texas. Their limited range, cargo capacity, poor maneuverability, and lack of night-flying ability made it difficult to envision them as covert infiltration aircraft. But here they were. The MH-47E was obviously better than its predecessors.

I guess the old bird has come a long way, Cohen thought as the last of the big choppers lifted off.

Switching off their strobe, he and Gomez slipped through the trees to their left until they came to a barely trickling stream. It ran out of the woods and turned left along the wood line. Twenty meters inside the woods, on the right, or east, bank, they would meet the Rangers' contact man. He would come to the wood's edge, hit the stream, and follow it until challenged. Lying prone behind a tree, Cohen and Gomez waited. A brilliant flash suddenly reflected through the forest from the west.

"They got one of the birds," Gomez muttered.

After the flash, two figures rose from the ground a short distance in front of them.

"Camel!" Cohen called softly.

The figures crouched. "Sandstorm," came the curt response. One man edged forward and knelt in front of Cohen. He was wearing a Ranger cap and BDUs in the desert "chocolate chip" pattern. His face was also camouflage painted.

"Sergeant Cohen," the LRRP whispered, offering his hand. "Welcome to the best show in town."

The man gripped his hand firmly. "Major Fulner. Let's hope it's a good show. You got a program guide for me?"

"Yes, sir. There's been no changes since our last report. We'll get an update from one of my men who's kept the objective in sight. He'll meet us at our objective rally point."

"How many men do you have?"

"Five, sir. One with me, one in the ORP, and two in the OP. How soon will your men be ready to move, sir?"

"We're ready when you are, sergeant. I want you with me at the point to lead the way. When we get close to your ORP, you can go ahead and make contact. Then we'll send in the company COs and platoon leaders to assign each platoon a perimeter sector. After that keep your team with my command group until we need you to guide us to the objective. Once in the attack position I'll turn you over to the security-element leader. He'll send you with the PZ security team. Did they tell you what your team was going to do after the attack, sergeant?"

"No, sir, I assumed we'd continue our mission."

"You're to be extracted with us."

"Damn!" sighed Cohen.

"Shit, man . . . sir!" Gomez piped up. "In one of those flying SAM magnets?"

"Relax, troop. It'll be too hot around here for you to stay on the ground. They're going to be sweeping the area looking for left behinds," murmured Fulner. "They always have before."

Fulner had expected these men to be jumpy. He had no idea on how long they had been back here. The Rangers always went in and got out, and it was always nasty, but surviving out here day in and day out, that was different. Even so, he had not expected them to be reluctant about coming out!

"Believe me, you don't want to be anywhere near here once this is over!"

"You're the boss, sir," grunted Cohen. "Let's do it!"

They followed the stream back to the clearing and then the wood line to the right. They were quietly challenged and recognized. Moving past two Rangers with an M60 Cohen suddenly felt disoriented. There were men everywhere! He could see them lying behind trees and kneeling beside bushes. He could *feel* them!

Get a grip on yourself, he thought.

It occurred to him that he had never been in the woods with so many men, except maybe during infantry training six years ago. In Company G they operated only as small teams. Even when they bivouacked as a unit during field training, each platoon was assigned a secluded area, and the teams set up their own bivouac sites. This was too weird!

The movement to the ORP was uneventful. Albert and Manning were in the ORP with Chappel. They quickly briefed the major and some other officer, making a sketch on the back of a map sheet with their blue-green filtered flashlight shielded by a poncho.

The Ranger officer disappeared to give his final orders. A sergeant came up, reporting he was from the security element. He would stay with them until they led the Rangers to the attack position and then take them to the PZ with the rest of his team.

After a short wait, Cohen's team was called to lead the way to the attack position. Again the movement went smoothly. Cohen was pleasantly surprised that this many men could move so quietly.

Fulner led Cohen to meet the security-element leader, a lieutenant whose name he didn't catch. Albert went off with the major and three other officers for a quick leader's recon. They were back in less than half an hour.

"Act Two, sir. It's your show now, and we exit stage left."

"I want to thank you and your team, sergeant. Half our problem has been getting to the right place to kick these shows off. You've made it easy up to this point. Thanks again!" The two leaders shook hands.

"See you at the PZ, sir. Lots of luck!"

"Roger that, sergeant," responded Fulner. "Now you be gone!"

The PZ security team, six Rangers, and Team 32 slipped through the woods to the extraction PZ, four klicks away. Thirty minutes later, they heard several muffled thumps followed by a rising crescendo of automatic-weapons fire punctuated by more thumps and booms. Cohen's watch, set on Zulu time, showed 0236 hours. The automatic-weapons fire swelled in intensity, sounding like hail on a tin roof. Flares left smoky trails as they hung over the stark landscape, drifting under their parachutes. The firing went on for the better part of an hour.

Another loud bang echoed down the tunnel followed closely by a concussion and more dust. The dust was worse than the darkness. It burned the eyes and lungs. The Spetsnaz kept spitting and sucking on their canteens, trying to clean out their mouths. They would quickly run out of water at this rate. Many had torn open their field dressings and tied them over their nose and mouth in an effort to defeat the dust. Most of the men had bloody noses, and a few had trickles of blood coursing down the sides of their necks, leaving a maroon track in the dust coating their skin.

Bodnya was having second thoughts about accompanying the assault group. Another blast boomed down the tunnel, stunning his battered ears again. After joining the reinforcing platoon, a smiling junior sergeant had handed him a cigarette. Being a non smoker, he started to decline but then saw the other Spetsnaz tearing the cigarettes in two and inserting the butts into their ears. He adjusted his own makeshift earplugs again and looked into the calm face of a dead partisan sprawled beside him. His dead half-slit eyes held a cunning stare.

A fusillade of automatic-weapons bursts rattled up ahead followed by warning shouts. Bodnya instinctively ducked his head behind the dead Kurd's body. The blast hit him like a wall, bouncing his dead companion into his face. Tracers streaked down the tunnel, careening off the walls. Another man screamed as a ricochet bullet found a soft target. He had not even heard the weapons fire on the heels of the demolition charge's deafening blast. A renewed fit of coughing followed from the assault group's survivors. Soon he would be forced to relieve the assault group and their recent reinforcements and replace them with a 2nd Company platoon, now waiting inside the cave's entrance. Wounded Spetsnaz were crawling or being pulled to the rear in a steady stream.

A dust-colored form emerged from the gloom and rolled in beside him. The acid smell of burned explosives and weapons fumes was almost overpowering.

"Comrade Commander," croaked Lieutenant Dubovik, "we are making no headway." There was no tone of apology, it was simply a hard fact. The officer propped his submachine gun atop the body they shared for cover. Dust and blood were smeared around his nose and mouth. Mucus laced with blood flowed freely from his nose, and still more blood traced odd tattoos below his ears. "There is a barricade of sandbags and rubble around a sharp turn in the tunnel! We cannot reach it with anything we have!" He broke into a fit of hacking coughs, and spit out a muddy ball of mucus. "I have lost five men, shot dead the moment they revealed themselves to fire a rocket or throw a concentrated charge!" More coughing. "We continue to take casualties from ricochets and their grenades!"

Bodnya looked into the young officer's pleading eyes. They said that his assault group had done enough. They had given their all and were totally spent.

"Send a lightly wounded man back as a messenger. I order Captain Shepelev to relieve your group with a fresh platoon. Do it now!"

Dubovik returned a single curt nod, unable to speak, and scrambled across the gravel floor into the dust. Bodnya coughed and spit again, rolling onto his back, his eyes blinking crazily in the dust-filled air. A series of rapid single shots rang down the tunnel, ricochets sparking on the walls.

Ricochets, thought Bodnya. His mind queried his far past. Ricochets. When stationed with the Soviet Military Liaison Mission in Frankfurt, West Germany, he had had many informal discussions with one of the American of-

ficers. One had been about how primitive societies had
conducted war. The discussion soon led to the American
West and their Indian wars. The conversation had become
interesting and most pleasant. Bodnya had refrained from
making the usual required accusations of America's sub-
jugation and genocide of the wild Indians. The American
officer had stressed that some of the Indian tribes were
considered the best light cavalry in the world. He spoke
of them with admiration. His stories of their ability to
wage guerrilla warfare against the U.S. Army's superior
strength and weaponry impressed the young Spetsnaz officer. Maybe there was something to learn from these wild
savages. Bodnya asked the officer if there were any books
available at a military library telling of the Indian Wars.

The officer checked out two books from the Frankfurt
Military Community Library and loaned them to Bodnya.
Both officers immediately reported the contact to their su-
periors, and both sides contemplated the possibility of
mounting a recruiting effort.

Bodnya was more interested in the history books, beside
which sat an English–Russian dictionary as he struggled
through them. Many incidents, perpetrated by both sides
in the brutal wars, impressed him with their savagery, but
one incident in particular was unique in its disregard for
human life.

A group of cavalrymen had discovered the hidden
stronghold of a band of Apache in 1873. The stronghold
was a cavelike cleft high in a cliffside above Arizona's
Salt River canyon. The Indians, whose band included
women and children, thought the position to be impreg-
nable and felt they would be able to hold off attacking
soldiers with little effort. The soldiers would have had to
fully expose themselves to attack the cave's mouth and
then have to climb a natural stone parapet. Rather than
spend the time needed to starve the Indians out, the soldiers began a steady, ceaseless fire aimed at the cave's
downward sloping roof. The ricocheting bullets were dev-

astating and killed or severely wounded many of the Indians. The soldiers finished off the defenders by rolling boulders into the cave from above. Almost a hundred Apache braves, women, and children were killed. Decades later, archaeologists found the cave littered with the Indians' bones. Bodnya thought the slaughter was brutal but innovative in the expedient use of terrain and the resources at hand and filed the incident away in his mind.

"Dubovik!" he shouted over the din of another volley of fire. "To me!"

The lieutenant soon appeared on hands and knees again dropping behind the body. "Has the messenger left yet?"

"Not yet, Comrade Commander," he panted.

"Excellent. Direct him to order the command group to send in the NSV machine gun, a full crew, and all the ammunition they have! Do it now! This second!"

"It . . ." Dubovik choked, fighting another bout of coughing. "It is done!" Both officers began coughing as Dubovik scampered off.

★ 23 ★

Hickey slowly scooted back against the wall, using BJ to cover his movement. The door guard glanced over momentarily but quickly turned back toward the firing. Hickey pulled his legs up under himself and slid his fingers over the canvas top of his right boot, feeling for the laces. He pulled the knots loose and worked the boot open. He slid two fingers down the material folded inside the boot until he found the single-edged razor blade hidden there. He pulled the blade out with his fingers and sat still for a moment, not wanting to draw the guard's attention again.

The door guard was halfway out of the room now, staring down the road. Hickey peeled off the cardboard blade protector and turned the blade over in his fingers. He pressed it against the nylon bonds, and they parted instantly under the razor's edge. When his hands were free, he slid his right hand out from under him and slowly cut the cords that held BJ's wrists. BJ nodded and took the blade from Hickey.

"Jinx," BJ whispered, "lean this way."

Jinx leaned back toward BJ and felt the nylon slip apart. In another minute, King muttered, "Uh huh," signaling that his hands were now free, too.

"So now what?" Hickey asked softly.

"Wait, I guess," Jinx answered. "Thanks, Hickey."

"No prob," Hickey whispered. "Old habit."

"Good habit," BJ agreed.

The door guard heard them speaking and turned, gesturing with his rifle.

"Silent!"

The prisoners nodded and settled back to wait for an opportunity. The wait was not long. Telebani came storming back in, followed by another Kurd soldier. He barked an order at the door guard and then strolled over to the captives who sat sullenly against the wall. The guards took up firing positions facing the main corridor.

"I was interrupted," he hissed. "Where was I? Oh, yes, your tongue!" He pulled his knife from his wide belt and leaned down, grabbing Jinx by the hair. "Now, Yankee, I . . ."

The movement was fast. Jinx's hand shot up and grabbed a big handful of Telebani's testicles, twisting them as Jinx stood up. Telebani, caught off guard, reflexively slashed down with his knife toward his crotch, seeking to cut off the hand that was crushing his genitals. BJ caught Telebani's wrist with both hands and twisted it. Hickey, back in possession of the razor blade, stepped up to Telebani and deeply slit the man's throat. Telebani screamed, but the sound got lost as the air whooshed out of his severed windpipe.

At the door, one of the guards caught the movement out of the corner of his eye. He glanced over, then spun, pulling his rifle to his shoulder.

Jinx, now up on one knee, was pulling Telebani's Makarov pistol from its holster as the guard looked over. Jinx thumbed off the safety and pulled the trigger as the guard brought up his rifle. The pistol roared twice in the small rock cavern. The guard fired, then spun backward, the thin chest strap of his Sam Browne belt cut by one of the 9mm slugs. Jinx felt the bullet from the guard's rifle rip through Telebani, splattering Jinx's face with the Kurd's blood.

The other guard spun and wheeled back against the wall. As Jinx fired, he could see the second guard's rifle center on him. He knew that he would not be able to pull the pistol around before the second man fired. Time went into slow motion. His mind was screaming at his hands to twist, to pull the pistol muzzle over to the second guard, to save his life. His hands were like lead. They stubbornly refused to budge. Jinx's breath caught in his throat.

The guard twisted to the left and slammed into the wall. A trio of slugs ripped into his chest, small dust puffs erupting from his jacket front as a spray of blood, bone chips, and tissue exploded from his back, painting the dull rock with some crimson cubism. Jinx's pistol was moving now, but there was no need. The man had collapsed. King was on his feet, running for the door as the second guard died. He scooped up the guard's AKM and flattened himself against the bloody rock, looking for any Kurdish reinforcements.

"Jenkins!" Tina's voice rang from the corridor, "do not fire!"

"Come on, Tina," Jinx called back.

The wounded guard, lying at King's feet, groaned and tried to move. The huge black man, hardly taking his eyes off the tunnel, bashed the guard's head with the butt of the AKM. Tina, standing in the door, winced as she heard the *klonk* of steel on skull.

Hickey and BJ rushed up to the other dead guard and scooped up King's M4. Jinx stood over a writhing Telebani as Tina came up beside him. The man was rapidly bleeding to death, a stream of crimson jetting up from his cut carotid artery, the belly wound oozing a steady stream. Telebani's hands were at his throat, choking himself in an effort to stop the bleeding there. He was trying to speak, the sounds gurgling in his throat. Tina knelt on one knee, watching the man die. Her expression was a combination of curiosity, loathing, and satisfaction that made Jinx's skin crawl.

In the movies, this would be where I explain to him the error of his ways, and he would spit in my face, Jinx thought as the pool of blood beneath Telebani spread toward Jinx's boot. But somehow, I can't think of anything profound to say. As the blood parted to flow slowly around his boot, Jinx stepped back.

"Adios, motherfucker," he said softly as Telebani's eyes rolled back and his hands went slack around his neck. The stream of arterial blood slowed to a thick trickle that oozed from the deep slash.

"Come on, Jinx," BJ called. "Let's get out of here."

"I know a way!" Tina said, jerking her eyes from the dying Telebani. "There is a back entrance to this cave system, an air shaft."

With King covering them from the door of the room, they made their way quickly toward the tiny fissure. Behind them the sound of combat became steadily louder.

"What about the launchers?" BJ asked as they neared the huge cavern that housed the two missiles. They stopped outside the entrance.

"I don't think there is much chance that they will get away," Jinx answered. "But we've got to get past the entrance. Sling arms and hands behind your heads. Tina, hold your gun on us."

The others quickly slung their guns on their left side and put their hands on their heads. Jinx nodded.

"Here we go, look captive. King, take the right side to cover the rest of us."

"Move, American dogs!" Tina screamed. The Americans shuffled along in front of her as they passed the huge opening. Inside, the guards were in firing positions, waiting to hold off any attackers. They laughed when they saw the captured Americans being herded by their leader's sister. She waved, they waved back, catcalling the Americans. King shuffled along the right, his bulk hiding the others. The blood across his back and shoulders caught their eyes. No one seemed to notice the Americans' weapons. The entrance was at least seventy-five feet across. Each step seemed to take forever. As they neared the far side, Tina jerked up her rifle and butt-stroked Jinx between the shoulder blades.

"Move, Yankee pig!" she shouted as the Kurds hooted their approval. No one moved to help her, she was obviously in control of the captives.

Once past the entrance, they all broke into a dead run, Tina leading the way toward the end of the tunnel complex. Behind them, the hammering of small arms grew louder, punctuated by the dull whumps of grenades and the loud bangs of RPGs.

A pile of dead Iranians marked the entrance to the fissure. The two dead Kurds lay off to one side. No one noticed that one was shot in the back.

"Up there!" Tina pointed up the narrow crack. BJ slipped into the fissure, peering upward. He scrambled up out of sight, his feet clattering against the stone wall.

"It's here!" he called down from the crack. "Looks like it comes right out the top!"

The others slung their weapons again and slipped into the crack, disappearing one by one into the rock until only Jinx and King remained.

"Go on," Jinx said to King jerking his head toward the fissure.

"Huh uh," King answered, "I'm last. I'm too big, if I get stuck, no one else gets out."

Jinx didn't have any answer for that. The man was right. Jinx holstered his pistol and slid up into the rocks. Turning back, he called down to King.

"Okay, Ty, come on."

King's face appeared below him, looking up at the rock fissure. The big man climbed up, following Jinx. He was nearly to the top when his shoulders stuck in the rocks.

"Fuck!" King bellowed, "I'm stuck! I knew this would happen!"

BJ slipped back down in the rocks to the choke point that held King.

"Come on, Ty, we gotta get outta here!" BJ said as he braced his feet in the rocks and pulled on King's wrists.

The two men grunted and groaned, but King was stuck tight in the rocks.

"Get back down, Ty, we'll blow it loose," BJ said, leaning back on the rock, trying to catch his breath.

"No!" King said emphatically. "You do that, all of 'em will hear it. You go on, I'll cover you."

"I'm not leaving anybody, King," BJ answered. "Everybody goes home."

"You take the team and split," King answered. "I'll wait till it's dark and then blow it myself," King smiled. "My natural camouflage will protect me after dark."

BJ started to protest, but King cut him off. "Here, give me a grenade. I got one. Two oughtta be enough to blow a hunk outta this rock. Come on, gimme."

BJ stared down at King's dark, smiling face. The man was right, but that didn't make it any better. The idea of leaving someone behind made his balls hurt.

"Okay," BJ sighed, "here." He pulled the grenade out of his pocket and handed it down to King.

"Good," King said calmly. "Now get outta here!"

BJ knelt down in the rock and stuck his hand down to King.

"See you tonight at the rally point."

"I'll be there," King answered as he reached up, shook BJ's hand, and then dropped out of sight back down the crevice.

Topside, there was nothing but long faces. They had all heard the conversation; all knew that King was right, and all hated it.

"OK, let's get out of here," Jinx said, pushing the men away from the hole. "We aren't out of this yet."

As the LRRPs started down the rock face, Tina took Jinx's arm.

"I, too, must stay," she said softly.

"What?" Jinx asked, amazed. "What are talking about?"

"These are my people," she lied. "My brother leads them. I cannot run away."

"Yes you can!" Jinx insisted, grabbing her arm. "You stay here, you'll get your butt shot off, and I'm kinda partial to your butt."

She laughed. "I know you are, but I have my job to do, too." Her eyes suddenly sparkled, and she clasped Jinx's restraining arm in both her hands. "I will cover your black man when he escapes tonight!"

Jinx just looked at her. It was obvious that nothing he was going to say was going to change her mind. Jinx stared at her, trying to etch her image into his brain. She pulled him down for a kiss, a soft kiss that said only good-bye.

"Go now," she whispered as she held him to her briefly, then pushed him away. Before Jinx could reply, she disappeared down the tiny hole in the rock. Jinx looked at the rock for a moment, then turned and followed his team.

At the base of the fissure, King started as the girl stepped down out of the rock into the cavern.

"What you doin' here?" he asked softly.

"I promised Jenkins I would take care of you," she answered.

King's laugh was drowned out by the sudden flurry of firing from the direction of the missile room.

King slipped down on all fours and crawled out to the dead bodies sprawled in front of the fissure. He quickly took all the weapons, ammunition, and grenades he found on the dead and crawled back to the fissure.

"Just in case," he said, smiling at the girl who just stared down the cavern, listening to the rising din of battle.

Tina listened to the firing, unsure of her next move. The Russian commander might know of her mission, but that was a big assumption, especially standing next to a huge, black American soldier. It would be better to escape and make contact later. In this charnel house, she could only die.

★ 24 ★

Dubovik flopped down hard beside Bodnya and immediately began to hack, almost gagging. Tears flowed down his cheeks. It was apparent that they would not be able to endure this subterranean hell much longer. But, reasoned Bodnya, the partisans had little choice. They would endure or die. He planned for the latter.

"The heavy machine gun is here, Comrade Commander!" Dubovik gasped amid more hacking.

"Have the crew follow me to the right wall." A grenade thumped loudly ahead, sending hot fragments whining down the tunnel.

The battalion possessed a single NSV heavy machine gun, used for headquarters defense. The NSV was normally mounted on tank turrets as an air-defense weapon, but they had been used effectively in Afghanistan on a ground tripod mount to engage long-range targets in the mountains.

The gunner and his assistant came forward in a crouch, one on either side of the heavy weapon. The gun mount's tripod legs were already extended. The gunner was on the right holding the butt stock, and his assistant on the left supported the barrel's carrying handle. Each had a bulky ammunition box in his opposite hand as a counterbalance.

Bodnya motioned the gunner, his eyes wide behind a scarce pair of goggles, toward the wall.

The goggles are a good idea, thought Bodnya. The gun was down, and several men came up behind it, depositing more ammunition boxes. The gunner and his assistant began to feed the big-belted cartridges into the machine gun as Bodnya dropped to one knee beside them. He aimed at a random point high on the far left wall where the tunnel curved sharply to the right and squeezed off a short burst. The tracers ricocheted toward the ceiling. Another burst's tracers flew off in a more acceptable direction but still too high. The third burst had the desired results as the tracers splanged sharply downward off the wall, disappearing around the turn. The gunner locked a bulky SLS night sight on the gun in place of its normal optical viewer. Another good idea, though it would help little in this thick dust and smoke. The young gunner would be rewarded for his initiative, reflected Bodnya, if he survived.

He tapped the gunner's arm, shouldering his submachine gun. ''Shoot where I mark and keep shooting until I tell you to stop or you run out of ammunition,'' he yelled. The assistant gunner was linking the fifty-round belts together end to end. Bodnya fired a burst and then another. The gunner nodded, jacked a long cartridge into the weapon's chamber, and pushed his shoulder tightly into the butt stock.

The NSV's 12.7mm bullets were a half inch in diameter, as long as a man's thumb, and weighed almost two ounces. The gun's rate of fire was high when compared with similar weapons, 700 to 800 rounds per minute, thirteen to fifteen bullets a second striking the target area. There were no standard solid-core bullets available for the machine gun. The ammunition belts were composed of carbide steel-cored, armor-piercing incendiary rounds, every fifth bullet a tracer. The first tentative burst of fire was a four- to six-round burst. A single tracer slammed off the wall, the bullets creating a shower of sparks as the incendiary composition ignited. The second burst was twice as long with several tracers bouncing off the wall and around the curve.

The gunner looked over at Bodnya. "Excellent, excellent! Now, do not stop firing!"

"But the barrel will overheat, Comrade Commander!" pleaded the gunner.

"Piss on it! Now shoot!"

The gun's screaming roar blasted through the cavern, its heavy belt leaping into the feed port. Empty cases cascaded from the opposite side. Its rate of fire was so high that it was difficult to differentiate between individual shots. It sounded like a large-caliber chain saw.

The continuous tracer stream hosed into the wall and spewed into the tunnel around the curve. The burning carbide cores, bullet jacket fragments, and rock splinters rained into the tunnel. Bodnya pondered how many times each bullet would ricochet. The gunner's goggles were slipping down his nose, the vibration was so severe. He released the trigger and poked the goggles back into place.

"Keep firing!"

The roar resumed. The hungry weapon gobbled up belts, and its barrel began to glow a faint pink. The hammering continued as the assistant snapped yet another belt onto the end of the disappearing one. The firing suddenly stopped with the echos continuing for some seconds, the barrel glowing like a dim orange-neon light tube.

"The gun is jammed," shouted the gunner. "It is overheated, and the headspacing is off! We will have to change barrels," he coughed. The assistant was already trying to unlock the glowing tube with protective gloves.

"How many rounds?" demanded Bodnya.

The assistant looked up from his task, his face lit by the glowing barrel. "Over seven and a half belts, almost four hundred rounds, Comrade Commander!"

"Perhaps enough—for now. Change the barrel and stand by," ordered Bodnya. "Dubovik!" The company commander appeared beside him, struggling to hold back another fit of coughing. There was no return fire, only a loud silence. "Send two scouts forward," he whispered.

Dubovik darted off. Behind him Bodnya heard a muted crunching in the gravel. The 2nd Company relief platoon materialized out of the dust and went into prone positions along both sides of the tunnel.

The main barrier had been overcome. Bodnya knew there would be more resistance, but he still had one last weapon in his arsenal.

Dusk was quickly giving way to dark as the LRRPs threaded their way through the rocks down the back side of the mountain. Overhead, helicopters beat the air. At each sound of rotors, the team hid, pressed against the rocks, using them to hide the heat signatures of their bodies.

Off to their left, the sound of small arms rattled through the rock canyons.

"How we gonna signal the other teams?" Hickey hissed in BJ's ear.

"We aren't," BJ whispered back. "We're just going to get outta here and see what happens." Hickey nodded and slipped back into the darkness. There was no other conversation for the next three hours as the team slipped through the dark mountains, headed for the rally point near the Kurd village.

The firing was close, and rock chips flew from the rocks high up on the wall as ricochets whined down the corridor above Tina's head. Down the corridor, a crowd of Kurds was firing around a corner at their attackers. Wedged into crevices in the rock wall, the Kurds were keeping the enemy at bay, suffering losses only from the Russians' grenades and rockets. Even so, they would not be able to hold the attackers indefinitely. It was time to get Ahmad out of the caverns, not to mention herself. The Soviets had no way of knowing her rank in the GRU. She didn't even want to think about being captured. If she was lucky, they would only kill her.

As Tina rounded the corner into the launcher room, one of the younger Kurds nervously fired, splattering three bullets off the rocks a meter from Tina's head. She screamed and fell to her knees. One of the other guards shouted at the young shooter and whacked him with a rifle barrel. The youngster looked sheepish but still panicky. Her knees hurt, cut by the rock, but the hot flash of adrenaline washed away the pain. The younger Kurd was babbling an apology, but she ignored him.

As she stood again, a high-pitched keening sound came from the back of the cavern, barely audible above the noise outside. Tina saw her brother and Moz, one of his bodyguards, bending over a crumpled form between the two launchers. It took a second for her to realize that the sound was coming from the small form at their feet. She hurried toward the men.

"Tadjii!" she called. "The Russians are very near! We need to . . ." Tina stopped when she got close enough to see what they were doing. Moz had his knife out and was using it to torture their Russian captive. She could not see precisely what he was doing to the wretched man, but she jerked her eyes away before she saw more.

"Great Bey," she began again, "the Russians are nearly into the corridor. You need to make an escape now, before the Russians cut us off."

Ahmad turned and walked toward her, mercifully shielding her from the grisly work. Another pitiful sound escaped from the ruined form, a pleading sound followed by a faltering torrent of words.

"Do not be concerned, my sister," Ahmad said quietly. "The Russian dogs will not have us today."

His tone made her nervous. Ahmad was a firebrand but not a fanatic. He knew when to break off and fight another day.

"If we remain much longer, they will have us dead or alive," she answered, looking back at the cavern entrance. "They have too many guns."

When she turned back to her brother, her blood chilled. He, too, was looking at the cavern entrance. The look on his face was one with which she was all too familiar. It was a radiant, happy look that made men's faces glow and women's hearts sink. It was the martyr look, the expression of joy at dying. Half the men in her family had died with that macabre smile on their face. The others had mostly just looked surprised.

"We shall give the bear a taste of fire, Fatima," Ahmad laughed. He turned back to Moz, who looked up, smiling and nodding. Tina could see a tiny line of blood across the man's cheek, a thin spurt from an open Russian vein. "The Russian is telling us now the secrets of his weapons," Ahmad continued. "We will set off the warheads here. The Russian dogs will learn. . . ."

A loud bang shook the cavern, the noise stabbing into her ears like hot ice picks. Even as she flinched, Tina turned toward the entrance, bringing her weapon up. A loud flurry of gunfire erupted at the entrance. The Kurds were pouring everything they had into the Russian attackers. Ricochets whined overhead, knocking rock chips off the walls and pinging off the steel launchers.

Tina dropped flat on the gravel floor and searched for a target. The mass of Kurds holding the entrance blocked any shot at the Russians, but holes were opening up in the line as one Kurd after another fell before the Soviet fusillade. The loud thumps and bangs of grenades punctuated the machine gun fire, the little black puffs of smoke drifting slowly back toward her from the crowded entrance.

"Damn!" Moz's voice cursed behind her. She cut her eyes back toward the men who now crouched over the Russian. The torturer slapped the crippled man in disgust and stood.

"He is dead, Great Bey," Moz spat. "He died while revealing the launch code."

The animal cry that erupted from her brother made her jump. His face was no longer wreathed in the martyr's smile. It was now awash with fury. He kicked again and again at the lifeless form at his feet, howling.

The sound of the nearby battle faded as she watched her brother's fit of rage. If the Russian had not been dead before, he surely was now. Finally, Ahmad stepped back and swung his rifle around. He fired a short burst at the dead Russian's head, nearly ripping it from the shoulders. A welter of blood and brains splattered against the front tire of the huge GAZ's tire. Ahmad looked up at the huge machine and spoke softly to Moz, who nodded and slung his rifle behind his back as he reached up for the metal handholds on the launcher's side.

The two men climbed quickly and stood atop the long green missile. Tina realized what they were doing. Unable now to detonate the atomic warheads, they were going to shoot up the missiles themselves. In the confines of the caverns, the explosion of the missile's solid-fuel propellant would have a nuclear effect.

"No," she screamed as she rolled over on her back and fired between her knees. Moz staggered, then caught himself against the missile's erector railing. He turned toward her, huge red stains already soaking his shirt, turning it a dark red that matched his cummerbund.

"Witch!" he called, swinging his rifle toward her. She pulled the trigger again, only to feel the rifle's hammer fall on an empty chamber. She clawed at her pocket, reaching for a full magazine. She knew she would never get to it. Moz's muzzle was pointing right at her for now. Before she got the magazine out of her pocket, he would kill her.

She flinched and shut her eyes when the shots rang out, but she felt nothing. When she looked up, Moz was dangling upside down from the railing. Ahmad stood two meters away, his AKM still leveled on his bodyguard's dying form. Ahmad had killed Moz to save her life, but why? He would not permit Moz to kill his own flesh and blood, but he was planning to set off the missiles and fry them both to death.

Ahmad smiled at her and began firing at the thick missile, firing a three-shot burst every meter or so. Tina jumped up and ran toward the launcher, firing at her brother as she ran.

A burst hit him in the upper thigh, and he fell out of sight. She was almost to the launcher when she heard his wild laughter and another burst from his AKM.

"Tadjii! No!" she screamed, climbing onto the launcher, clawing her way up to the missile. She gained the top as another burst roared.

"Tadjii!"

The launcher seemed to move, then the world turned yellow.

"Ready?" Bodnya asked the energetic young squad leader as his chemical squad set out the last of the pots.

"Yes, Comrade Colonel," the junior sergeant replied, nodding vigorously.

Bodnya pulled his protective mask out of its canvas case. "Begin!" he ordered as he pulled the rubber mask up over his face.

The sergeant barked the order to his troops, which struck the matchhead igniters on the round YaD-11 smoke pots. Two seconds later, the pots poured out a thick cloud of yellow-white smoke that moved quickly down the corridor on the breeze that seemed to flow continuously into the tunnel complex. The smoke contained chloroacetophene, a form of tear gas. Each pot would burn for about five minutes.

Bodnya doubted that the defenders had any chemical protection. The smoke would hide his troops and incapacitate the enemy. The chemical squad had been slow in arriving, but now that they were here, Bodnya would use them to their fullest.

"How much smoke do you have, Comrade Sergeant?" Bodnya asked, his voice muffled by the rubber protective mask.

"The entire BRDM is filled with pots, Comrade Colonel," the sergeant replied, "enough for more than two hours of continuous smoke."

"Very well," Bodnya nodded. "You and your men will move up behind the lead attack elements. I want your smoke to precede us down these corridors."

"Just so, Comrade Colonel!" the sergeant answered, motioning one of his soldiers over. "We will give you . . ."

The light breeze carrying the smoke into the tunnel suddenly became a gale blowing in the opposite direction, and the sound of gunfire was drowned out by a roar. Everyone in the tunnel turned as the smoke billowed and swirled around them, obscuring the tunnel. They were all still peering through the acrid smoke when the fire swept over them.

Bodnya felt himself picked up by the blast and flung against the wall. The chemical sergeant and his other soldier landed on Bodnya, pinning him to the ground and knocking the breath out of him. Around them, the world was on fire. Bodnya could hear the two soldiers on top of him screaming, felt them writhe as they were roasted alive above him. Bodnya felt like he was in an oven. He jerked his hands underneath him to keep them from the flames. The fire lasted for twenty long seconds that seemed like years. As suddenly as it had come, the fire vanished. Bodnya felt the temperature around him drop. Now the roar of the fire was replaced by the screams of the burned troops caught in the fiery blast.

He struggled to move the two soldiers off him. They were very still now, dead still. When he finally managed to push their lifeless bodies off and rise to one knee, he was revolted by the sight of them. Their uniforms had

been burned off one side, and their charred skin and muscles attested to the intense heat. Their protective masks
had melted to their faces and bubbled up, giving them a
grotesque reptilian look. Bodnya had seen burned bodies
before, but the sight of these two made him gag. He struggled to his feet and stumbled away from the two charred
corpses who had saved his life.

The wind had shifted again, the expended fire pulling
air back in to replace the burned oxygen. The toxic smoke
pots were still burning, scattered around the tunnel. Their
thick smoke swirled back down the tunnel. It will not be
necessary now, Bodnya thought, there is no one alive in
there. There was no more sound of battle from the tunnel.
Defender and attacker alike were cinders, cremated by the
destruction of the missiles.

Bodnya had thought for a second that the atomic warheads had detonated. Obviously, they had not. Most likely
the missile propellant had exploded. As he staggered by
the burning hulk of the BRDM, he realized that his mission was accomplished. Around him, those soldiers still
able to move were dragging the other wounded toward the
tunnel entrance. Another BRDM was moving down the
tunnel, picking up as many wounded as it could hold.

As it passed, the private driving it saw Bodnya's rank
and slammed the vehicle to a stop. "Comrade Colonel,"
he called, "are you wounded?"

Bodnya turned to answer. The driver was opening his
door, his face wrinkled with concern. Bodnya spoke, but
no words came out.

Where are the words? he thought as the tunnel suddenly
spun and the dark floor leaped up to grab him.

The firing was much closer now, the reverberations of
grenade and RPG explosions sending shock waves down
the corridor. King scrunched back into the crevice, trying
to hide his substantial bulk in the narrow chimney. He
looked up again at the too-small hole.

A series of explosions boomed down the corridor. For the first time, King could hear the screaming of wounded men.

"Where are you, girl?" he muttered to himself. "It's time to go."

He slung the rifle from his shoulder and climbed up the chimney, using the palms of his hands and his knees to wedge himself in the rocks as he moved up to the hole at the top. He stuck his head up quickly through the hole, looking for any sign of danger on the outside. There was no one in sight.

King slipped the rifle off his shoulder and hung it by its sling on the rocks outside the hole.

"Now the hard part," he whispered. He pushed up through the hole until he stuck again, then dropped back down and turned his body this way and that, looking without success for some permutation that would ease him up through the small opening. Below him, the sound of combat continued unabated.

"Shit!" he swore. "There has to be a way to get my large, heroic ass outta this hole." A fleeting memory of home flashed through his mind, something his sister Georgia had said after she had had her first child, something about her baby being too big to get out. Yeah, that was it. One shoulder after the other, she had said, that baby just shouldered his way out.

Maybe that would work for him, too. He braced his feet in the rocks and twisted his body, pushing his arm and right shoulder up through the hole. When his chest stuck in the rocks, King exhaled as hard as he could and pushed up with his legs, forcing his chest up into the hole. A mental picture flashed through his mind, a picture of him trapped in the hole, unable to breathe because of the wall of rock around his chest. He banished the fatal vision and pushed even harder with his legs. The rock dug into his left shoulder, digging at the skin under his uniform shirt.

As he struggled in the tiny opening, King felt a trembling in the rock itself. Around his chest, a breeze whistled through the gaps in the rock, the whistling sound getting louder as the breeze grew in strength and velocity. A hammer hit from beneath him. King felt himself blown up through the hole. Pain seared his left shoulder and arm. He fell next to the hole and slid down the slope. With his right arm, he grabbed the rifle and hung on to it as a gout of flame roared up out of the hole, singeing him with its sudden fierce heat.

"Motha fuck!" King screamed as the big blowtorch of flame roared a few feet away. The flame went out as suddenly as it had come, and King could hear the air being sucked back into the hole. A smell like burned rubber hung in the air.

"Shee-it!" King gasped, still hanging from the now smouldering sling. He flipped over on his stomach and crawled up a bit to get a better hold on the rocks. Around the hole, the rock was too hot to touch.

King sat up and gingerly fingered his aching shoulder. Any movement of his left arm sent stilettos of pain through his shoulder. Most likely, it was broken. Dislocated at least. King reached over and took his left wrist, pushing his hand inside his shirt between the last two buttons. The pain was awful, but it felt better once he had it in the shirt. He dug into the cargo pocket of his BDU pants and fished out the plastic-wrapped bandage, ripped open the plastic pouch with his teeth, and pulled out the muslin dressing. Using his teeth and his good hand, he fashioned a strap out of the dressing and strapped his injured arm against his chest, immobilizing it. The simple operation hurt like hell, and by the time he had it done, he was out of breath and shaking. King leaned over the hole, holding his breath against the acrid smell that still drifted up. There were no more sounds of fighting.

Guess they went up after all, he thought as he leaned back to take a breath, whatever blew, the fight's over now.

Time to get my black ass out of here. Wonder what happened to that girl?

King gathered up the rifle and slung it across his chest. It would be nearly useless with just one hand, but better to have it, anyway. Slowly and awkwardly, King made his way down the slope, following after his team.

"Did you see that?" Bendel blurted. "Shit!"

Fire had belched from the entrance of the cavern, scorching the rocks and leaving black sooty streaks on the rocks.

"Hey, look at that," Loggins pointed at a black smoke ring that rose over the crest of the ridge behind the caverns. "Must be an entrance back there, too."

"Gentlemen, this does not bode well," Randell declared. "I think we need to get the fuck out of here real soon. Mitch, send a message, tell them the launchers are believed destroyed by Soviet action, and we are leaving the area."

"Roger, dodger."

★ 25 ★

A thin line of pale yellow light was just visible between the mountains as BJ held his hand up to signal a halt. No one spoke, their mouths were too dry from the long walk to waste any spit on conversation.

Jinx slipped up next to BJ and leaned close.

"How much farther?" he croaked.

BJ shook his head and held up two fingers. "Two maybe three klicks," he rasped.

"What'sa matter, BJ, cat got your tongue?" a voice said from the rock. BJ almost jumped out of his skin at the sound. The voice chuckled. "Not too stealthy, fearless leader," Al Parker said from his hiding place. "We heard you coming a mile off." Shadows moved in the darkness as Parker's team emerged.

"Water!" BJ said softly as the other LRRPs joined them. Canteens appeared, and BJ's team drank greedily.

"Thanks, Al," BJ said when he had taken a swallow. "We were pretty dry. Had to leave our gear."

"Lucky you got out with your ass," Parker answered. "We watched the Sovs go in after you guys, musta been a battalion at least. King get it?"

BJ shook his head. "Stayed back. We'll wait for him."

"Not for long," Parker said. "We already called for extraction."

"When?" BJ snapped.

"Dawn, 0600 hours," Parker answered. "We thought you guys weren't comin' out."

"Where are the others?"

"They followed you to the caverns," Parker explained. "We figured you might need some backup." BJ started to protest the disregard of their orders, but changed his mind and merely nodded.

"You want us to try to call some air on those Kurd fuckers?"

"Naw, no point," BJ shook his head. "They're just caught in the middle anyway. Either way, they get screwed."

"Serves 'em right," Paterson snapped. "Bastards were gonna kill us!"

"Let it go, man," Hickey said. "Let it go."

"Anyway, we can hardly call in air on our valiant allies, now can we?" Jinx added dryly. "Especially since they accomplished the mission."

Paterson scowled, "Fuck the mission!" He shrugged and looked away.

"Bad Karma, this is Free Ride." The voice on the radio only lasted a second.

"Free Ride, come to one hundred ten degrees."

The V-22 popped up over the low rise, skimming just above the rocks, masking itself in the folds of the mountains. It was an Air Force search-and-rescue ship, not the usual special-ops bird. It came in from the east, hiding in the rising sun. Littlejohn had a panel marker out, snapping the marker open and shut to flash its orange panel at the approaching tilt rotor. The others crouched in the rock crevices, waiting for the plane to get closer, watching for any unwanted guests.

Randell's team had heard the transmission and was moving north to the pickup zone. There was little need for stealth, nothing had moved in the area, not even any birds.

* * *

"Somolov, did you hear about the man who had saved up enough money for a new car?"

Somolov was slowly sweeping the binoculars across the horizon. "No, Comrade Ensign."

"Well, his name was Ivan, and he took his money to the People's Automotive Collective in his village and ordered his new car," Kovpak began. "The clerk told him that his new car would be delivered in four years."

Somolov turned to Kovpak and grinned, then turned back to the glasses as Kovpak continued. " 'Four years, eh?' Ivan asked the clerk. 'Will it be delivered in the morning or the evening?' The clerk looked at Ivan and said, 'What difference does it make if it is morning or evening if it is four years from now?' Ivan threw up his hands and said, 'Because the plumber is coming that morning!' "

The section all laughed at Kovpak's ancient but all-too-truthful joke.

"Listen!" Somolov interrupted.

The drone of an aircraft was barely audible to Kovpak's ravaged ears, but Somolov seemed to hear it plainly.

"There!" Somolov pointed to the south. "Down there!"

Kovpak motioned his section forward. An aircraft, he thought, and us with no missiles! An SA-14 would bring down any allied aircraft, but they had none. The RPG-16 was the only real firepower the section had. Well, it would have to do.

The men were moving well, their movements quick and sure. All of them were veterans of the Battle for the Liberation of Germany. Their very existence was a tribute to their skill. Like wisps of vapor, the six Spetsnaz slipped through the rocky terrain. The sound of the engines was louder, though still just a distant hum.

The Osprey slowed as it approached the panel, then turned around 180 degrees, its big engine pods rotating up to their helicopter positions. The ramp was down, facing the men who now appeared from the rocks and ran bent over toward the hovering ship. The first LRRP ran aboard just as the plane settled onto the gentle slope. One hundred meters to the left, another group appeared and darted toward the ship. Behind the ship, one of the LRRPs and a man dressed in native clothes stood watching the others approach.

The four men were fifty meters from the plane when the Russians opened up on them. Randell and Pius went down first, caught in a single burst. Loggins and Bendel dropped, rolled, and came up shooting. They were caught out in the open, though, and first Bendel and then Loggins was stitched by the ambushers. In less than four seconds, the entire team was dead within sight of the plane that would have whisked them to safety.

"GO! GO!" Jinx screamed as the tracers jumped from the rocks toward the Osprey. The pilots had seen the tracers, and the engines were howling now, picking the craft up and straining to get it moving forward. Jinx and BJ sprinted to the ramp and threw themselves onto it.

The left door gunner was firing, the sound of his minigun a rasping roar over the noise of the engines. Bits of steel and carbon fiber chunks whipped around the cargo bay as rounds from outside hit the composite walls of the V-22. The ship lurched as the wall just behind the door gunner blew in with a loud *whummp!*

The cargo bay was filled with smoke and sparks from a burned electrical box that snapped and crackled on the far wall. The right side-door gunner was slumped against a seat, his Nomex suit smoldering where the jet from the shaped charge had burned through his body, torching the contents of his chest.

Flames were flickering from the electrical box. Shannon Hickey was yanking loose a fire extinguisher as Moser beat on the box with his field jacket. Hickey finally wrestled the extinguisher out of its bracket and sprayed the nearly invisible Halon at the blaze. The flames disappeared, but the box still smoked and sparked.

The V-22 lurched forward, and for a second Jinx thought they were going in, but the pilot had power now, and he was dropping the rotors forward, picking up speed. The ship was hit badly but still flying.

The door gunner had been stunned by the blast, but he was back on his gun now, searching for the attackers. He jerked his gun down and back as he spotted the dust cloud from the RPG's back blast. He thumbed the gun to high rate and poured 300 rounds of 7.62mm into the rocks.

"A hit, Comrade Ensign!" Somolov screamed. He stepped in front of Kovpak, who handed Somolov the launcher to reload. Kovpak pushed past Somolov to see the damaged plane. He had hit it all right, there was smoke pouring from the side, but it was still flying.

"Reload! Quickly!" he screamed at Somolov. The man already had the new round in the tube. Kovpak shoved it into place as Somolov thumbed down the hammer again to shoot at the fleeing plane.

"This time!" Somolov shouted as he lined the plane up in the RPG's Christmas tree sight. On the side of the plane, a gun flashed. Somolov pulled the trigger just as three rounds from the whirling minigun hit Kovpak's left leg and left side. The rocket went wild and arced over the fleeing plane. Next to Kovpak, Somolov went down, an American slug in his face. Other *ikhotniki* were hit, too. One was dead, two others wounded. The wounded men were still firing at the plane that now picked up speed, skipping low over the rocks. In a few seconds, it was gone.

In the tilt-rotor plane, chaos reigned. The fire was out, but the smouldering box still poured acrid smoke into the cargo bay. Jinx pulled the dead gunner onto the bench seat as BJ did a quick head count to see who was still alive and who was wounded. The door gunner was screaming, holding down the firing switch on his minigun. The six barrels were a blur, the muzzle end of the gun a ball of fire. In seconds, the ammunition ran out and the gun whirled silently. Finally, the gunner dropped the handles and slumped back against the wall, his eyes wild and glazed. The barrels of his minigun glowed red. Smoke from the overheated barrels streamed back into the cargo bay to mix with the swirling smoke from the fire.

Jinx slipped the dead gunner's headphone off and tugged it over his own head.

"Simpson, Wallace, what's your status?" the pilot was calling.

Jinx thumbed the intercom switch. "This is Jenkins. Starboard gunner dead, some wounded back here. We got the fire out, but there's a hole in the port side six feet aft of the gun. What's your status? Are we going to make it?"

"Looks good," the copilot answered. "We took some hits, and we lost some hydraulic pressure, but we'll make it. How's Simpson?"

The dazed gunner pressed his mike switch. "Okay, sir, just got excited there for a second. Port gun is out of ammo."

"Okay, Simm, take it easy. Get some ammo from the starboard gun if you can."

"Roger."

The gunner made his way aft, playing the intercom line out behind him. He bent over the hole, looking for damage, then moved over to the still smoking electrical box, pulled off its cover, and examined the burned wiring inside. He spoke into his mike and went back forward to throw some circuit breakers set in a small panel on the bulkhead. This done, he pulled the lid off the starboard side ammunition storage and broke a link on the belt. He pulled out several arm lengths of ammunition, broke the belt again, and began reloading his gun on the port side.

"How we doin', BJ?" Jinx asked.

"Okay, I guess," he answered. "Some fragments, some burns, but no sucking chest wounds."

Jinx just nodded and slumped down in the nylon seat. The Osprey was pitching up and down, following the terrain, but the motion did not make him queasy as it often did. This time, it made him feel better, protected somehow. The wind was whistling in through the hole in the fuselage, but they had nothing to patch it with, so everyone was ignoring it. He pulled the field cap out of his shirt and wiped his face with it.

Jinx could hear the pilot on the radio.

"Iron Rifle, this is Free Ride. We have Bad Karma."

On the nylon bench seat, Jinx was just beginning to relax, letting the weight of fear and excitement slip off him when the Osprey suddenly slid sideways, its huge propellers rotating, slowing the big tilt rotor as it slid sideways in the air. The gunner held his mike close to his face and spoke quickly into it, unbuckling his belt.

He stepped over to Jinx and leaned close.

"They see one of your guys!" he shouted above the noise of the engines. "Black guy." The gunner then continued on his way back to the ramp.

The LRRPs all looked at Jinx, who cupped his hands in front of his mouth and shouted, "They found King!" He pointed downward.

"Alive?" BJ screamed back.

Jinx held his palms up and shrugged. He hadn't thought to ask.

The Osprey's ramp opened with a loud whoosh as the plane settled just above the ground, hovering. BJ and Hickey were on the ramp, craning their eyes around, searching for their friend.

"Got him!" Hickey shouted as he stepped out onto the ramp and dropped off the back onto the ground. BJ was right behind him.

King was still on his feet, staggering toward the V-22,

feebly waving at his teammates. As BJ and Hickey dropped to the ground and ran toward him, the big man collapsed, half sitting on the stony ground, holding his useless left arm to him.

"Come on, Ty," BJ said as the two LRRPs scooped King up off the ground. King winced, gasping with a sharp cry of pain.

"Watch that side!" King rasped. "I think it's busted."

"It's okay, man," Hickey reassured him. "We're on our way home."

Back inside the Osprey, the other LRRPs made a place for their wounded friend on the bench seat. They buckled King in with three sets of seat belts, and BJ put his rolled field jacket under the wounded man's head for a makeshift pillow. The V-22 lurched forward and picked up speed, streaking for the safety of the Allied lines.

After King was settled, had a drink of water, and a shot of morphine for his wounds, Jinx sat on the floor next to him.

"What happened to Tina, King? The girl who helped us."

"Don't know," King mumbled, the morphine starting to numb him. "She went back in. Never saw her again."

Jinx nodded and patted King's good shoulder. As he sat back on the seat and buckled in, BJ leaned over.

"What'd he say about your girlfriend?" BJ shouted.

Jinx just shook his head. BJ screwed up his face in disappointment. "Sorry, guy!" he shouted at Jinx.

"Yeah, me, too," Jinx answered. The two men lapsed into silence. The mission had been costly to everyone. BJ had lost a team. Jinx had lost his whole weird little army. And Tina. He looked down the bench seat at the others. Most of the LRRPs wore a thousand-meter stare, the expression of exhaustion, fear, and guilt so common to soldiers.

Jinx dropped his head back onto the nylon seat back and tried hard to switch off his brain.

★ 26 ★

Bodnya held his breath as he reached inside the mask and wiped the fog from the lenses. As he snugged the mask back in place, he blew out his breath to clear the smoke and fumes from the inside of his mask. Around him, other masked figures scurried with litters bearing the wounded. Others lugged shelter capes that carried the dead. Many of the dead were burned so badly they were hard to recognize as human beings. Under his coat, Bodnya's back still burned, the pain a dull ache made sharp by the chafing of the wool coat.

Even with the burn, he had been lucky. Those two poor bastards that had been on top of him were dead, roasted alive by the blast. His throat hurt, too. He had not inhaled any flame, as so many others had, but the hot fumes had burned his nose and mouth as he later pulled himself out from under the two charred Spetsnaz. The protective mask had saved him from inhaling any toxic fumes.

The launchers and their deadly payloads were destroyed utterly. The nuclear warheads had not gone off, but lay scattered around the still burning interior of the cavern. Only nuclear technicians would be allowed into the cavern to recover the damaged warheads. They would not arrive for some time. Bodnya wondered how much radiation he and the other survivors had been subjected to after the

blast. It hardly mattered now. There was no treatment and
they all were still much more likely to die from battle than
from uranium poisoning. He would ask that the 800th
Guards Special-Purpose Battalion be pulled back to the
rear, but that might very well not happen. Even as chewed
up as they were, Spetsnaz were still vital. Bodnya shook
his head and turned back toward the entrance. It was not
a soldier's task to question his orders, but this fight, this
slaughter, left ashes in his mouth. He had lost men in
Germany, but there they had fought the Americans and the
British. To have his men killed fighting these *Basmachi*
made him sick. It smelled too much of Afghanistan.

As he walked out of the cave entrance into the sunlight
and pulled off his mask, a radio operator called to him.

"Colonel, it is Ensign Kovpak," the senior private explained. "He has intercepted an enemy aircraft."

Bodnya stopped, tipped back his head, and laughed out
loud. "Has he stolen it?" Bodnya asked, laughing again
and greatly confusing the earnest young radio operator.

"What the fuck? Over," BJ shouted above the engine
noises. He pointed out the tiny window. The V-22 was
streaking over the green waters of the Gulf. Jinx unbuck-
led and made his way forward, motioning for the gunner
to give him his headphone.

"Pilot, this is Major Jenkins," he said, thumbing the
talk switch. "Where are we headed?"

"Saudi," the pilot answered. "We just got revectored.
The Reds broke through down south. We're pulling everything back to Saudi."

Jinx handed the headphone back to the gunner and
stumbled back to his seat.

"What's up?" BJ asked.

"Looks like we gettin' our ass whipped again!" Jinx
shouted back. "We're pulling back to Saudi."

BJ's incredulous expression said it all. Jinx shook his
head and shrugged.

At least we're alive, he thought, that's not much, but it beats the alternative. He looked out through the blast hole. The bright sunlight shafted in through the two starboard windows. Beneath them, the Gulf glowed emerald green.

"Truly another shitty day in paradise," Jinx observed.

"Two dead, Comrade Colonel," Kovpak answered, his voice strained with the pain of his wounds, "four wounded, myself included."

He shifted a little farther up the slope and propped himself up against the rocks. "The enemy tilt rotor was damaged, trailing smoke. It flew off to the south." He nodded, listening. "In no way, Comrade Colonel. We will mark our position for the helicopter. Yes, Comrade Colonel. Eugen One Three out."

Kovpak hung the receiver back on the radio and slumped against the rocks, gasping for breath. The exertion of merely talking on the radio had sapped his strength. Below him, the remaining members of the section were bandaging the wounded. The two dead men were wrapped in shelter capes nearby.

Wounded again, he thought, wincing. I seem to be a magnet for bullets. For a man of peace, a pacifist at heart, this is not right.

The two Mi-17s rumbled over fifteen minutes later. As one of them set down on the flat spot below them, Kovpak could see that it was already filled with wounded men, some burned black. Overhead, the other helicopter continued on, banking eastward. A man's arm dangled from the open door, the hand fluttering like a leaf in the wind. Kovpak struggled to his feet and used the empty RPG launcher as a crutch. A rifleman gathered up the radio and slung it on his back as he went down to help the wounded onto the chopper.

Grenalli Varennikov idly scanned the cockpit instruments one more time. He had already done a preflight inspection of his Su-25 ground-attack fighter, but he had little else to do until the armorers finished loading the ten weapons racks. He and his wingman, Valentin Dapkus, would be carrying a mix of rockets and bombs today. Their target was a native village in a remote mountain pass. Dapkus was in the latrine again, still fighting an intestinal bug he had acquired two days ago.

I wonder if he will finish the mission today without another accident, Varennikov chuckled. Dapkus had been very unpopular with his ground crew after the mission yesterday. He had emerged from the reeking cockpit loudly proclaiming, "This whole war is the shits!"

Varennikov was running a final electrical check on the rocket pods when Dapkus walked up. The young pilot's face was pale, almost gray. His flight suit was unusually bulky around the hips. Varennikov assumed that the stricken pilot had a towel wrapped around his butt in anticipation.

"So, Comrade Senior Lieutenant," Varennikov asked casually, "are you finally ready to fly?"

"Just so, Comrade Captain!" Dapkus answered with a snappy salute that belied his ashen color.

"I tell you, Valentin," Varennikov complained, "we will never make Sniper Pilot at this rate. Raids against mud huts earn no medals."

Dapkus nodded. "True, but for myself, I have one enemy inside; I need no more outside." The young pilot walked past Varennikov's plane and climbed the ladder into his own cockpit. His wrinkled nose told Varennikov that the ground crew had not been too conscientious in cleaning the cockpit.

"Remember," Varennikov called, "first pass high and slow for the bombs, second pass fast and low to finish off!" Dapkus nodded and gave a thumbs-up sign as his engines coughed to life.

What crap, Varennikov thought as he cranked shut the canopy, stuck flying reprisal raids with a sick wingman when I could be blasting American armor units! Pathetic! Even the targets were pathetic. Varennikov had never even heard of Kurds until this morning's briefing. It was too frustrating. This war would be over before he got in on the real fighting. This was the time to win rank and medals. He would never be able to do that bombing peasants.

At least the mission would be short. He and Dapkus would flatten this Kurd village and be back before the noon meal. Perhaps when they returned, he would go over to the medical subunit and see if that pretty technician was on duty. Dapkus would probably go back to bed.

"Comrade Commander, I have made contact with our support unit," the radio operator said hesitantly. "They report that they have been attacked by an American Ranger unit." The young radioman waited to gauge his commander's mood before proceeding.

"And?" Bodnya replied, fixing him with a cold stare.

"And they have suffered heavy losses," the radioman stammered. "They are unable to fully support us but will send as many BTRs and Feldshurs as they can spare!"

Bodnya nodded and waved the radioman away. No use punishing the messenger for the message. It hardly mattered, anyway. Those wounded in the blast would not likely survive their burns, and the other wounded were being treated now by their own medical team. Bodnya's parched throat reminded him. He turned to the radioman, who hovered a few meters away.

"Send this message to the support group. Bring all available water supplies." The radioman snapped a quick "It is done!" and bent over his radio set.

Poor old Kovpak, wounded again, Bodnya chuckled to himself. I hope he is not shot in the ass again.

A red-faced sergeant standing in the turret of an M1 tank looked over at the motley group seated on the tarmac and laughed. He keyed his mike, and a second later another helmeted head popped up to gawk at them.

BJ looked up and saw the two tankers laughing. He

lunged to his feet and screamed, "What the fuck are you laughin' at, assholes?"

Neither tanker could hear him over the noise of the tank's turbine engine. They clanked off, chuckling.

"They're laughin' at me," Jinx said placatingly as he stepped over and put a hand on his friend's shoulder. "Why not? I look like some Casbah pimp."

There was some truth in that. Jinx still had on the baggy pants and Kurdish cummerbund. The borrowed BDU shirt he wore made the outfit even more incongruous.

"I don't care," BJ fumed. "Those pukes don't need to laugh at their betters!"

Both men laughed, watching another C-141 Starlifter land on the long strip of concrete. Hickey came up behind them.

"You guys heard the latest latrine-o-gram?"

"No," Jinx answered, "tell us."

"Looks like the Reds have asked for a cease-fire," Hickey explained. "Pulled right up to the Gulf and shut 'er down."

"Makes sense," Jinx agreed. "Iran's what they wanted."

"So what did we do?" BJ questioned Hickey further. "Are we goin' for it?"

"Beats me, but considerin' that our stuff's fucked up like Hogan's goat since we pulled back across the Gulf, I bet we will."

"Perfect," BJ snapped, "just perfect. We take it up the butt again! We ought to change our motto from In God We Trust to Bohica!"

"Bo-what?" Hickey asked. Jinx grinned. He knew Bohica.

"Bohica," BJ answered, a grim smile pulling up the corners of his mouth. "It's an acronym for Bend Over, Here It Comes Again."

The crew of another passing M1 tank stared at the three odd characters standing on the tarmac, laughing their heads off.